MURDER
YET TO COME

BY ISABEL BRIGGS MYERS

CENTER FOR APPLICATIONS OF PSYCHOLOGICAL TYPE, INC.
GAINESVILLE, FLORIDA

Original copyright 1929 Isabel Briggs Myers

Originally published in 1929 by A. L. Burt Company, New York/Chicago,
 by arrangement with Frederick A. Stokes Company.

Published in 1995 by
Center for Applications of Psychological Type, Inc.
2815 N.W. 13th Street, Suite 401
Gainesville, FL 32609-2815

CAPT gratefully acknowledges the assistance of
Production Ink, Gainesville, Florida,
for the design, production, and printing of this title.

Printed in the United States of America.

Library of Congress Cataloging-in-Publication Data

Myers, Isabel Briggs.
Murder Yet to Come/by Isabel Briggs Myers.
p. 254
ISBN 0-935652-22-1
I. Title.
PS3525. Y427M8 1994   93-49476
813 .54—dc20   CIP

FORWARD TO 1995 REPRINT OF
MURDER YET TO COME
BY ISABEL BRIGGS MYERS

The original publication of *Murder Yet to Come* was the result of a young Isabel Myers winning a mystery novel contest by *New McClure's* magazine in 1929. It was published by Frederick A. Stokes Company, and translated into several languages. Not incidentally she bested a young Ellery Queen to win the contest.

Myers' writing of novels and screenplays was just the beginning. The work begun by her mother and carried forward by Isabel would far outweigh her early accomplishments.

That "work" was the creation of the Myers-Briggs Type Indicator®, the operationalizing of Dr. Carl Jung's complex theory of Psychological Types. With incredible intelligence and persistence Myers forged what has become the most popular normal psychology instrument. The importance of her work should not be overlooked; Myers made self-awareness, appreciation of differences, and a lifelong developmental model available to the common person.

The characters in *Murder Yet to Come*, are beautifully consistent with type portraits, and those readers who know type will enjoy "typing them" as the mystery progresses.

It is with a sense of deep admiration that we at CAPT make available this early work of Isabel Myers. We hope it gives the reader much enjoyment as well as a glimpse of Isabel Myers herself.

The Center for Applications of Psychological Type was founded by
Isabel Briggs Myers and Mary McCaulley in 1975.
This book is being published to celebrate the 20th anniversary of
CAPT. Through research and education, CAPT continues to make the
vision of Isabel Myers a reality.

To

CLARENCE G. MYERS

*in grateful appreciation of
the keenly critical judgment and unfailing
resourcefulness which were invaluable to me
in the concoction of this tale.*

CONTENTS

PART ONE

CHAPTER   PAGE

1 The Curtain Goes Up 1
2 A Lady in Distress 11
3 The Vengeance of Kali 21
4 The Other Door 33

PART TWO

5 Possibilities 49
6 Pieces in the Night 57
7 Two Years Too Late 67
8 Jerningham's Cup of Coffee 79

PART THREE

9 Jerningham Cross-Examines 97
10 The Wrath of Kali 107
11 The Wine of Disaster 115
12 Murder Yet to Come 127

PART FOUR

13 Knowledge at a Price 141
14 A Method of Coercion 149
15 Jerningham Sticks by His Guns 159
16 Consequences 169
17 "Forgive Me—Linda" 179

PART FIVE

18 The Scream in the Night 193
19 The Servant of Kali 203
20 Through the Crack of the Door 213
21 The Opening of the Last Act 221
22 Curtain 229

PART
1

1
THE CURTAIN
GOES UP

If you frequent the theatre at all, you have watched the curtain rise on at least one play from the pen of Peter Jerningham. If you missed "Butter Side Down," you certainly saw "Storm." And if you haven't already seen "Challenge," you will before the year is out. The critics agree that "Challenge" is the best thing he has done.

I know better. Being his secretary,—and more than that, his friend,—I have good reason to know better. The finest proof of Jerningham's genius is something the critics never heard of,—his solution of the murder of Malachi Trent.

It was Jerningham's wish that no one should ever hear of it. And we who had shared with him those three perilous days—and nights— at Cairnstone House, recognized his right to dictate. We agreed that no one but Jerningham himself should ever lift the curtain of secrecy behind which the grim drama had taken place. And having so agreed, we fled—thankfully—from that house where Death had made him-self at home.

Jerningham and I, too weary for speech, came back together through the November dusk, to the peaceful sanctuary of Jerningham's bachelor apartment in New York. We had been expected. There was a roaring blaze of hickory logs awaiting us in the great fireplace. With-out a word, we made for the two huge chairs on either side of the hearth, and stretched out at ease, to let the warmth and the security and the blessed sanity of the place soak in to the chilled marrow of our bones.

I watched Jerningham's face in the glow of the fire. One by one the lines etched there by the last three days softened. The tiny muscles around his eyes began to relax. His mouth lost some of its grimness. But even his favorite pipe could not banish the air of deadly fatigue that enveloped his long, lounging figure,—nor the bandage that crossed his forehead,—nor the black silk sling which took the weight of his right arm from his broken collar bone.

"Mac," he said at last, with a deep breath of satisfaction, "there's nothing like a roaring blaze to exorcize the Powers of Darkness. Cairnstone House is fading already. In three weeks I shall doubt if it ever existed."

"Then I'll hire you a stenographer tomorrow morning," I declared, "so you can record what happened while it's still fresh in your mind. If we wait till my hand is fit to run a typewriter, you'll have forgotten a lot of the fine points."

Jerningham frowned.

"And why," he inquired, "do I want a record of this damned business?"

"Because some day you'll need it—badly!" I prophesied. "The story will come out sooner or later, and if it doesn't come out exactly straight there'll be the devil to pay. In your shoes, I'd publish it immediately, and be done with it."

All the grimness had returned to Jerningham's face.

"I'll take my chances," he said. "If we publish it, we'll never hear the last of Cairnstone House. We'll see it on the front page of every paper, meet it on the lips of every acquaintance, eat it at every dinner table, hear it in the intermissions of every play, and dream it every night! No, thanks! I've had all I can stand—now!"

"You're taking it too hard," I protested, amazed at his vehemence. "There's no need to feel like that."

"Perhaps I won't, after a month or two," he half apologized. "I'm going to do a lot of intensive forgetting. Pretend to myself I never watched the blood running from your finger-ends, or staked other people's lives on my own hunches, or heard a scream in the night! Lord!"

In spite of the fire, he shivered in his chair.

"You see?" he commented wryly. "It's lucky 'Challenge' has two more weeks of rehearsal, and I'll be so immersed in the details of it that I shan't have time to think. Perhaps I'll come out of Jordan cleansed of my foolishness and readier to follow your advice. But in the meantime———"

He half grinned at me, but there was an undertone of appeal in his voice.

"In the meantime, if you don't want to see me in the psychopathic ward, don't mention Cairnstone House in my hearing."

"All right, old man," I promised.

But in that agreement we reckoned without the gentlemen of the press.

It was three days later that we returned through the early dusk from a rehearsal, to find a young man awaiting us in Jerningham's apartment. He introduced himself as Collins, of the Associated Press. Jerningham's face stiffened, and I saw the two men taking each other's measure.

"Mr. Jerningham," Collins said without preamble, "I want to know who murdered Malachi Trent."

"Who murdered him?" Jerningham questioned curiously. "That's an exaggeration, isn't it? How do you make a murder out of an old man's fall from his library ladder?"

"I have strong reasons to believe he was murdered," the young man persisted gravely. "You were there. You must know all about it. And I want the straight of it from you before I stir things up."

Jerningham laughed and shook his head.

"I know those 'strong reasons'," he returned. "You compound 'em of one part hunch to nine parts hopefulness. Of course a murder, even a murder that never happened, makes a better story than any accident. But I'm too busy with my own brand of invention just now to help you out with yours."

"It's not invention, Mr. Jerningham, and you know it," Collins objected a trifle sharply. "I went up to Cairnstone House yesterday, on the chance that there might be a human interest story connected with the death of an eccentric old millionaire. Nobody else had interviewed the local people, so I had the field to myself. It was a rich field.

The local doctor, for instance, told me he'd been called to Cairnstone House on four different errands within three days after Mr. Trent's death."

He glanced significantly at Jerningham's bandages and mine.

"Yes?" said Jerningham. "That was Dr. Lampton, of course. But Dr. Lampton himself certified that Mr. Trent's death was caused by the fall."

"He did—at first," conceded Collins. "But he had since come to consider it extraordinary and—er—illuminating, that so many other— shall we say, accidents?—have followed on the heels of the first one."

"Extraordinary, perhaps," Jerningham admitted, "but why illuminating? Just what light do my broken collar bone and broken head cast upon Mr. Trent's death?"

"That's what I'm asking you," Collins declared candidly. "Nothing sheds much light, so far. But a lot of facts cast significant shadows."

"For instance?" Jerningham prompted.

He seemed positively to be enjoying his inquisitive young visitor, and I gave silent thanks that three good nights' sleep and three engrossing days of rehearsals had so nearly restored him to his old self.

"For instance," Collins responded, "the fact that Cairnstone House is closed, and every member of Trent's household has disappeared without leaving a forwarding address. And the fact that Trent's attorneys declare he died intestate, and have already taken out letters of administration, in spite of the strong rumor that he made a will just before his death."

"Nothing very dark so far," Jerningham commented.

"It gets darker," Collins said. "There's talk in the village of witchcraft practiced at Cairnstone House,—of unexplainable things,——"

"Any ghosts or goblins?" Jerningham suggested helpfully.

"There's another rumor," Collins continued, undisturbed, "about an enormous ruby which Trent swore he'd keep as long as he lived. His attorneys, however, haven't found it. At least, it's not mentioned in the inventory of his goods which they've filed. Finally——"

He paused significantly.

"Finally, there's Dr. Lampton's story,—and the stories of the two clergymen of the village. Taken all together, they make an incredible tale."

I groaned inwardly. Collins was in a position to put two and two together, and make at least a dozen.

"I fear," Jerningham said dryly, "you have been inciting some otherwise virtuous people to gossip. The clergymen should have given you a test from Proverbs. 'The simple believeth every word, but the prudent man looketh well to his going.' "

"I've done a lot of looking," Collins assured him. "The more I look, the darker the thing gets. The darkest fact of all is that Malachi Trent's death was followed so soon by another death—under the same roof."

Jerningham's face was inscrutable.

"The second death," he observed calmly, "was a suicide."

"You mean," Collins corrected, "you told Dr. Lampton it was a suicide. Just as you told him Trent's death was an accident. Whereas, candidly, both the accident and the suicide were—murder."

There was a little silence.

"Candidly, and not for publication," said Jerningham at last, "they were."

Collins drew a long breath.

"Gosh!" he murmured reverently. "The Murders at Cairnstone House! It'll be the scoop of a lifetime!"

"If you get it," Jerningham amended.

"You're going to give it to me," said Collins simply.

Jerningham's mouth quirked again at the corner.

"When I didn't even give it to the police?"

Collins nodded gravely.

"Yes. For the sake of the story, if for nothing else. If you won't give me the inside dope, of course, I'll have to go ahead on my own. I'll spring the best murder mystery I can concoct from what I know. An after me—the deluge. Sunday editions—tabloids—special features— sob stuff—and none of it probably, within a hundred miles of the truth."

He was watching Jerningham's face with keen appraisement.

"You're a craftsman," he finished. "You won't enjoy seeing a fine yarn garbled. You'd rather give me the whole tale and let me tell it straight."

Jerningham laughed in spite of himself.

"True," he said. "And only a straight story will satisfy the police. Still——"

He fell silent, considering, but Collins was no respecter of silences.

"Why did you keep it from the police in the first place?" he inquired.

"Because I thought," Jerningham answered, almost absent-mindedly, "that it was our one chance to prevent the second murder."

"What!" Collins cried. "You mean you saw it coming?"

"From a long way off," Jerningham replied. "We didn't know who the murderer would be, or the victim. But we did know there was murder yet to come."

"And when it came," Collins demanded, tensely, "Why didn't you report it then?"

Jerningham's mouth grew stern.

"We saw justice done," he said, shortly. "There was no need of the police."

A moment's silence. Then Collins leaned forward.

"If you don't give me that story," he said, "you'll have me committing murder myself—right here on your hearth rug."

"All right," Jerningham decided suddenly. "You can have it on one condition."

"Just name it!"

"I'll trade you the story for two weeks' peace," Jerningham offered. "I'm in the last fortnight of rehearsals on my new play, and I can't be bothered now. But I'll have a full written account of what happened ready for you in two weeks, if in the meantime you keep the papers off the subject—and off me. Is it a bargain?"

"Gosh, yes!" Collins promised fervently.

"Only remember," Jerningham warned, "if you get impatient and let the thing break too soon, I'll hunt up your worst enemy and spill the whole tale to him.——And now make yourself scarce till the morning after our first night!"

"Scarcer than bow legs in the 'Follies'," Collins agreed jubilantly, and took himself off.

"Hard luck," I commented, as the door closed behind him. "None the less, I'm glad you're going to write it."

Jerningham calmly lit his pipe.

"I haven't the slightest intention of writing it," he returned imperturbably.

"What?" I demanded. "You can't go back on a promise like that!"

His mouth twisted in mild irony.

"Listen to the 'Keeper of the King's Conscience'," he drawled, with the affectionate insolence which is the accolade of his deepest intimacy. "You're stepping out of character, Mac. What the devil did I engage you for?"

"Lack of sufficient sales resistance when I asked you to," I hazarded with a grin. "I don't know why else!"

The question carried me back of a sudden to a day three years before, when "Butter Side Down" was rocking Broadway with laughter. After distant hero-worship of "the most brilliant of the younger dramatists," I had gained entrance to this room at last, and watched Jerningham lounging in this same big chair, and asked no more of my luckiest stars than to be chosen as the assistant in the workshop of this man's mind.

Jerningham snorted.

"Don't be an idiot," he bade me. "You've always known I couldn't get along without you. You must have known it from the looks of this place that first day you tracked me to my lair!"

He swept a glace of wry reminiscence about the great comfortable room, which only my continual vigilance saves from continual inundation. When Jerningham is alone, the rising flood of books, papers, magazines and personal belongings, engulfs everything, and the bills from his morning mail and the manuscript from his midnight labors go down into oblivion together.

"Utter chaos you found, didn't you?" He chuckled, remembering. "And me swamped in the midst of it, yelling for help. I knew what I needed, all right. Somebody to type my stuff and answer my neglected letters and clear my desk. Preferably somebody who could drop everything and listen when I wanted to talk,—and then go off and attend to the catankerous details of life when I was through. If I were very lucky—somebody with tact enough to bull the market of my self esteem in times of depression———"

He broke off to laugh at my guilty expression.

"Oh, I know exactly how you do it, but that doesn't make it any the less consoling. And I know just how you deflate me when I'm too dangerously pleased with a new idea. Well—that's what I wanted— and you're letter-perfect in the role. *But*———"

His deep-set gray eyes twinkled beneath the jutting brows as he returned to the attack.

"Did I, or did I not, engage you to hound me into doing my duty against my will?"

"You did not," I admitted. "You most explicitly engaged me to take your duties out back somewhere and wring their necks."

"Exactly," said Jerningham.

"But just the same———" I persisted doggedly.

"Sometimes you're astonishingly dense, Mac," he interrupted. "I've been trying to break it to you gently that you're going to write the tale yourself."

For a moment I was speechless.

"But I can't!" I got out at last. "I———"

"Oh yes, you can," he returned heartlessly. "Better than I! We've got to give 'em every last, least detail, or they won't believe us. And that's your specialty. You have a most extraordinary faculty for remembering the irrelevant and the trivial, as I may perhaps have mentioned before———"

"Yes! You've mentioned it every time in the last three years that I've had to remind you of a fitting at your tailor's or a luncheon engagement that you didn't want to keep!"

"Quite so! I've always regarded a memory for details as a frightful waste of gray matter. But I here and now apologize. Your memory saved the day for us at Cairnstone House. And it's going to save the day for me now."

"Thanks," I said dryly. "But you've got a memory yourself, you know."

"Not a photographic one like yours, with every detail of the background neatly filed for reference. I only remember the most important figures, silhouetted against whatever I was thinking at the time. When I try to put in details, half of 'em are pure invention."

I laughed in spite of myself.

"I must admit," I said, "that your recollection of anything is always better than the truth."

"Or worse," he amended. "And this time, the truth is bad enough. No, Mac, the job is up to you. Get everything in—get everything straight—make 'em believe it—and the half of my kingdom is yours!"

So I have done my best—alone, for Jerningham would not even be consulted. I have put down everything, just as it happened. I can swear to all the facts before a grand jury if need be. But whether or not it sounds like the truth, I do not know.

A LADY IN DISTRESS

I t was early in the evening of Armistice Day, 1928, that Malachi Trent was killed at his country estate of Cairnstone House, some eighteen miles out of Philadelphia along the Baltimore Pike. Had he died on any other date in November, Jerningham and I would never even have read the news of his death, for "Challenge" was in rehearsal and we had forgotten temporarily that newspapers existed.

But Jerningham had had for ten years a standing engagement for Armistice Day, and he was determined to keep it this year as usual, whether "Challenge" ever reached its opening night or not. So the evening of Sunday, November eleventh, found us driving down the Baltimore Pike on our way back from a three day hunting trip with ex-top-Sergeant Carl Nilsson, Jerningham's erstwhile comrade-at-arms in the 83rd Company of the 4th Marines. And since all three of us were ravenous from a day spent in the open, we stopped about seven o'clock at a small tea room, five or six miles from Wawa.

While we waited to be served, I contemplated with silent enjoyment the contrast between the two men, whose friendship is only strengthened by the difference between them. They were dressed substantially alike in corduroys and high leather boots, hunting shirts and leather jackets, but there the resemblance ceased. Jerningham is six feet one, with the lean and lazy grace that comes from beautiful muscular coordination, and the keen gray eyes and mobile face that suit his eager spirit and eternally questing mind. Nilsson is one of the Vikings, a superbly built blond giant, broad in the shoulders and lean in the waist, blue-eyed and square of chin, slow of movement except in emergencies, slow of speech except in wrath, slow of thought as compared with Jerningham, but moving steadily forward from one solid conclusion to another—and impossible to halt unless by the force of logic better than his own. Nilsson admires tremendously, without admitting it, Jerningham's quickness of insight that is forever running rings around his own plodding mental processes. Jerningham pays reluctant tribute to the smashingly effective action which follows inevitably on Nilsson's solid, slow decisions.

This mutual appreciation, of scout plane for armored tank and armored tank for scout plane, dates back to some of the worst terrain between Belleau Wood and Hill 204, and when, after the Armistice, Jerningham left the service, he and Nilsson swore by all the gods of A.E.F. to foregather on each anniversary of Armistice Day, no matter how far apart their paths might have diverged in the meantime.

As a matter of fact, Armistice Day, 1928, found them only as far apart as New York and Philadelphia. Nilsson had remained with the Marines for six years after the war. When General Butler took charge of the Philadelphia police in 1924, Nilsson was in command of the handful of Marines stationed at the Broad Street terminal to discourage the too popular practice of robbing the mails. His enlistment expired that year, and judging that man-hunting offered more action than peace-time duty with the Marines, he asked the General for a chance on the homicide squad of the city's police force. In the four ensuing years he won rapid promotion, and in the storm of criticism to which the Philadelphia police were subjected in the fall of 1928, Nilsson's record of integrity and achievement made him the outstanding figure on the detective force.

In the three days of our hunting trip, he had renewed his annual argument with Jerningham as to the relative merits of their respective professions, and as we began our supper, the battle was still raging.

"It stands to reason," he argued, "that it's better sport to solve a real murder on the front page, than to sit over a typewriter and invent stuff that never gets beyond the theatre section no matter how exciting you make it."

Jerningham chuckled.

"Nilsson," he chaffed, "you don't know how much satisfaction a man can get from working things out in his brain—provided, of course, he has one."

"Meaning," boomed Nilsson, "that the police don't have any? Well, sometimes we don't use what we've got. And sometimes we do, and it doesn't show in the results. But we're dealing with facts in our business. When we get stuck, we can't just step back into the first act and change things around to suit our convenience. It's no job at all for *you* to work things out!"

Jerningham snorted.

"And how long would an audience stand for a plot that was arranged 'to suit my convenience'? They'd say, 'Pooh! Nobody would have done that!' and walk out of the theatre. No, you're the one who's got it easy. You only have to figure out what people really have done. Every least fact is a finger pointing to the answer, and you can get bearings on the truth from twenty different angles. But my job is to start cold and figure out what imaginary people will do, and that's ten times harder. As I said, though, it's fun. I can't help practicing it even on the real people. For instance——"

He cocked an eyebrow toward a man who, a moment before, had entered the tea room and made straight for the telephone.

"For instance, look at the man across the room. There's a high tension about him that's going to be discharged in action pretty soon, or I'm no judge of characters."

We followed Jerningham's gaze. The man in question was gripping the telephone with baffled intensity.

"But why not?" He was demanding of the impassive instrument. "But where are you sending her? . . . But why? . . . But . . ."

A sudden helpless silence on the stranger's part told us that his party had hung up. He stood staring at the telephone for a moment, then replaced the receiver with intense deliberation. Presently he flung up his head in a gesture of resolution, turned and scanned the nearly empty dining-room with a searching eye.

We were too interested by that time to look away.

His gaze met ours squarely, his fact lit, and he came directly across to our table.

He was a man who would have arrested attention anywhere—

well-built, well-groomed, with well-cut features so darkly tanned that his eyes seemed oddly light. But the remarkable thing about him was his manner. There was no swagger to the man, but no emperor ever stepped forth to review his conquering armies with more dynamic self-confidence. Not only was he confident. He conveyed the assurance that his confidence was justified. Nevertheless, as he stopped at our table and I saw his tight-clenched fingers, I knew he was not reviewing his armies. He was sending them into battle.

"Luck is with me," he began, with grave eagerness. "You're Peter Jerningham, are you not? My name is Ryker. I met you once at a Lambs' Club dinner which you have, no doubt, long since forgotten."

Jerningham waved him into our fourth chair.

"I remember your face," he said, "but I'm a hopeless dub at names. These are my friends, Carl Nilsson and John MacAndrew. Nilsson saved my life ten years ago, and Mac saves my reason every week."

Ryker included us both in a brief smile that hardly stirred his dark face.

"Then I've come to the right shop," he said. "I need help tonight in a matter where both life and reason may be at stake. When I recognized you just now," he turned to Jerningham, "I thought perhaps your professional interest in queer situations might make the experience repay you for the risk involved."

He had guessed right. Jerningham was learning forward upon the table, his deep-set eyes bright with interest.

"What sort of help do you need?"

"A quite medieval sort," Ryker answered, his eyes upon us. "Two or three stout fellows at my back to rescue a lady in distress."

Jerningham's face kindled.

"Bravo!" he said. "And who is the dastardly caitiff against whom we ride?"

"Malachi Trent," answered Ryker gravely, "the former copper king."

We all three nodded at the name.

"This distressed lady of mine is his niece,—his great-niece, rather, —a lovely child of seventeen, named Linda Marshall. She has lived for the last ten or twelve years at Cairnstone House, his country estate, and he's never let her set foot outside the gates. She has no other relatives, no friends, not even an acquaintance—except myself."

"How long have you known her?" Jerningham inquired.

"I met her a week ago. She bewitched me at first sight, and I had to tell myself sternly that she was too young for love-making. Then I began to find out the truth."

"Which is——?" Jerningham prompted.

"That for some reason Cairnstone House is a horror to her. That she's not only utterly alone, but desperate with some fear which she won't confide. I could think of only one way to help her. I urged her to marry me without delay, so that I could take her away. She accepted gladly, and Trent, to my surprise, gave his consent. The ceremony was to be tomorrow."

He drew a long breath.

"This afternoon," he resumed, "I went to Cairnstone House on some business of Trent's and found him unusually cordial. When I asked for Linda he said, rather oddly as I look back, that she was resting in her room and wasn't to be disturbed. I came away without seeing her. Before I'd driven far, it dawned on me that the hour of the wedding hadn't been definitely fixed, so I stopped off here to telephone."

"Then it was Trent you were talking to on the phone?" Jerningham asked.

"It was," Ryker affirmed grimly. "I asked to speak with Linda, and he refused. He said she was leaving Cairnstone House tonight — that I'd never see her again. And he laughed as he hung up. Something about his laugh turned me cold. There's some ghastly catch in that 'leaving Cairnstone House'. He would speak like that—and laugh like that—if Linda were dead and going to be buried tonight."

He stared straight ahead for a moment, then shook himself like a man shaking off a bad dream.

"Of course he hasn't killed her. He wouldn't dare do anything so crude as that. But there are a hundred subtler ways——"

He hesitated.

"The man's a devil," he said in a low voice. "Whatever it is that's going to happen tonight, I can't leave that pitiful child alone another hour."

"What can happen?" Jerningham asked quietly.

"Anything," Ryker answered slowly. "To a girl alone in that house —anything! And I haven't seen her since yesterday afternoon. 'Resting in her room,' he said. How do I know what he meant by that? Locked in? Ill? Out of her head with fear?"

He broke off, and it was plain that his composure cost him a bitter effort.

"I don't know what can happen. I wish to God I did," he went on. "But Linda knows, and the terror of that knowledge has been driving her over the edge."

"You mean——" Jerningham hesitated.

"Insane," Ryker answered, and the word hung in the air between the four of us, like a blue haze of horror.

Nilsson leaned forward and spoke for the first time.

"What are you going to do about it?" he demanded.

"Go and get her and marry her tonight," Ryker answered bluntly. Nilsson shook his head.

"She's only seventeen, you said. You can't marry her without his consent. If you do, he can have it annulled and get her back."

Ryker reached in his pocket and spread a sheet of paper upon the table between us. It was a license for the marriage of Heldon Ryker, 39, and Linda Marshall, 17.

"Trent had the license clerk come to Cairnstone House and issue this," Ryker explained, "the day he gave his consent to the marriage. Tomorrow it will doubtless occur to him to call up the Marriage Bureau and have it revoked. But it's perfectly good for use tonight!"

Jerningham rose to his feet.

"All right," he said. "Tell us the rest on the way to Cairnstone House."

We all piled into Nilsson's touring car. Ryker's roadster could hold only three, and he thought it unwise to split the party. At Nilsson's suggestion, Ryker took the wheel.

"Well, what would you like to know?" He asked, once we were started on the six mile drive.

"Cast of characters first," said Jerningham. "What sort of man is this Malachi Trent?"

"You've probably heard a good bit about him indirectly," Ryker responded. "Whatever you heard, it wasn't exaggerated. He's very eccentric, very much the recluse, but he has a wide range of financial interests which he still controls. I've been his agent for years in various matters, most of them personal investigations of projects in out-of-the-way corners of the earth. In business he's keen, level-headed, and shrewdly ingenious. But he's a neurotic, with a ruthless streak of cruelty and an abnormal passion for domination, which he has indulged all his life. He can't bear to have anyone even suggest a decision to him, and judging from his behavior when he's thwarted I have some doubt of his sanity."

"For instance, two years ago he took me along on a trip into Upper Assam, on the edge of the Eastern Himalayas, up under the Roof of the World. At Dibrugarh he heard rumors of an extraordinary ruby which no white man had ever seen. It belonged to the temple of a Hindu goddess, up in the sacred gorge of the Brahmaputra,—the Temple of Kali the Destroyer. Native pilgrims, on their way to worship Kali at her annual festival, said that this stone,—'the Wrath of Kali,' they called it,—was the biggest ruby in the world, but wasn't famous because it could never be shown except on this one night of the festival and then only to true believers."

The man was talking rapidly, almost casually, but there was an undertone of strain in his voice. I guessed that he was telling us the tale to keep himself from thinking of what he might find at Cairnstone House.

"Trent was in a bad mood,—his plans had miscarried,—and he swore we'd go and see the 'Wrath of Kali' for ourselves, believers or not. We had a frightful trip, for the Brahmaputra was still swollen from the rains, but we reached the temple in time for the festival— and of course we couldn't get in. Trent was beside himself with fury. I don't think he cared a straw about the ruby, but he went into one of his cold, deadly rages over the 'affront'. He promised a couple of native ruffians a whacking price in gold if they could steal the 'Wrath of Kali' for him, and somehow they managed to do it—right under the noses of the worshippers. (Trent has a gift for laying his hand on an efficient scoundrel when he needs one!) He paid their price and we started back to civilization. We barely got out with our lives. News of the sacrilege went down the Brahmaputra faster than we did, for all our haste, and Trent still has a handful of poisoned arrows that some of the wild little hill hunters sprayed into our boat as we went past. One of the boatmen was shot in the throat and died in five minutes from the effects of the poison."

"And what became of the 'Wrath of Kali'?" I asked.

"Oh, he has it still. Makes rather a fetich of it because of the triumph it represents. He even has in his study a little image of Kali which he bought at Chittagong so that he could flaunt his victory in her face. A mad business! It's a fearful thing sometimes to see such a man wielding the power his millions give him. If you once thwart him, he goes any length to smash you. If I get Linda tonight, he'll go after my hide, but anything's better than wondering what's happening to Linda."

The car wheeled into the driveway of an estate hidden behind high brick walls, and stopped before the great gates that barred the way. The lodge-keeper stepped out, recognized Ryker, tipped his cap and opened the gates for us to pass.

"Point one in our favor," Ryker commented. "Trent hasn't yet given orders to keep me out. That's the advantage of striking at once. As Lord Bacon said, 'When things have once come to the execution, there is no secrecy comparable to celerity.' "

He switched off the headlights and throttled down the car's speed, and we crept slowly up the long winding drive, feeling our way through the starlit darkness.

"Hasn't anyone ever told him where to get off?" Nilsson asked hopefully.

"Linda's mother did," Ryker answered. "If she hadn't, Linda would have been my daughter instead of Harry Marshall's. Eighteen years ago this fall—I'd asked her to marry me, and Trent butted in and told her she must. She simply walked out of Cairnstone House and married Marshall. I couldn't blame her—it was her right, and my misfortune.

. . . Of course that's why I lost my heart to Linda. She's her mother all over again,—except for what Cairnstone House has done to her."

His voice grew remorseful.

"The worst of it is, I'm partly to blame. When Linda was six or eight years old, her parents were killed in a railway accident. Trent sent me to bring the child back to him. I found there were some friends who wanted to keep her. No wonder! She was a lovely, proud, upstanding little thing. Entirely too much like her mother ever to knuckle under to Trent. And I made the ghastly mistake of suggesting the perhaps he'd better let them have her. He thought I meant he couldn't manage her. That sealed her fate. He kept her at Cairnstone House. But he never spoke of her, I never saw her when I was there on business, and I assumed he'd sent her away somewhere to school—until I met her a week ago."

"What happened in those years I don't know. Linda won't talk about it. Apparently he set out from the start to break her spirit, and when he found he couldn't, it grew into an obsession with him. Her mother had defied him. He couldn't stand it from the daughter too. The longer she kept her courage, the more he hated her. And now at last he has found a weapon that is reducing her to abject terror—and worse. I've got to get her out of his hands tonight, if I break my neck—and yours—doing it."

He turned the last curve of the driveway, and stopped the car. We stepped out quickly and stood an instant gazing at the huge, dismal, menacing bulk of Cairnstone House, black against the stars. There was not a light visible except a sickly gleam through the dark red glass of the transom over the front door.

It was Jerningham who first shook off the spell of silence.

"Let's go," he said. "Which battlement do we climb?"

3
THE VENGEANCE
OF KALI

We start," Ryker answered, "by ringing the bell at the front door. If it's answered, two of you lead the way in and insist on seeing Mr. Trent. He'll be in his library, at the left as you go in. He's always there, except when he's at the table or in bed. All you have to do is to keep him there, with talk if you can, by blocking the door if you have to. The third man goes with me to find Linda and get her out the of the house before you release Trent. Then we go. Perfectly simple—if it works!"

"Jerningham and Mac had better take the old man," Nilsson suggested, as we mounted the steps of the front porch. "I'm not so much on talk, but if they've locked your little Linda up I've got a good shoulder to lean against her door."

Ryker fumbled for the bell, and found it, and we stood silent for several moments, listening for footsteps in answer. It was pitch dark beneath the porch roof, only our faces showing dimly in the faintly diffused light from the stained transom. Ryker stepped back from the doorway.

"Dark as a pocket," he commented, "but it'll be lighter as soon as the door opens. Jerningham, perhaps you'd better be the spokesman. Give them a couple more rings, and then if no one comes we'll have to try Nilsson's shoulder."

Another long silence. I suppose it was a minute and a half.

"Sounds like an empty house," Nilsson offered, at last. "How many people are there in it tonight, anyhow?"

"Should be four," Ryker responded. "Linda and Trent, and an old crone of a housekeeper named Mrs. Ketchem, and Ram Singh, a Hindu servant Trent picked up the day he got the ruby, to expedite our departure out of Kali's neighborhood. The man is a curious——"

That sentence was never finished. From inside the closely shrouded library windows on our left came a crash loud enough to wake the dead. It did not sound like the crash of a revolver shot. It sounded like the smashing fall of some heavy object. Indeed I felt the jar in the floor of the porch beneath my feet. And then, before the reverberations had died, there came from inside the same shrouded windows a sound that stopped the breath in my throat,—the sound of a girl's voice, in a single cry of horror.

None of us spoke. We only flung ourselves as one man against the great door,—once, and again, and again. It shook on its hinges before our onslaught, creaked, yielded, and swung open with the crack of a splintering lock, precipitating us pell-mell into the dimly lighted hall.

We did not stop to look around. A shaft of light was streaming from the open door upon our left. With one accord we rushed through that door into the brightly lit, silent room, and then halted in our tracks, stood blinking and staring at the two motionless figures standing before us—the girl we had come to rescue, and the man who faced her—who was not the man we had thought to see.

We had reason afterward to remember every detail of that scene. The library was a large room, lined with books from floor to ceiling. The wall of books was broken in only three places—at the rear of the room where a huge stone fireplace held a dying fire, at the front end of the room where heavy curtains of black velour evidently covered a long bay window, and in the center of the long wall opposite us where similar black curtains, veiling another bay window, served also as a background for our first glimpse of Linda.

The picture she made would have tempted the brush of a master. Her slender golden loveliness, startling against the somber black, was set off by a quaint gown of a fashion long gone by, a gown with a slim bodice and billowing, ruffled skirts. The gown was strange to my eyes, but in that first moment I passed over its strangeness, as I passed over

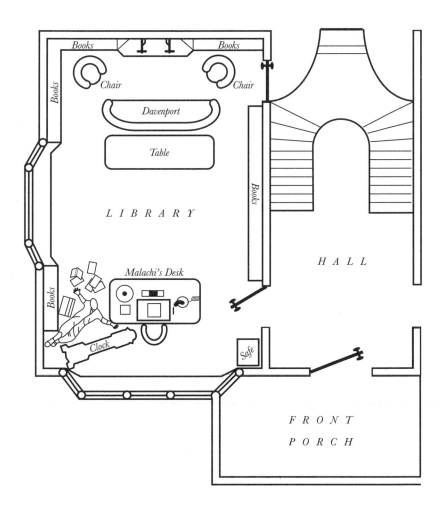

GENERAL PLAN OF LIBRARY

the unexpected presence of the white-faced, red-headed, young man who stood at the extreme front of the room.

For what riveted my attention was the expression on the faces of these two. They were both frozen, fascinated, staring—staring at something on the floor between them, something hidden from our sight by the large desk that stood in the middle of the room.

Slowly the four of us moved apart, to right and left around the desk, till we could see what thing was behind it. On the floor, at the foot of a small stepladder, lay the body of an old man in a dressing gown, his head askew at a horrible angle, one motionless hand outflung toward the wreck of a tall grandfather's clock which lay on the floor beside him.

While we still stood and stared, a tall man in a white robe brushed past us—I dimly remembered having seen him at the head of the stairs as we rushed through the hall—and Trent's Hindu servant, Ram Singh, crouched above his master, feeling his wrists, his temples, groping beneath his dressing gown to catch the least fluttering beat of his heart. When the Hindu rose again to his feet, his dark face was a mask.

"It is the vengeance of Kali," he said. "Trent Sahib is dead."

We all had known it before he spoke, but the words seemed to break the spell that held us. Ryker put a swift arm around Linda to steady her as she swayed.

"Are you hurt?" he demanded gently, urgently. "What happened?"

She seemed utterly bewildered.

"I don't know," she faltered. "I can't remember,—I heard him coming, and I was afraid—and I hid——"

"Where did you hide?" Ryker prompted softly.

She flung a hand behind her toward the bay window in the long wall.

"On the window seat, behind the curtains. But that was a long time ago—just after dusk—I waited hours, I think, for him to leave the room, and he didn't—And then it's just a blank—I can't remember——"

"Did you faint, do you think,—or go to sleep?"

"Sleep?" She turned a dazed face to his, as though she had never known the meaning of the word. "I don't see how I could have slept—I haven't slept for days——"

"And then what happened?"

"There was a crash that brought me back—a crash in the room, I thought—and the first thing I knew, I was standing right here—and I looked—and saw——"

She caught Ryker's sleeve with clinging fingers.

"There really was a crash?" she begged. "I didn't dream it? I'm not dreaming still? Oh no, he isn't dead. I don't believe it."

"He is," Ryker assured her, and shifted his position to hide from her sight the horrible sprawling body on the floor.

She drew a long tremulous sigh.

"Then I don't have to do anything more," she murmured to herself. "Or plan any more, or fight any more, or be brave any more. I can—rest."

She swayed a little on her feet.

"You can go to bed and sleep for a week, dear child," he answered with forced lightness, "and I think you'd better go this minute and leave everything to us. Where's Mrs. Ketchem? I'll tell her to tuck you in."

Following the direction of his glance I turned and saw, in the doorway by which we had entered, a withered old crone with sunken jaws and pointed chin, who might have been one of the Weird Sisters. It struck me as pitifully significant of Linda's situation, that there was no woman to comfort her except this grim old witch. Perhaps Ryker too doubted the old woman's maternal instinct, for he gave her minute instructions as to Linda's care. Linda submitted passively. Only at the door she turned back for an instant to look at the young man who had faced her across Trent's body.

"You didn't go!" she said.

"I couldn't," he answered gravely.

I thought relief flared for an instant in her face, but she turned without another word and followed the old woman up the stairs.

When she was gone, the four of us who had come to Cairnstone House to rescue her from the man who was dead, turned with one accord to the young stranger. I realized for the first time that if you could forget his hair, there was in his thin face an unmistakable resemblance to the hawklike features of the dead man.

"You are David Trent, Mr. Trent's grandson, I suppose," Ryker said. "Can you tell us what happened?"

"He must have fallen," David Trent answered. "I didn't see it. I was in the room across the hall waiting for Linda to come downstairs, when it happened. Right after the crash, I heard Linda's voice inside the room and I came in here on the run. I found him lying there on the floor at the foot of that little stepladder, with the grandfather clock on the floor beside him and books scattered all over the place. Just the way he is now. I didn't see anything that you didn't. I just saw it all a second or two sooner. I hadn't even felt for a pulse when you came in. He didn't look—as if it would be any use."

"No," Ryker agreed, "he's dead. But we'll have to call a doctor just the same."

The tension under which we had all been laboring was relaxed. Nilsson began to wander about the room in apparently idle curiosity, drawing back the black curtains and examining the enormous bay windows at the front and along the far side of the room. Jerningham was studying David Trent with undisguised interest. Ram Singh had withdrawn to the far end of the room and was impassively waiting for orders. Ryker picked up the telephone from Trent's desk.

"I'm calling from Cairnstone House on the Baltimore Pike," he informed the operator. "Can you tell me who is the nearest doctor? . . .Lampton? Will you call him, please? . . . Dr. Lampton? This is Mr. Ryker, calling from Cairnstone House on the pike. Mr. Trent has met with a fall, and we think he is dead. Can you come at once? . . . Thank you."

He set down the phone, and turned to the silent Hindu.

"Do you know anything about the accident, Ram Singh?"

"Nothing, sahib."

"Where were you when we rang the bell?"

"Lost in meditation, sahib."

"Did you hear Mr. Trent fall?"

"While descending the stairs I heard a crash—and afterward the noise of the strange sahibs entering in great haste."

As though reminded of something, Nilsson turned to David Trent.

"By the way," he said, "when the crash came, was the library door open or shut?"

"Shut and locked," young Trent answered.

"Then it was you who broke it open?"

"Yes. It gave on the second smash. I was in a hurry."

"Evidently," Nilsson said.

Young Trent stepped over to look at the door, Jerningham and I following him. It had not been locked with a key. There was indeed no key in the lock. But screwed to the door itself was an old-fashioned sliding bolt, shot to its full extent. And on the door casing were three screw holes in splintered wood, which showed where the socket had been.

"Where's the socket gone to?" David Trent asked.

"Over here," Nilsson said, pointing to where it lay on the carpet near the desk.

"Well, nobody's going to bolt that door again in a hurry," David Trent remarked, with a tinge of satisfaction.

"Nor the front door," Ryker told him. "It's stouter than this, but it didn't hold up long after we heard Linda. Of course we didn't know you were here——"

If the statement implied a question, young Trent ignored it. Ryker shrugged and turned again to the body on the floor.

"And the last thing in the world we expected to find was this," he finished, and knelt to straighten the sprawled limbs.

"Better leave him as he lies," Nilsson said, "till the doctor's seen him. He has to make out a death certificate, and he'll want to know just how it happened.

We can be surer of the facts if we study things exactly as they are."

"It's pretty plain," Ryker pointed out. "He must have toppled backward off that little ladder, and struck the back of his neck against the sharp edge of the desk. There's nothing else within reach he could have hit."

Nilsson was eyeing the loaded bookcases that lined the walls to the ceiling. On the top shelf, directly above the ladder, a number of books were missing.

"There's the reason he climbed the ladder," he supplied. "He wanted those books, took too many, lost his balance, and fell with 'em in his arms."

"In one arm," David Trent amended. "He must have had his left hand free to grab at the grandfather clock when he felt himself going. Sickening sensation—to snatch at something to save yourself and have it simply tip over on top of you!"

He raised the clock,—it was as tall as he was,—to an upright position, then gave it an experimental push, caught it as it toppled forward, and eased it down to the floor again.

"No stability," he commented. "Tips over at the merest touch. No wonder it didn't save him."

Jerningham was stooping above Trent's body, his fancy caught by the task of reconstruction.

"What do you suppose broke his glasses, Nilsson?" he inquired.

"Hard to tell. Probably got mixed up with the clock or the books in falling."

"The books?" Jerningham repeated, thoughtfully.

He stooped lower to read their titles without disturbing them.

" 'Manual of Astronomy,' 'The Human Body,' 'Principles of Rhetoric,' 'Elementary Physics,' 'Latin Grammar,' 'Advanced Algebra.'— Funny set of properties for a farewell appearance! They aren't the books I'd expect a man like Trent to break his neck over. College texts, every one, and out of date by twenty or thirty years. What did he want of an armful of antiquated textbooks, Nilsson?"

"Hanged if I know. There's a blank sheet of paper on his desk, and a fountain pen and a bottle of ink. He was going to write something. Must have wanted the books for reference."

"Not good enough," Jerningham demurred. "No one who's once passed his final exams is ever again seized by sudden thirst for the rudiments of astronomy, algebra, physiology, grammar, and physics, simultaneously. It doesn't make sense."

"Well, *he* didn't always make sense," young Trent said suddenly. "I think he was half crazy."

But Jerningham had straightened up, and was regarding the scene with frowning concentration.

"Which step of the ladder was he standing on?" he inquired slowly. "If it hasn't been dusted too recently, there may be tracks."

Nilsson bent close.

"No tracks," he said. "No dust at all."

"What about the edge of the desk, where his head hit?"

"No dust there, either."

Jerningham turned carelessly to Ram Singh, motionless and silent in the far corner of the room.

"Was Mr. Trent very particular about having his study kept dusted?" he asked.

Ram Singh shook his head.

"It was his custom to forbid all to enter," he answered calmly. "He did not desire disturbance of his papers and his possessions."

"I could have told you that, Jerningham," I said. "Everything in the place is thick with dust."

"Is it?" Jerningham inquired, and thrusting his hands in his pockets he began a leisurely circuit of the room. He cast one casual glance at the dusty library table, another at the dying embers on the hearth, another at the odd little arrows tacked to a piece of bark cloth upon the wall above the mantel. And presently he halted, there at the rear of the room, and bent to scrutinize the lock on the other door,—a closed door which obviously led into the hall.

"Here's another thing that's half crazy," he told young Trent as he straightened again, his hands still in his pockets and his head on one side. "With two doors—both leading to the hall—why did your grandfather bolt one door and not the other?"

Nilsson glanced up quickly, and opened his mouth to answer, but a peal of the doorbell interrupted him. Ram Singh moved silently to answer it, and in another moment Dr. Lampton entered the library.

He was a plump, gray-haired, little man, with cheeks like winter apples, and childlike blue eyes that seemed untouched by the experiences of his fifty years. He came in hurriedly with an air of genuine concern, but his first examination of Trent's body told him his errand was a useless one.

He looked up regretfully, as he knelt beside the body.

"I'm sorry," he said. "You were right. He is dead. It is very sad."

No one seemed able to produce an appropriate reply.

The little doctor tried again.

"Very sad indeed," he said. "A great loss to his family and friends."

Something had to be said. Jerningham stepped into the breach.

"You knew him?"

"Oh, no," returned the little doctor, "but I can sympathize with you who did."

There seemed to be nothing to say to that.

"Such an unexpected death," mused the little doctor. "Here in this quiet room, in the midst of his scholarly pursuits."

He picked up one of the scholarly volumes that lay beside the dead man. It was the "Advanced Algebra." He put it down with some haste.

"What would you say caused his death, doctor?" Jerningham asked deferentially.

The doctor looked faintly startled.

"Didn't you see it?" he asked.

"It happened just before we entered the house," Ryker explained.

"Oh, I see," said the doctor. "Why, it was undoubtedly the fall that killed him. You can see that he was on the ladder with an armful of books, and he must have struck the back of his neck against the desk as he fell. A tragic mischance! The back of the neck is such a fragile spot. Even a slight blow may dislocate a vertebra and prove fatal. His death must have been instantaneous. There would have been nothing I could do, even had I been here at the moment."

He rose to his feet, and with young Trent's help, lifted the body on to one of the cushioned window seats, and pulled together the heavy black curtains, hiding it from view.

"I shall attend to the death certificate, of course," he said. "Can I do anything else for you?"

"You might be of service to Mr. Trent's niece, Miss Marshall," Ryker suggested. "She's hardly more than a child, and this has been a shock——"

"A young girl in this house?" The little doctor stared. "I never knew that. She must be an extraordinarily stay-at-home young person. Poor child! What a difference this will make to her!"

"It will, indeed," said Ryker. "Ram Singh, will you inquire if Miss Marshall will see the doctor?"

But even as Ram Singh started for the door, Mrs. Ketchem appeared on the threshold, a bent old figure in rusty black, with gray witch locks straggling at the back of her skinny neck.

"She's asleep," she reported, in a croaking voice. "Dead to the world."

And off she hobbled without evincing the least curiosity as to her late employer's fate.

So the kindly little doctor went his way. When he was gone, Ryker turned to us warmly.

"I owe you chaps all the thanks in the world," he said. "Chivalry isn't dead. But I won't impose upon your time any further. My little Linda no longer needs a rescue. She's safer tonight than I dreamed she could be."

Jerningham shook his head, and something in his face made me catch my breath.

"I wish I thought so," he said gently. "But you see, this wasn't an accident tonight. It was murder."

4

THE OTHER
DOOR

"Murder?" David Trent cried, in sharp consternation.

"Murder?" Ryker echoed, incredulously.

"Murder?" said Nilsson, and his eyes narrowed.

He turned squarely to Jerningham and focussed all his attention on his friend's face, as if to read there more than could be said.

"I thought of that possibility when we first came in," he said slowly, "and I couldn't find a scrap of evidence to bear it out. Why do you call it murder, Jerningham?"

"Because as an accident it doesn't make sense."

"You don't think he fell?"

"I don't think he fell. I don't think he was on the ladder at all."

"Then how could he have struck the desk hard enough to break his neck?"

"He never struck the desk. He was murdered by a blow from behind, and the 'accident' was made up out of whole cloth to cover the deed."

"And the clock?"

"The murderer pushed it over," Jerningham said slowly, "to furnish the crash for the fall that never happened."

There was a dead silence in the room.

"That's a damned ingenious theory," Ryker said at last, reluctantly. "But I can't believe it."

"Neither can I, without proof," Nilsson agreed slowly. "Where's your proof, Jerningham?"

"There's proof in the titles of those books," Jerningham answered. "There's proof on the surfaces of the ladder and on the edge of the desk. There's proof in the dust on top of the grandfather's clock."

Nilsson stooped promptly to look at the top of the prostrate clock. "But there's nothing there," he said. "Nothing at all."

"Exactly," Jerningham agreed. "If a man caught at that clock to save himself from falling, he'd grab it by the molding on the top. He'd have to. And he'd leave fingermarks a quarter inch deep in the dust. There are no fingermarks. Therefore, nobody pulled the clock over in falling. Q.E.D."

"All right," agreed Nilsson, frowning. "What proof do you gather from the ladder and the desk? There's no dust on *them*."

"No. But there ought to be. In the whole room, the only surfaces that aren't dusty are the two vitally important ones, where marks in the dust would have proved—or disproved—Trent's accidental death."

"You aren't maintaining that the murderer dusted 'em are you?"

"I am. When he had the scene all set, he noticed the dust on the ladder. It didn't show the prints of Trent's carpet slippers. It showed the murderer's own footprints, made when he climbed up to get the books. So he had to dust the ladder. And then he had to dust the desk because it didn't show the marks of Trent's fall. But he never thought of the top of the clock!"

Jerningham finished on a note of such elation that Ryker laughed aloud.

"Jerningham," he said. "I take off my hat to your powers of invention. Malachi Trent was murdered, and the proof is that two pieces of furniture have been dusted and a third has not! No wonder your plays are ingenious."

Nilsson looked dubious.

"You certainly haven't got anything yet that would convince even a coroner's jury," he declared. "What's the point about the titles of the books?"

"Their irrelevance," Jerningham answered. "Trent couldn't possibly have chosen such a miscellaneous hodge-podge of school books for the sake of their contents."

"He might," Nilsson insisted, stubbornly.

"Well, then," Jerningham argued, "supposing he did, for some obscure purpose, want an algebra, an astronomy, a grammar, a physiology and a physics text, is there one chance in a million that he'd have found them all side by side on the same foot of shelf? No, they weren't chosen for content. They were chosen as properties,—part of a stage setting. And it was Trent's murderer,—not Trent himself,— who needed them for that."

"Trent may have wanted something that was hidden behind 'em," Nilsson contributed thoughtfully.

"That's shrewd," Jerningham applauded. "I admit I hadn't thought of that. Go ahead and verify it, Nilsson. If you find anything hidden there, you knock my theory flat."

I wasn't converted to Jerningham's theory, but I watched with breathless interest as Nilsson mounted the little stepladder and peered through the gap in the row of books. After one look, he began removing the books on either side, to get a wider view.

"What luck?" Jerningham demanded.

"None at all," the big man answered, with some disappointment. "There's nothing here. And he didn't take anything out, for the dust hasn't been disturbed. And he wasn't putting anything in, or we'd have found it lying on the floor beside him. So that idea's a dud. Go on with your fairy tale, Jerningham."

"All right,—if you admit there's no sense to Trent's taking those particular books. But suppose it was the murderer who took them down, after the crime. He had to take them from the top shelf, to explain why Trent climbed the ladder. He had to take a whole armful, to show why Trent lost his balance. And finally, he had to take them from the extreme left end of the shelves, within reach of the clock. So there you are."

"And that's all there is to your case?" Nilsson asked.

"For the present."

Nilsson shook his head, with mingled relief and disappointment.

"Indictment dismissed! It's too thin, old man. Two pieces of furniture dusted and one not, as Ryker says. And an argument that a man couldn't have taken certain books off his own shelves! I vote with Ryker,—it's a damned ingenious theory,—but that's all!"

"It's a theory that happens to be true," Jerningham insisted quietly. "Where I'm going to need ingenuity is in convincing you of the fact."

"Just a minute," David Trent interposed, with sudden anxiety. "Do I understand that you're actually serious in this?"

"Dead serious," Jerningham assured him.

"Then you haven't counted the cost."

Jerningham's eyebrows went up.

"What cost?"

"The cost to Linda," young Trent returned doggedly. "Ryker said you broke down the front door tonight to rescue her. Is that true?"

"Naturally," Jerningham assented.

"Then at least you knew she needed rescue. And you saw tonight how close she was to the ragged edge. She didn't half know what she was doing." His voice was rough with pity. "She can't stand anything more. She's got to have a chance to rest and play and lie in the sun,— and forget the very name of Malachi Trent."

"Granted," said Jerningham.

"And now that he's dead," said young Trent bitterly, "she'd have her chance—if it weren't for you."

"I don't quite get you," Jerningham answered slowly. "You don't believe—you can't believe—that the solution of the murder would implicate Linda?"

"Lord, no! There won't *be* any solution," young Trent retorted impatiently, "because there wasn't any murder. But the bare charge of murder will implicate everybody under this roof. It won't matter how abjectly you repent it later. You can't lay the suspicion for a murder till you make somebody the goat and convict him. You'll put Linda at the mercy of every yellow tabloid. You'll let her in for police investigation, grilling, perhaps even a courtroom experience. And then she'll *never* have a chance to forget. She'll be 'the girl in that Cairnstone House murder' as long as she lives. And you came here tonight to rescue her!"

He flung the words bitterly in Jerningham's face.

"I haven't forgotten that," Jerningham answered gently. "You think the best thing for Linda would be for us to clear out and leave the matter an accident?"

"By all means."

Jerningham stood for a moment, considering.

"I can't agree," he said at last. "There *has* been a murder here, even if I'm the only one who sees it. And there's been some horror hanging over Linda. Until we get to the bottom of those two mysteries, we can't judge what's best for Linda. I don't want to decide in the dark. I want to be sure."

"So do I, if it's possible," Ryker agreed heartily. "But young Trent here has the right idea about protecting Linda. We can't bring in the police."

"No, we can't," Jerningham admitted. "We're going to have to solve this thing ourselves."

"Then you're counting on my help," Nilsson chuckled, "in tracing a murder that wasn't committed to a murderer who doesn't exist?"

"I'm counting on your help," Jerningham assented. "And if you don't convince yourself, right here tonight, that this murder does exist outside my imagination, I'll chuck the whole business."

"That's fair enough," Ryker commented. "But why make Nilsson the judge?"

"Because," Jerningham answered, "he happens to be the crack man on the Philadelphia homicide squad."

"The homicide squad?" David Trent said slowly. "Then you *have* brought in the police."

Nilsson shook his head.

"I'm not here officially," he declared. "I'm not on duty at all. I'm on a shooting trip—until tomorrow morning."

He turned curiously to Jerningham.

"How is it that I'm to be convinced in spite of myself?" he asked. "I heard you predicting something of the sort."

"I want you to accept my theory for just one hour," Jerningham explained. "Assume you know positively that Trent was murdered, and devote the hour to finding out how and why. I'm willing to stand or fall by what you find."

"All right," Nilsson agreed. "I'll give you my best professional services. The first step is to chase the whole lot of you out of here before you muss up the evidence."

"Nothing doing!" Jerningham retorted. "I'm going to watch."

"Can't we all?" Ryker asked. "We're all concerned."

"Very well, but keep hands off! I'll start with Trent's body, and when I'm through you can take it up to his bedroom and then park yourselves on the window seats out of my way."

It was obvious that Nilsson was undertaking Jerningham's program in good faith. His face was grimly intent as he drew back the heavy draperies from the window seat where lay the body of Malachi Trent, removed the rest of the dead man's clothing, and bent to an exhaustive examination which put Dr. Lampton's efforts to shame.

"No marks of any injury," he reported at last, "except the one across the back of the neck. That was made by something pretty heavy, with a dull square edge. The skin's not broken except right over the dislocated vertebra. I don't find anything else but a slight cut high on the left cheek and a small black smudge beside it."

Jerningham moved over to look at the dead man's cheek.

"What do you make of those?" he asked.

"The cut is probably from his glasses when they broke," Nilsson replied. "The smudge could be ink,—or soot from the fireplace."

He touched the mark with an experimental finger.

"Perfectly dry—won't smear. Probably ink."

He turned his attention to the contents of the dead man's pockets. They seemed to be undisturbed. A billfold in a trouser pocket contained five or six hundred dollars.

"Assuming it's a crime, it's an amateur's work," Nilsson commented. "A professional would have taken that money—or most of it, anyway. . . . Well, I can't learn anything more from the body. Carry it upstairs to his bedroom. Next thing is to tackle the 'scene of the crime'."

When Ryker, David Trent and I returned from the trip upstairs with our gruesome burden, young Trent was mopping his brow.

"Whew!" he remarked, as we reentered the library. "It's hot as hell in here."

"So it is," Ryker agreed, and stepped over to look at the thermostat on the wall beside the door. "Trent always did like a tropical temperature. He's got the thermostat set for 76 degrees as usual, and an open fire besides. No wonder the thermometer's up to 80."

Nilsson paid no attention. He was on his knees beside the spot where the body had been found, studying the position of Trent's broken eyeglasses among the books on the floor. But Jerningham was interested.

"Did you say thermostat?" he asked. "What is the heater, an oil burner?"

"Yes. It just suited Trent to be able to control the house temperature without so much as stepping out of the room. The maximum of heat was his notion of comfort."

"With a minimum of fresh air, apparently," Jerningham added, struggling vainly to open a window. "He's got all his windows locked and battened down so tight I can't budge a one of 'em. Why anyone should choose to live in a hermetically sealed room——!"

"Jerningham," Nilsson interrupted with mild exasperation, "sit down on that window seat and keep your hands to yourself. If I hadn't already looked those windows over, I'd break your neck for tampering with 'em."

"I'll be good," Jerningham promised, subsiding on the window seat, and the rest of us followed his example.

Nilsson was still on the floor, picking up the eyeglass fragments with the utmost care and examining each against the light, hoping for fingerprints and finding none. When he had collected them all, he laid them on a magazine and brought them to me.

"Fit these together, will you, Mac," he requested, "and see if they're all there. You can thank your stars that the clock didn't have a glass face, or your job wouldn't be so easy."

It proved very easy. The right lens was unbroken, and the half dozen fragments of the other fitted readily into place.

"There's one piece missing from the center," I reported, and presented the reconstructed lens for inspection.

"Hm! Got to find that," he grunted, and began a minute search of floor and rugs. When that failed, he extended his hunt to include the desk top, the desk chair, the easy chairs, the davenport, the library table, the cushioned recesses of the window seats, and finally every surface in the room.

It took him a long time, for side by side with the search for the scrap of glass, he conducted a hunt for fresh fingerprints on every suitable surface. He met with no success whatever, and with each new disappointment his expression grew more dogged.

Only once did he volunteer a remark. That was when he halted before a stoutly built cabinet in the corner of the room nearest the front door, and inspected the black marble statuette that stood upon it.

"Well!" we heard him mutter. "I'll be eternally demoted!"

"Found it?" Jerningham demanded eagerly.

"No," Nilsson replied, his eyes upon the weird black carven figure. It was a naked dancer with four arms, a sword in one hand, and a necklace of human heads about her throat. "No, I've found something else. I don't know what you'd call it, though."

"Oh, that's Kali," Ryker answered casually. "I told you Trent brought her home from India."

But Ram Singh answered also, as though the other had not spoken.

"Kali the Eternal, Kali the Unapproachable, Kali the Destroyer," he said ceremonially, and I had a sudden impression that Ryker had spoken lightly of a terrible thing.

"Kali the Destroyer?" Nilsson repeated in an odd tone. "You may be right, at that. Jerningham, this statuette has been picked up, and set down again,—and dusted! What do you make of that?"

Jerningham was across the room in three strides.

"And the base has a dull square edge," he declared. "And the body makes a perfect handle. A very convenient weapon. Nilsson, you're beginning to be convinced!"

"I'd a lot rather find that confounded piece of glass," Nilsson grumbled, and took up the hunt again.

"What's the importance of the glass?" Ryker asked curiously, when a search of every square inch of the room had failed, and Nilsson was painstakingly ransacking the dressing gown and other garments of the dead man.

"Can't tell yet," Nilsson answered. "It all depends on where I find it. If it's in some spot it could naturally have reached when Trent broke this glasses falling, it won't prove a thing. If it's some place it *couldn't* have reached naturally, it'll mean a lot. It'll prove, not only that Trent didn't break his glasses in falling, but that somebody deliberately placed the fragments beside him to make it appear that he did. In other words, somebody was faking something. And that—" he glanced at Jerningham, "would pretty much prove your wild and melodramatic theory."

"It might also tell us where Trent actually was killed," Jerningham suggested. "Look in the desk drawers. He may have been sitting at his desk with a drawer slightly open when he was attacked."

Nilsson looked, but found no glass. The top drawer disclosed a jumble of pencils and paper clips and rubber bands, a jar of paste, a ball of green cord, a pair of scissors,—and a blued steel revolver, with all the chambers full.

"Didn't see his fate coming, did he?" Jerningham commented musingly.

Another drawer, full of papers, revealed three unopened letters addressed to Linda Marshall. At sight of them, young Trent swore viciously beneath his breath.

"No wonder she didn't answer," he finished. "The damned old skunk!"

"Recognize the letters?" Nilsson inquired.

"Ought to. I wrote 'em."

"When?"

"This last week on my way to Chicago and back."

Nilsson turned to Ram Singh, standing impassive by the door.

"Know anything about these letters?"

"No, sahib. It is forbidden that any save Trent Sahib shall touch the mail. He caused a letter slot to be put in that window, that all letters might come direct to his hands."

We looked where he pointed, and saw that the window which gave on to the front porch was indeed equipped with a letter slot in the lower rail of the sash. It was eloquent testimony to the completeness with which Linda had been cut off from the outside world.

But Jerningham did not seem greatly interested in the letters. His gaze returned to the objects on Trent's desk,—the telephone, the metal lamp, the metal ash tray, the big leather-mounted desk pad crisscrossed with recent blottings, the sheet of blank paper that lay upon it, the uncapped fountain pen, the tightly corked bottle of ink,—and I saw his face light with sudden exultation.

"Tell me, Mac," he said, in suppressed excitement, "was that ink bottle corked when we first came into the room?"

"I don't know," I said. "I didn't take time to look around till Linda went upstairs. It was corked then."

"And have any of you touched it since coming in?"

Nobody had.

"Eureka!" he exclaimed. "Nilsson, look in the ink bottle!"

Nilsson reached out a big hand for the bottle, twisted off the cork, poured out the ink into the capacious ash tray, and shook out on the blotter something inky and shining and angular,—the missing bit of glass. He turned to Jerningham with reluctant admiration.

"What the devil made you think of that?"

"The smudge of ink beside the cut on his cheek," Jerningham answered. "He was sitting over his desk, of course, with the ink bottle open before him. The murderer struck him from behind with the statue of Kali,—struck him hard enough to drive his face down upon the ink bottle and break his glasses. Naturally, when the murderer moved Trent's body and arranged it at the foot of the ladder, he placed the broken glasses beside it. And he never dreamed, as he corked the ink bottle, that he was sealing up inside it the perfect evidence of his crime."

"By George, that's neat!" Nilsson declared. "A servant might have a queer system of dusting, or a man might have a queer taste in books. But no little piece of glass is going to jump into an ink bottle and cork itself in!"

"Then you admit Trent was murdered?"

"Have to, I guess." Nilsson's voice grew very thoughtful. "Murdered at his desk, as he was getting ready to write something. . . . I wish we knew what he was going to write."

He gazed thoughtfully at the blank sheet of paper on the desk. Gradually his eyes narrowed.

"Look here!" he said. "He did write something. You can see the imprint across the top of this page. He must have taken out two sheets of paper, and the words he wrote printed through on the second sheet!"

He picked up the page and tipped it this way and that beneath the light.

"By jingo!" he cried, in mounting excitement. "*You can read it! This—is—my—last—will—I—devise—and—bequeath——*"

"Go on!" Jerningham cried impatiently. "What's next?"

"Nothing!" Nilsson said heavily. "The murderer came up behind and read it over his shoulder,—and killed him before he could write another word."

They looked at each other in blank disappointment.

"Well, we mustn't quarrel with our luck," Jerningham said with a sigh. "We've got the why of the murder, anyway. Somebody objected to Trent's making a will, and killed him, and destroyed the unfinished draft. The question now is—who?"

The atmosphere in the room was suddenly electric. We had been too busy proving the murder to speculate about the murderer. But now the echo of Jerningham's "Who?" seemed to fill the silent room.

Nilsson turned brusquely to David Trent.

"If your grandfather died without leaving a will," he demanded "who gets the estate?"

The young man flushed.

"I do," he answered, with some defiance.

"And after you, who's next in line?"

"Linda," he answered in a low voice. "We're the only relatives left alive."

"Ever hear of your grandfather's making a will?"

"No."

"Have you, Ryker?"

"No."

A thick silence took possession of the room.

"Suppose," Nilsson at last said pointedly to young Trent, "you tell us all you know about what happened in this house tonight."

The young man moistened his lips and answered slowly.

"I came here about twenty minutes to eight this evening. Mrs. Ketchem came to the door, and I told her I had to see Linda. Then I waited in the room across the hall for about ten minutes, watching the stairs and the door of the library, till Mrs. Ketchem came down again.

She said that Linda's door was locked and Linda wouldn't answer, but she had called through the door that I was here, and she thought Linda would be down presently. So I waited another ten minutes or so. Finally I heard a crash in the library and Linda's cry, and I broke open the door. My grandfather was lying dead on the floor—and Linda was staring at him. That's all I know."

Another silence. Then Jerningham took up the questions.

"How long did you say you waited across the hall?"

"About twenty minutes."

"Did you hear anything in the library?"

"No," David answered automatically. Then he added quickly. "The wind was making a lot of noise. I wouldn't have heard ordinary small sounds."

"Would you have heard two people talking?"

"I don't know."

Jerningham hesitated, then continued with an odd expression on his face.

"Did you see Linda enter the library while you were watching outside the door?"

"No, of course not," David answered indignantly, "Didn't she tell you she was asleep on the window seat?"

"She didn't say she was asleep," Jerningham corrected. "But never mind that. Did you see her enter?"

"No!"

"Couldn't she have entered while you were looking the other way?"

"Not a chance. I had a full view of the door, watching every minute!"

"Did anyone else enter or leave through that door?"

"Not a soul."

"Could your swear to that?"

David stiffened.

"Of course!" he said. "But there's the other door,—that you found unlocked,—that opens out of sight behind the stairs. A dozen people could have gone in and out the way, without my knowing."

He looked Jerningham squarely in the eyes.

"As a matter of fact," he added, "the murderer *must* have got out that way while I was breaking in."

"And if he didn't?" Jerningham demanded steadily.

His tone was so strange that young Trent stared.

"And if he didn't?" Jerningham repeated inexorably.

"If he hadn't," David Trent answered, "we'd have found him here."

"Exactly!" said Jerningham. "We did."

I felt a chill along my spine.

"What do you mean?" faltered David.

The color was draining from his face.

"I mean," Jerningham answered, "that nobody at all went out through the other door."

"Why not?" cried David sharply. "You said it wasn't locked!"

"It wasn't," said Jerningham. "But the door is nailed shut."

Something that was almost panic came into David's face.

"It—can't be!" he protested, desperately.

"It is," Nilsson affirmed. "I noticed it at the start. There's a molding nailed to the floor. See for yourself!"

Mechanically, David walked to the other door and tried it. He saw for himself. He turned accusingly to Jerningham.

"Then you lied when you said it was left unfastened!" he charged. "Why did you lie?"

"I didn't," Jerningham answered gravely. "I made the statement in good faith. Afterward when I saw the door was nailed, I did—purposely—hold my tongue."

"But why?" David demanded, hoarsely.

"To find out what you would tell us before you knew. Before you learned that the door you watched was the only door. Before you knew that the whole case would turn on what you said."

"And what did I say?" asked David, his voice unsteady.

"You said you could swear that nobody left the room."

"God forgive me!" said David, bitterly. "So I did."

PART
2

5
POSSIBILITIES

In the silence that followed David Trent's remorseful cry, my heart sank lower and lower. His testimony given in his ignorance that the other door was nailed shut, meant that Linda had been alone with Malachi Trent in the locked library when the murder occurred. Could that be true, or was David lying to save himself? His remorse read either way. And either way, it was a black business.

"In the light of the facts as you know them now," Jerningham said at last, "do you want to swear to a different story?"

The young man's face darkened with a painful flush.

"No, damn you! I took your word about the door, and you made a Judas of me with your questions. I retract all I said, and you can go to the devil!"

He stalked away from us, to stand staring out the black front windows.

"Judas?" Ryker said softly, with a deadly thrust in his voice. "Judas? You—you mean you betrayed—with a kiss?"

Young Trent whirled round, his face black with rage.

"It's none of your infernal meddling business what I mean!" he cried. "If you haven't enough respect for Linda——"

The two men glared at each other, sudden hatred in both faces.

"I have so much respect for Linda," Ryker interrupted with cold fury, "that I do not consider your story implicates her in the least. It merely shows you up as a liar and a coward, trying to shift your own crime on to a girl's shoulders."

Young Trent started in Ryker's direction with a vicious lunge. Nilsson stepped between.

"Hold on," he snapped. "We haven't time for a private scrap, even if you both are crazy about the same girl. She's in a bad jam. We've got to work this out as reasonable men."

"Reasonable hell!" David Trent retorted. "Call me a murderer, a liar, and a coward,—and then ask me to be reasonable!"

"I ask you to hold your horses and help us get at the truth. And not blow up at the suggestion that you committed the murder."

David Trent's face hardened.

"I don't know that I mind particularly being credited with the murder," he flung at us. "Whoever killed my grandfather did a public service!"

"I'm inclined to agree," Ryker said coldly. "The point of my remarks, however, concerned a liar and a coward."

Nilsson grunted his impatience.

"Better ease up on the personalities," he advised Ryker. "When he told his story, he didn't know that he was clearing himself at Linda's expense."

"He knows it now," insisted Ryker implacably.

There was a heavy silence. David Trent looked defiantly from one face to another, then turned his back upon us all.

"Imagine what you like," he said sullenly. "I don't give a damn."

"I'm not going to imagine," Nilsson took him up sternly. "I've got to know,—got to know a lot. For instance, what did Linda mean when she said, as she left the library, 'You didn't go'."

No answer.

"Where did she think you were going?"

No answer.

"When was the last time you saw her?"

No answer.

"You aren't making things any easier for yourself or for her by this sort of conduct, you know."

David Trent shrugged his shoulders.

"Nor for you," he commented shortly.

"All right," Nilsson said brusquely, and reached for the phone. "If you won't help us, the local authorities will."

David Trent came suddenly to life.

"Good Lord!" he cried anxiously. "You wouldn't turn this mess over to them!"

"I'll do just that—if you don't behave yourself," Nilsson promised grimly. "I'm putting my official neck in the noose by not reporting this at once. For Linda's sake I'm going to stop, look and listen first. But I won't stand for any hindrance. You'll promise to give me a free hand, stay within reach, and answer questions—or I'll call the District Attorney of the county—now."

"You win," young Trent admitted. "I'll promise whatever you like—but I don't answer any more questions tonight."

"You won't need to," Jerningham intervened. And then, with a hint of a quirk at one corner of his mouth, "But we'd appreciate an invitation to stay at Cairnstone House."

"Compulsory houseparty?" asked David Trent, almost cheerfully. "Very well. I think you're a bunch of damned meddlers. But as between you, or the local police and the newspapers,—better the devil I know than the devil I know not. Ram Singh, will you prepare rooms for these gentlemen?"

"No hurry. We're not ready to turn in for a while yet," Jerningham told the impassive Hindu, who was already moving to the door. "Better fix young Mr. Trent's room first. We're going to dispense with his assistance for the rest of the evening."

Young Trent hesitated visibly. Jerningham sent him a glance of shrewd kindness.

"I'd advise you to go," he said, in a mater-of-fact voice, "You need to figure out the answers to the questions we'll ask tomorrow."

"And how!" young Trent agreed fervently.

He followed Ram Singh through the door, then turned for a last word.

"I hope," he said with cordial venom, "you all climb out your windows in your sleep and break your damned necks."

When the two of them, new master and old servant, had disappeared up the stairs, we four "meddlers" drifted with one accord into the davenport and great chairs around the dead fire, and reach into our pockets for our characteristic smokes. Nilsson and Ryker brought out cigarettes, Jerningham and I, our pipes.

"Well, what do you make of it, Nilsson?" Jerningham demanded after the first puff.

The big man was unconscionably slow about answering, and Ryker's cigarette hung unnoticed between his lean brown fingers as he waited.

"I'm sure of only one thing," Nilsson answered at last. "Linda didn't do it."

Ryker began smoking again.

"What about young Trent?" Jerningham pursued.

"Well, he's either lying or telling the truth. If he's lying, I'm satisfied he's the murderer. If he's telling the truth, then there must be another way out of this room. And we'll have to find it."

"I hope there is," Jerningham mused, "but I doubt it—very—much."

"Thing to do is find out," Nilsson growled, and tossing his unfinished cigarette into the fireplace he tackled the job forthwith. The method, patience, and ingenuity which he brought to the task were amazing. When he finished his measurements and scrutiny of walls, ceiling and floor, Saint Thomas himself could have felt no further doubt.

"Well, that settles it," Nilsson said at last with decision, as he sank again into one of the big chairs. "There's no other exit. So young Trent's lying. He did it himself."

Jerningham seemed a bit troubled.

"If young Trent killed Trent—Confound it, there are too many Trents in this. Let's call the young one David and the old one Malachi.— If David killed Malachi, and his story is a lie,—then who broke in the library door?"

"David—before the murder," Nilsson answered, thinking aloud. "Malachi suspected something wrong and refused to open when David knocked, and David busted in."

Jerningham slouched lower in his corner of the davenport.

"That's no good," he disparaged. "Whoever killed Malachi came in peaceably without disturbing him—or else so softly Malachi never heard him at all."

"Where do you get that?" Nilsson demanded skeptically.

"It's obvious," Jerningham retorted. "The bit of glass in the ink bottle established that the old man was killed by a blow from behind while he was sitting at his desk, presumably leaning forward over the will he was writing. He wasn't in the least apprehensive, or he'd have dropped what he was doing and faced his visitor, revolver in hand if necessary. He certainly wouldn't have sat with his back turned so carelessly on a man who had just broken in his library door."

Nilsson looked slightly nettled.

"If the door wasn't broken in after the murder, as David says, or before the murder, as I say, when was it done?"

"It was faked," Jerningham declared. "Faked like everything else—to furnish the final proof that Malachi's death was an accident. The last thing David did, in setting his stage, was to yank that bolt-socket off the door casing. Then he pushed over the clock, and rushed for the hall, planning to be found by the rest of the household in the act of struggling with a bolted door, which would yield to his efforts just as the others came on the scene. Not so bad, either!"

"Then why didn't we find him in the hall outside the door?" Nilsson demanded.

"Something upset his plan," Jerningham answered. "I suppose it was the sudden appearance of Linda. Of course he hadn't known she was there at all. If she came to life before he got out of the room, he never had a chance to play his little door-breaking scene."

"Mm! Maybe, but that isn't the only hole in your theory!" Nilsson pointed out with friendly malice. "How could David break down the door from the inside? With nothing but a door knob to grab, and no chance to throw his weight against it?"

"That's easy enough," Jerningham countered. "It would only take a minute or two—and a penknife—to start the screws that held the socket, and turn them halfway out. Then he could yank the socket loose with one or two good jerks at the door. Anything else?"

"No, I guess not," Nilsson conceded reluctantly. "It's another one of those theories of yours! Just plausible enough to fit all the known facts, and defy contradiction,—though I'm convinced it's all wet!"

"I'll admit there's some basis for your feeling judgment this time," Jerningham said, his eyes following the smoke from his pipe. "There's one fearful hole which you haven't mentioned."

"That's honesty for you! Well, out with it!"

"Why did David arrange all this elaborate hocus-pocus about a bolted door, to establish that the room was locked tight,—and entirely neglect to lock the other door?"

"The other door was nailed shut," I put in.

"Yes, but David didn't know it. Whether his testimony tonight was true or false, he certainly gave it in the belief that the other door was unfastened. So—if he wanted to establish a locked room, why didn't he turn the key in the other door?"

Nilsson pondered the question, frowning.

"Give it up," he said at last.

"So do I," agreed Jerningham, gloomily. "And it knocks the theory galley west."

Ryker lit a fresh cigarette and leaned forward.

"I don't see that," he objected. "Why let one unexplained detail upset all your deductions?"

"Because it has a perfectly good explanation,—which points the wrong way," Jerningham answered, regretfully. "Here's the problem— one door locked, one door unlocked. What's the obvious conclusion? Why, that the person who locked the first door knew he needn't lock the other, because it was nailed shut. Which practically proves that the first door was locked by Malachi Trent."

"Or by someone else who lives in the house," Nilsson added reluctantly. "Linda, of course, knew it was nailed shut. But she's out of the question."

"I'm thankful you take that view," said Ryker earnestly. "Of course anyone who knows her, knows she'd be incapable of a thing like this. But I wasn't so sure you'd see it."

Jerningham's eyebrows went up with a hint of a frown between them.

"I'm not sure," he observed with extreme deliberation, "that I see it as clearly as the rest of you. Why is she incapable of a thing like this?"

Ryker stared at him, hunting for words.

"If the fact isn't self-evident," he said at last, "there's not much use trying to prove it. She simply isn't the sort——"

"You mean she hasn't the nerve?" Jerningham probed. "You said she was plucky and high-spirited before Malachi broke her."

"Of course she's plucky. But that's an entirely different quality from the sheer brutal nerve it would take to step up behind a man and murder him in cold blood. You're crazy!"

"No. Merely open-minded," Jerningham demurred. "In my business, I look at all of a character's possibilities before I throw any of them away. Seems to me Linda has more possibilities than you give her credit for. Do you think if she had a revolver in her hand and was being attacked by a brute, she'd be too ladylike to shoot?"

"No," Ryker returned in exasperation. "She'd be too sensible not to. And she'd shoot straight. But that's pure self-defense!"

"Granted. But how do you know this wasn't self-defense tonight?"

Ryker stared.

"Are you implying that an old man writing at a desk is comparable to a brute bent on assault?"

"He might be much more deadly," Jerningham said thoughtfully. "I don't pretend to know how. That's one of the things we've got to find out—exactly what sort of menace Malachi was to your little Linda. But you've said he was ruthless. You've said he was subtle. You've said he hated her. You've said that fear was driving her to the verge of insanity. How do you know what passed between them? How do you know she didn't find herself, in this room tonight, facing a crisis in which her only salvation was his death?"

"Another one of your plausible theories," Ryker muttered. "God forbid!"

"Amen. And help us to disprove it," Jerningham added, not irreverently. "That's one theory I'd like to smash to kindling, but I need some facts to do it."

"Well, here's one fact," Nilsson said, with an irritation that betrayed how deeply he was moved. "Take it quick, and knock your crazy theory on the head with it. Malachi was killed with an unfinished will on the desk before him, and the will has disappeared. There's only one reasonable deduction from that—a mercenary motive on the part of the murderer. And even your prolific imagination will have a hard time picturing Linda murdering anybody for his money!"

Jerningham stretched himself with a sigh of relief.

"Right you are," he said. "That's a consoling thought and I'll sleep the better for it. Lucky you discovered the ghost of the will!"

"Mighty lucky," Nilsson answered grimly. "And that will points directly at David Trent. Tomorrow, if you'll take charge here, I'll go back to headquarters and get my leave extended a bit. Then I'll get all the dope I can about our friend David. And after that—we make him answer questions."

"Sounds like a full day tomorrow," said Jerningham. "When do we turn in?"

"Now," Nilsson decided. "We've pulled this clever little case all apart. We'll pick up the pieces in the morning."

And we all assented, not knowing we were destined first to pick up some pieces in the night.

6
PIECES IN THE NIGHT

nilsson's resolution of adjournment adopted, I went out to the car to bring in our scanty baggage and our guns. When I returned, heavy laden, I found the others debating how to lock up the library for the night.

Jerningham was turning over the little pile of objects from the dead man's pockets.

"The key ought to be here," he said, picking up the keyring. "Yes, here's one that looks like it,—and fits like it."

He twisted it off the ring and dropped it carelessly in his own pocket. Ryker switched off the ceiling light.

"Suppose we leave the desk lamp burning," Jerningham suggested. "If there should be any disturbance in the night, we'd appreciate a little light down here."

"What sort of disturbance are you looking for?" Nilsson asked cheerfully. "Think Malachi's ghost is going to walk?"

"Not literally, perhaps," Jerningham responded with unexpected seriousness. "But Mark Antony said, over the body of Caesar, you remember, that the evil men do lives after them. Malachi planned a lot of evil before he died, and I'm inclined to think some of it is still hanging in the atmosphere of this house, very much alive."

"Just a trifle superstitious, eh?" remarked Nilsson.

"Call it that if you like," Jerningham answered. "Just the same I'm dubious about the likelihood of a long undisturbed night's sleep under this roof, with Malachi Trent's body in one bedroom and his murderer in another. It's not my notion of a peaceful setting."

"Well, then lean your shotgun by the head of your bed," Nilsson advised him. "You don't need to worry about any evil that's merely hanging in the air, and a gun will take care of any that walks into your room on two legs."

Jerningham shrugged his shoulders.

"All right," he said. "But in that case, we'd better not come strolling unannounced into each other's rooms in the dark."

"Naturally," Nilsson grunted. "That's a fool thing to do anywhere, any time,—let alone here. If you get any inspirations in the night, keep 'em to yourself till morning."

However, we left the desk lamp burning when we filed out of the library, and from the expression on Jerningham's face as he locked the door and returned the key carelessly to his pocket, I was not so sure he would take Nilsson's last advice to heart.

As we reached the head of the stairs I realized for the first time the general plan on which Cairnstone House was laid out. The wide hallways of the place were T-shaped, the stem of the T being the main entrance hall, while the arms of the T stretched right and left to the rooms in the wings. The main entrance hall, which was two stories high, was largely given over to a gracefully curving stairway, and all bedrooms on the second floor necessarily opened on the transverse hall. The stairway that led to the third floor was situated at the rear of the house.

There were eight bedrooms on the second floor, the four largest occupying the main portion of the house, the other four being situated in the wings. Ram Singh was waiting for us in the upper hall, and reported impassively that the four rooms in the wings had been prepared for our use. Of the two huge front bedrooms, the one over the library, he said, was Trent Sahib's, the other now belonged to young Trent Sahib.

We chose our rooms at random, Jerningham and Ryker taking each a room in the east wing, Nilsson and myself a room apiece in the west. A chance question brought the information that Linda's room was just behind Mrs. Ketchem's on the third floor of the east wing, and the Ram Singh's own room was over Nilsson's on the third floor west.

It was after one o'clock when we parted for the night, and I was tired, if not sleepy, so that I did not lie long awake. My sleep, however, was uneasy, shot through with more and more fantastic dreams until at last I found myself in hell. Not the conventionally lurid hell of fire and brimstone, but a far more dreadful place of intolerable darkness and smothering heat that turned my bones to water. To cap the horror, I heard going past me through the void, one whom I knew to be Malachi Trent, since he said with a cackling laugh that he had leave from the devil to go back to earth and finish a particularly choice bit of evil he had left half done.

The desperate, fruitless effort I made to stop him, woke me from the nightmare, but even lying wide-eyed in my bed I found myself not much better off than in my dreams. The darkness was as impenetrable, the heat as suffocating, the sense of boding evil as strong. I got out of bed. The windows were open, but the wind had fallen to nothing, and the air in the room was stifling. I groped my way to the door and opened it noiselessly. The atmosphere of the hall was even more oppressive. From somewhere in the house came a faint droning hum. I strained my ears for a long minute, and could hear nothing else, except—did I hear it, or imagine it?—the faint ghostly echo of the footsteps of Malachi Trent.

I am not proud of the folly which ensued. Only the sheer impossibility of remaining passively in my stifling room, drove me forth to meddle with the unknown. I groped about for my dressing gown and slippers, picked up the gun which Nilsson considered so efficacious against evil, and felt my way cautiously along the pitch dark hall past Malachi Trent's door,—was he or was he not still lying there where we had laid him?—till I came to the stairhead. There I stopped and failing to find the switch which should govern the lights, I stood and listened again, holding my breath while I strove to detect the slightest sound from the hall below.

This time I was rewarded. There was—no doubt about it—a not quite utterly silent hand, human or ghostly, turning the knob of the library door.

I had a choice of three evils. To go back—impossible! To wait on the top step through all eternity—unbearable! To go on groping in the dark—utter folly! I went on.

I suppose my heart continued to beat, I suppose I even drew a breath or two, during my stealthy decent of the long, curved stair-case,—but I have no recollection of either fact. What I do remember is that it seemed to me completely possible that the hand on the knob belonged to someone who could open the door without unlocking it—nay, worse, could pass through the door without opening it, and hence without allowing any blessed, comforting streak of light to shine out into the hall from the lamp on the desk inside the room.

By the time I got to the foot of the stairs I was praying wordlessly that I should find a flesh and blood hand upon the knob of that door.

I groped along the wall, found the door, reached for the knob.

I touched a hand. A strong hand—very much alive. The instant tensing of its grip upon the knob gave glorious reassurance that the fingers in my grasp were as much flesh and blood—and as much startled—as my own. But the owner of the fingers made no sound. Instead he sent a thrust of power along his arm, and the door swung suddenly, softly open. A streak of light knifed the darkness, widened, swept up his arm to his shoulder, to his face.

The man was Jerningham.

In another instant we were both inside the library. Jerningham shut the door with silent swiftness, and we stood staring at each other, each confronting an absurd replica of himself. Pajamas, dressing gowns, slippers, shotguns and rumpled hair, all corresponded. Only I know that my face wore no such expression as adorned Jerningham's. For while my feeling was one of pure relief,—something like that of a puppy who has unexpectedly discovered his master,—Jerningham had the look of a man at the utmost limit of exasperation. When he spoke, however, it was in the barest breath of a whisper.

"You unmitigated idiot!" he breathed, so softly I had almost to read his lips.

My spirits were rising.

"Idiot yourself!" I retorted in the same fashion. "What are you doing down here? I'd never have come down if I hadn't heard the doorknob creak."

"What would I naturally be doing?" he hissed. I knew he wanted to snort, but you can't snort satisfactorily in a whisper. "I came down to see what's given this thermostat lockjaw. It's kept the furnace going full blast with a forced draft for an hour. Don't you know when you're roasting in your bed?"

For the first time, the connection between that faint droning hum and the oppressive heat that had given me my nightmare, percolated through my thick head.

"Then go ahead and look at it," I returned, "and shut it off, or fix it, or whatever it needs."

He looked, and turned back to me with his lips pursed in a soundless whistle of amazement.

"The setting's been changed," he whispered rapidly. "Somebody's been in here and shoved the pointer over so as to give the highest possible temperature. Now why in the name of the incomprehensible did anyone want to do that?"

His brows twisted in a frown of concentration that looked odd beneath his wildly rumpled hair. Presently he shook his head in irritation.

"Can't make head or tail of it," he complained in a jerky whisper. "Think, Mac, think! What's the good of making the house into an oven? Think of any reason, no matter how wild!"

I did my best, but all I could suggest was a desire to set the house on fire and I had to admit there were many quicker ways of doing that. At last he threw up his hands in impatience.

"Well, suppose heating the house wasn't the point! Think me up a reason why anyone should want the thermostat shoved over—or the motor running all this time—or the oil flame burning——"

He broke off, smitten with sudden enlightenment. Then his face fell.

"Lord, how dumb I am!"

"Got the answer?" I demanded.

"Got it half an hour or so too late," he answered, in a whisper that was freighted with gloom. "Somebody wanted to burn something in Malachi's oil-burning furnace, and shoved the thermostat over to keep the blaze going. If only I'd thought of that at the start——"

"I don't see that it's too late," I argued. "Let's go down cellar and take a look anyway. We ought to find enough traces to give us a lead."

"You're right," he agreed instantly. "I'll go down and find out what was burned, and you'll stay here and find out who burned it."

That was more than I had bargained for.

"How the dickens will I do that?" I inquired, dubiously.

"Park yourself behind the curtains on one of those windowseats, and watch to see who sneaks in here and turns the thermostat back to normal. He'd probably have done it long ago if he hadn't found somebody prowling around. The minute he thinks the library is empty and the road clear, he'll come."

"He'll know it's not empty," I objected. "If he's watching, as you think, he'll have seen two people enter and only one leave."

Jerningham shook his head.

"Possibly. But I doubt if he knows there are two of us. From a little distance down the hall, he would merely have seen the flash of light from the opened door,—not our two separate figures as we came in. We came pretty fast. At any rate it's worth trying."

"All right," I yielded. "What do you want me to do if he comes? Challenge him?"

"No. Sit tight and keep your eyes open. After he's gone, wait twenty minutes or so before you come up to my room, and don't forget to use your own special knock on my door."

He handed me the key to the library.

"Lock the door after me as quietly as you can, and put the key in your pocket. Good luck!"

I locked the door behind him, and stepped up on the window seat opposite the door. The heavy black velour curtain had been pushed back, but not all the way, and there was plenty of room for me to stand or sit at the end of the window seat and still be sheltered from the sight of anyone entering the room.

I tried standing at first, but the upper layers of air in the room were stifling hot, and I was forced to sit. I had to keep an eye glued to a crack between the curtain and the wall, which soon became a wearisome business. I found I could ease the strain a bit by leaning my head against the wall. The air of the room was very hot—very close—very drowsy——

It was a slight click from the latch that warned me. I came out of my half doze with a start, and focussed eyes and ears upon that door which must in another instant open and give up the secret of the night prowler's identity. Would it be David—or the slender golden Linda—or Ram Singh, performing some last act in his dead master's service—or the old witch of a housekeeper upon some unhallowed business of her own——

Barely, faintly, I heard a key grate in the lock. First the latch—then the lock—surely now it would open—now—now——

It did not open. It did not open at all.

The seconds piled up upon each other—tantalizingly—dismayingly. An age-long minute went by—another minute. And as the absolute silence beat upon my ears I realized suddenly that the faint droning hum of the motor-driven fan in the basement was missing. The forced draft had been shut off. A sickening suspicion swept over me, drove me from my hiding place to look at the thermostat. It had been set back to seventy degrees. Which meant——

I had slept at my post. I had missed my chance. The prowler in the night had come—and gone!

Sick at heart over my inexcusable carelessness, I waited the twenty minutes Jerningham had recommended before I let myself out of the library and, feeling very like a puppy who had earned a spanking, made my way silently to his room. I dreaded to tell him, but the sooner it was over the better.

"Well?" he demanded eagerly, as he shut the door behind me. "Any luck?"

"I muffed it," I answered bitterly. "Had the solution right there and let it slip through my fingers."

He heard me out with grave attention, making no comment. At the end he gave me his most consoling grin.

"Cheer up," he advised. "You never know your luck. It may be all to the good that you missed him. Suppose he wasn't the murderer after all. Then seeing him would have sent us barking up the wrong tree. As it is, we go ahead with open minds."

"Too darn open, if you ask me," I grumbled, but was comforted none the less. "Did you draw a blank, too?"

The suppressed excitement in his eyes answered me.

"Thought I had, at first. There was a bare poker thrust across above the flames, and some burnt paper lying below the burner, on what was left of the old grates of the furnace. That looked to be all. But it occurred to me to explore the ash pit, beneath, and I found— this!"

"This" was the remains of a book, its pages gutted by the fire, its covers blackened and bent.

"Can you tell what it is?" I asked, beginning to share his excitement.

"A diary, a five year diary," he answered. "If only we could have had it intact! Apparently it was hung open across the poker so that the pages would burn, and they mostly did. There's nothing left that's legible except in the first three quarters of an inch nearest the binding. I suppose that would have burned too, in time, if the book hadn't fallen off the poker."

"But what good is three quarters of an inch?" I asked, puzzled. "That would barely give you the first syllable of each line."

"Hardly even that," he answered. "Malachi left a pretty wide margin. But here and there, when he had more to say than would go on the allotted five lines, he turned the book around and wrote in the margins, from the bottom to the top of the page. And those are the only sentences that survived the fire."

"Worse than the Sibylline Books!" I commented ruefully. "Do they make any sense without the context?"

"A couple of them do."

He handed me a sheet of paper on which he had copied perhaps a dozen sentences, with dates attached.

"These two," he said, pointing.

The first of the two was under a date two years back.

"Ram Singh is extraordinarily anxious to return with me. He may be very useful."

The second entry was only six months old.

"Have found at last the perfect way to dispose of L. Expensive, but I shall not be the one who pays."

There was something malignant in the very look of the words, even copied as they were in Jerningham's friendly scrawling hand.

"If that last makes sense," I asked uneasily, "what sense does it make? I suppose the 'L' refers to Linda."

"There's only one occasion, ordinarily," Jerningham suggested, "when a man can do something very expensive and leave it to some-one else to pay for."

"Meaning?"

"When he makes a will," Jerningham answered. "A will in which he does something fantastic with his property which robs the natural heir."

"But he wrote that he had found a way to 'dispose of Linda'," I objected. "No matter what sort of a will he made, it wouldn't 'dispose of Linda'."

Jerningham frowned.

"Wouldn't it?" he mused. "If we could see inside his head—If we could know what sort of a will he was going to write last night before he died——"

I looked at him curiously.

"You and Nilsson both attach a lot of importance to that will, but you don't seem to agree any too well."

"No," Jerningham admitted. "Nilsson thinks it proves Malachi was murdered for his money. My hunch is that the money was the least of it. If we knew what Malachi was going to write—and why—I'll wager we'd have the key to the whole business."

"Hard luck!" I said. "Because Malachi is taking that secret to his grave."

Jerningham nodded perplexedly.

"I suppose so. But I have a notion we're being very dense about that will. Overlooking something terribly obvious. Or forgetting some common, simple fact that would put the solution in our hands."

I recognized this frame of mind of Jerningham's, having seen it a hundred times.

"I know what's the matter with you," I said. "You think your subconscious mind does see the obvious thing you're missing, and does remember the simple fact you've forgotten, and is holding out on you."

"That's just it," he admitted. "And there's nothing more exasperating. To feel I've got the answer in my own head, right there for the taking—and not be able to take it!"

"Well," I said, with an involuntary yawn, "if the diagnosis is correct, here's the prescription. Treat the problem as you do the stubborn spots in your plays. Worry about it a while before you go to sleep, and then forget it—and the answer will pop up into your mind tomorrow morning over your cup of coffee. Just about the time you put in the second spoonful of sugar!"

Jerningham laughed.

"All right," he said. "Go on back to your room, and I'll try to get in both the worrying and the sleeping before dawn. If your prescription works—it will be an interesting cup of coffee."

7

TWO YEARS TOO LATE

As it turned out, Jerningham did not get his morning cup of coffee until after Nilsson had departed in search of whatever incriminating facts he could discover about David Trent. We all woke rather early, and half past six found everyone except David and Linda already downstairs. Mrs. Ketchem and Ram Singh seemed to be busy about breakfast. Ryker, Nilsson, Jerningham and I, avoiding the locked library by common consent, gathered in the billiard room, where some comfortable chairs offered the only informal lounging place in the whole great house.

Nilsson got down to business promptly.

"I'm going after David's scalp today," he said. "I'm convinced that he came here peaceably, found he was being cut off by Malachi's will, and killed the old man on the spur of the moment to keep from losing his inheritance. But that's almost too cold-blooded to credit unless there were some special circumstances to make him desperate."

He turned to Ryker.

"Know anything about him?" he inquired. "Where he lives and what he does? Or has he been living on his grandfather?"

"Far from it. He belongs to a small stockbroking partnership in Wall Street. Dolliver and Trent." Ryker smiled. "I deduce that you haven't been reading the financial page."

"Nope," Nilsson grunted. "That and the Social Register are two things I don't have to worry about."

"Well, it may have a bearing on your job this time, if special circumstances are what you want," Ryker said thoughtfully. "There have been some queer doings this last week, involving David and his grandfather and the corner in Galera Copper. Galera isn't a big company, you know, and Malachi pretty much controlled it. Last Wednesday David told his customers he had Malachi Trent's word for it that Galera Copper was in bad shape and would have to skip its next regular dividend. The news spread, of course, and while the other coppers were going up in the 'Hoover Market' there was a heavy raid on Galera, with a lot of short selling. Next day, Galera declared its regular dividend and a special extra dividend into the bargain. The stock began to skyrocket. All the shorts rushed to cover—and found there wasn't a share of Galera to be had. Nobody knew, for sure, who had cornered it. But it wasn't hard to guess."

He shrugged his shoulders.

"Most of the people who had sold short on David's information lost the shirts off their backs before they could settle up. Saturday noon it became definitely known that it was Malachi Trent who had cornered Galera, and David promptly found himself the best hated man in Wall Street. I suppose he and his partner made a lot of money out of the coup, but it was a short-sighted policy if they wanted to stay in the brokerage business."

Nilsson took a small notebook out of his pocket.

"Let me get this straight," he said. "David's firm is Dolliver and Trent. They fooled a lot of their customers into going short of Galera Copper. Malachi cornered Galera and squeezed the shorts. And David is in bad. That right?"

Ryker nodded. Nilsson frowned at his notes.

"Who were Malachi's brokers?" he asked. "He didn't deal through Dolliver and Trent?"

"No, they had no dealings so far as I know," Ryker answered. "Malachi never spoke of his grandson, that I remember, except to grumble about young cubs coming into money they hadn't earned. I had the impression he hadn't even seen David in years."

"What about that partnership? David's pretty young for that! Any chance that Malachi bought it for him to start him out in business?"

"No, I'm sure Malachi hasn't staked David to any capital," Ryker replied. "I think David inherited the partnership from somebody on his mother's side of the family. Dolliver probably inherited his half of it too. They're both very young."

Nilsson snapped his notebook shut.

"Thanks," he said briefly. "I think I'll run up to New York and have a talk with David's partner. He'll know more about what's happened than anyone else. I want all the facts I can get for ammunition the next time I tackle David. The only way to clear Linda entirely is to make him come clean."

"More power to you," Ryker said grimly. "Sorry I don't know more that would be of use."

"You've given me a good lead," Nilsson said. "I'll just have a word with Mrs. Ketchem and then I'll be off."

We sent for the old housekeeper, and she came from the kitchen, wiping her hands on her apron. Her old eyes were bright and crafty as she scanned our faces.

"Mrs. Ketchem," Nilsson asked, "how long have you worked for Malachi Trent?"

"Forty years," she answered, in the cracked voice that grated so unpleasantly on my ears.

"You've known all the Trents, then?"

"Known 'em all and all about 'em," she cackled. "Sweet lot, they are."

"What do you mean by that?"

"All possessed of devils," the cracked old voice informed us with obvious relish. "Some of 'em have the noisy, ramping kind of devil. Some of 'em have the sly kind. But they've all got 'em, every one."

"I don't want superstition," Nilsson told her brusquely. "I want facts. How long have you known David Trent?"

"Twenty-five years," she croaked. "Twenty-five years ago he was a squalling little brat in this house. A noisy devil he had, from the day of his birth. But he didn't stay here long. There never was three Trents could stay under one roof."

"You mean there was a quarrel?"

"Quarrel's no name for it. 'Twas a free for all fight! The old man stamping and storming and saying never to darken his door again.

And his son flinging his words back in his teeth. And David squalling as he always did. Heh! Heh!"

She cackled with horrid laughter at her memories of that far-off day.

"Did any of them ever come back?" Nilsson asked.

"Not they. I've seen Mr. Trent quarrel with every relative he had in the world, one after the other, and none of 'em ever came back. The Trents never forgive and they never forget and they never make up. I knew when I saw David Trent at the door a week ago there'd be trouble."

"A week ago? Monday?" Nilsson asked.

The old crone nodded.

"Monday he came, for the first time in twenty-five years. Mr. Trent wasn't here, and he said he'd wait half an hour. Then he saw Linda and stayed all the afternoon. Heh! Heh!"

"With Linda?" Ryker demanded.

"Who else?" the old crone countered, her bright eyes mocking him. "You think, because she gave you her promise that morning, she had no eyes for David Trent that afternoon? Ah, but the devil in that girl is a sly one!"

Ryker's face darkened.

"You keep your foul tongue off from her!" he ordered. "Miss Marshall is entitled to talk to whom she pleases."

"To whom she pleases! Aye, she pleased him well enough! Heh! Heh!"

"Hold on," Nilsson interrupted. "Is Monday the only time he came here?"

"No, he came again Tuesday," she said, with a malicious glance at Ryker. "Came early, and found Mr. Trent at home, and sorry he was to find him, too!"

"Did you learn what his business was with Mr. Trent?"

The old crone shrugged.

"How would I learn it? Listen at the door?"

Her bright eyes studied us wickedly.

"You must at least know whether they kept the peace."

She chuckled.

"For a quarter of an hour perhaps. Then the old devil found he had a young devil to deal with, and when he couldn't shout him down he drove him out of the house."

"Did he come again?"

"Saturday he was here for two or three minutes and talked with Linda in the hall. Ram Singh let him in, and didn't hear what they said—the fool!"

"What about Sunday?"

"He came about twenty minutes to eight, with a message for Linda and coaxing words for me. Said he had to see her. I told him her door was locked, but I had delivered the message. I didn't tell him her door was locked on the outside. Heh! Heh! He said he'd wait. A long enough wait he would have had!"

For a moment Nilsson was diverted from the subject of David.

"Locked on the outside?" he asked. "Then how do you account for our finding her in the library at eight o'clock?"

The bright old eyes regarded us aslant with malice.

"I'm not such a fool," she told us, "as to take upon me to account for her comings and goings—nor yet for her doings and undoings. I told you she had a familiar devil—a sly devil. Maybe he unlocks the doors for her. Maybe he teaches her the lies she tells. How should I know?"

It struck me as I watched her and listened to her malicious tongue, that if ever I had seen a human being possessed of a devil, it was this old woman herself. I began to discover a fellow feeling for Cotton Mather.

Nilsson's impatience was undisguised.

"Cut out the stuff about devils, and stick to facts," he said brusquely, and opened his notebook again. "Your facts are that David Trent hadn't been at Cairnstone House since he was a child, until last week. He was here all Monday afternoon, talking with Linda. He was here Tuesday morning, and quarreled with his grandfather. He was here Saturday for a few minutes—at what time? Two o'clock?—and saw Linda? He came last night at seven forty, gave you a message for Linda, and said he'd wait. That's all you know?"

"Oh, I could tell you plenty more about the Trents. There isn't a one of 'em you can trust——"

"Never mind," Nilsson interrupted, and snapped his notebook shut. "I'll check this stuff by questioning the gateman as I go."

She gave him a crooked smile, and vanished in the direction of the kitchen. Nilsson turned to Jerningham.

"I won't wait to see Linda. You talk to her when she comes down, and get her to tell you what she knows about David. It may fill in some of the gaps."

Jerningham sent his friend an odd glance.

"I'll try," he said. "But I don't think the important thing to get from Linda is her knowledge of David."

"What else?" Nilsson demanded.

"There are a dozen things I'd rather know," Jerningham answered. "How long she had been locked in her room—and why—and how she got out—and when? And what she was doing in the library when Malachi came back and surprised her. And what if anything she knows—or suspects—or has reason to fear—about his last will. And exactly how well she slept last night."

"What's that got to do with it?" Nilsson asked.

"If she thought Malachi's death was an accident, she ought to have slept like a log," Jerningham said, catching my eye. "If she knew he was murdered, I doubt if she had a very restful night."

"Well, I don't know what sort of a night you had," Nilsson rejoined pointedly, "but it doesn't seem to have cleared your brain. I suppose if you see circles under her eyes this morning, you'll call it evidence that she's a murderess. Try to keep your imagination in leash till I get back, old man, or you'll have us all sentenced to the chair."

He stopped on the threshold.

"Better prevent David from seeing Linda alone," he advised. "He might try to tamper with her story."

"I'll see to that," Ryker promised, rather grimly, and I knew that if David was to have a word alone with Linda, he would have to fight for it.

"And there's one thing more," Nilsson said. "What about the news-papers?"

"We'll have to send in Malachi's death notice at once," Jerningham said.

"Yes," Nilsson agreed. "And when they ask for details, we'll have to tell 'em something that'll hold 'em till we're ready to spring the truth."

"The whole truth," Jerningham amended. "And we're a long way from that ourselves."

"Are we? Well, give 'em a good story about accidental death, and hold the fort till I get back this afternoon."

He went, and Jerningham fell to drafting a statement on the back of an envelope. Before it was finished, we heard Linda's step descending the stairs. Ryker went to meet her, and brought her in to where we waited in the billiard room.

She was even lovelier in the cold gray light of morning than she had been the night before. She was wearing another gown that dated back fifty or sixty years, but its quaintness only added to her charm. Her hair was a warm gold, there was a delicate color in her face, and she acknowledged Ryker's introduction of us with a quiet grace and self-possession that would have done credit to a woman of twice her years.

Involuntarily I glanced at the faint circles beneath her eyes, but it would have taken a keener eye than mine to judge whether they were the result of a sleepless night or merely the sign of a long-continued strain.

"I hope you slept well after your difficult experience," Jerningham said warmly, as he took the hand she offered him.

"Quite well, thank you," she answered with composure.

But even as she spoke, her eyes were searching the room for someone who was not there. Jerningham caught the look.

"David has not come down yet," he said casually.

A bit more color came into her face.

"Mrs. Ketchem tells us," Jerningham went on before she could speak, "that after having been a complete stranger to this house for years, David has become a daily visitor!"

"On, no," Linda protested with gentle dignity. "There were a number of days when he didn't come."

"Wednesday to Friday?" Jerningham asked teasingly. "But no doubt he made up for lost time on Saturday?"

Her face was very still.

"No," she said quietly. "He only came on Saturday to say goodbye."

"Goodbye till Sunday?"

"Goodbye for five years," she answered soberly.

"Where was he going?"

"South America, he said. His boat was to sail from New York this morning."

"Then why did he come back here last night?"

"I don't know. I thought we were never going to see him any more."

"Then that was what you meant when you said to him last night, 'You didn't go!' "

"Why yes. What did you think I meant?"

She looked round at us, wonder dawning in her eyes.

"Why do you care what I meant?" she said.

"It makes a difference," Jerningham said gravely. "We need your help in discovering whether other people have been telling us the truth."

She stared at us, her eyes growing wider and wider. Her face went slowly white.

"The truth about what?" she asked at last.

"We have to have the truth about everything," he told her gently. "We know that Malachi Trent was murdered in his library last night. We don't know yet whose hand struck the blow."

"You know that he was murdered?" she repeated slowly. "When? How?"

"Some time between seven thirty or thereabouts, when Ryker talked to him on the phone, and eight o'clock, when we broke in the front door and found him dead. He was struck on the back of the neck with the statuette of Kali while he was sitting at his desk writing a will."

Her hand went involuntarily to her heart.

"How do you know he was writing a will?" she faltered, her voice barely audible. "Did you—did you—find it?"

"We found only the ghost of it," Jerningham answered. "The original has been destroyed—or taken away."

"The ghost of it?" she asked. "What do you mean?"

"The imprint of the words on a sheet of blank paper that remained on his desk."

"You could read it?" she asked, almost shivering. "How much could you read?"

"Only a couple of lines," Jerningham told her. "No farther than 'devise and bequeath'."

A wave of relief swept across her face.

"Did you know his intentions?" Jerningham asked slowly. "Could you tell us what he meant to write?"

"No—oh, *no!* How—how could I know?" She repressed a shiver. "How could anyone know what he meant to write?"

"The murderer knew, or thought he knew," Jerningham said.

She brushed a hand across her forehead.

"I don't understand," she said. "I saw him lying on the floor at the foot of the ladder. I thought he fell. I thought I heard him fall."

"We all thought we heard him fall," Ryker answered her gently. "We were meant to think so. Apparently what we heard was the crash of the grandfather clock, which the murderer pushed over. The whole thing was made to look like an accident."

"But then who—who was the murderer?" she asked, just above a whisper.

"We don't know," Ryker answered.

I saw his eyes meet Jerningham's, and saw the two men mutely agree that she should be spared knowledge of the story David had told.

"That's what we have to find out," Jerningham explained, "and that's why we want you to help us by answering a few questions."

She nodded slightly, her eyes fixed on his face.

"You were locked in your room yesterday?" he began.

"Yes."

"Since when?"

"Since Saturday afternoon."

"Did you know why?"

She hesitated for a second before answering.

"Yes. Mr. Trent was angry because I—because I had disobeyed him."

"You disobeyed him on Saturday?"

"Yes."

"In what way?"

The color came back to her cheeks as she hesitated, this time longer than before.

"I—I can't answer that."

"I beg your pardon," Jerningham said.

He paused, considering.

"Tell us how you got out of your locked room," he said.

"Through the window," she confessed, with a little shiver.

"Isn't your room on the third floor?"

"Yes, but there's a ledge under the third story window that runs all the way around the house. About six o'clock when everybody was at supper, I walked along the ledge to Mrs. Ketchem's windows and in through her room."

"And down to the library?"

She nodded.

"What was your errand in the library?"

Her hand went up to caress a bit of jeweled gold that hung from a slim black ribbon about her neck.

"I wanted my mother's locket," she answered slowly. "He snatched it away from me and flung it among the ashes in the corner of the fireplace when I—when he got so angry at me. I had to get it back. I knew it was risky, but I couldn't go without it."

"Go?" Jerningham caught at the word. "Were you going somewhere?"

She bit her lip.

"Yes," she admitted in a low voice. "I was running away."

"Very sensible of you, I think," Jerningham said. "Where were you running to?"

"Just away," she asserted. "I—I didn't know of any place to run."

"Haven't you ever been away from Cairnstone House since you came?" he inquired curiously.

Her face went white again.

"No—no!"

Jerningham regarded her with eyes grown suddenly intent.

"Not even when Mr. Trent went on his long trips?" he pursued with friendly interest. "Two years ago, for instance, when he was in India. What did he do with you then?"

It seemed to me that she could hardly shape the words with which she answered him.

"I was—right—here—all the time," she said.

"Alone with Mrs. Ketchem?"

"Yes."

"Pleasant," he commented. "I wonder you didn't run away then."

"I—couldn't" she said.

She faced his scrutiny for a moment, then went on, with a resolutely controlled voice.

"You can't run very far in your great-grandmother's clothes, you know," she said, her slender fingers flicking the ruffles of her voluminous skirt. "And I've never been allowed to have anything else."

She managed a pale smile.

"I suppose the theory was that their influence would make me as meek as my great-grandmother. But it never worked. I ran away over and over—as a child. Of course I was always caught and brought back. The last two years—I haven't tried it. What was the use?"

"Then last night," Jerningham said, "you thought your chances were better?"

"No," she said simply. "The chances were no better. My necessity was greater. That was all."

"Now we have come to the point," Jerningham said, gently. "Why was your necessity greater? We want very much to know."

She did not answer.

"We *must* know."

She shook her head.

"I'd rather die," she said, passionately, "than tell you that."

"We only want to help you," Jerningham said.

"Nobody can help me but myself," she answered. "I made up my mind to that—Saturday. I've been a coward too long."

She was looking him in the eyes, a half smile on her lips.

"I read the saying in some book," she said, "that every man carries his fate on a ribbon around his neck. Well—this is mine!"

She laid her treasured locket in his hand. He glanced at the jewels, turned it over and read aloud the inscription on the back.

> "He shall be master,
> Who scorns to be slave.
> The wine of disaster
> Strengthens the brave."

"A valiant creed," he said gravely, as he returned it. "But I should like to spare you the wine of disaster—if I could."

"You come too late," she said steadily. "Two years too late."

A croaking voice interrupted us.

"Your breakfast is waiting," said Mrs. Ketchem.

We looked around and saw her in the doorway. David was standing just behind her. How long they had been listening, I never knew.

8
JERNINGHAM'S CUP OF COFFEE

As Linda led the way down the long hall to the huge dining room, where breakfast was set for six in a room that would have held sixty, Jerningham and I loitered at the end of the procession. There was deep discouragement on his face.

"Was that my fault?" he asked under his breath.

"Was what your fault?"

"The way I bungled things with Linda. A more skillful man might have won her confidence and learned everything he wanted."

"Not on your life," I said. "She's made up her mind not to tell certain things. You got about five times as much as she meant to tell you—and twice as much as she thinks she told."

Jerningham shook his head.

"I got fragments of facts. She knows, or dreads, something about Malachi's will. But what? She was away from Cairnstone House during Malachi's trip to India. But where? She made Malachi furious on Saturday by standing up to him. But what about? And Malachi's weapon, whatever it was, is still a living menace to her. But how?"

"I wish we knew," I admitted.

"We've got to know," Jerningham fumed. "And that child could tell us—and won't."

"She has her reasons, of course," I said. "You can see it's a fearfully serious matter to her."

"A desperate matter," Jerningham agreed. "And she's done her efficient little best to keep us in the dark. For the moment I can't see a single step ahead.—And Nilsson thinks all he needs to do is to look up David. Sometimes I envy his singleness of mind!"

In that mood he took his place with the rest of us at the great table and ate the grapefruit which awaited him there. It was excellent grapefruit, but I knew that so far as Jerningham was concerned it might as well have been sawdust and vinegar. He had not the slightest notion what he was eating.

He sat staring across the table at Nilsson's empty chair while Ram Singh brought our eggs and toast and coffee. Mechanically he poured the cream into his cup and reached for the sugar. And then, with a heaping spoonful poised in mid-air, he stopped. His eyes lit with the incredulous delight of a man who sees his beaten team snatch victory from the jaws of defeat. I gave him a minute alone with his new idea, then jogged his elbow.

"Have some sugar, Jerningham," I suggested.

He dropped it in his cup and turned to me with an elated grin.

"Thanks, Mac," he said. "Thanks a heap. Your prescriptions are A, No.1."

The instant breakfast was over, Jerningham made for the locked library. On the threshold he paused and turned to me.

"There are some telephone calls to be made before we start anything," he said, reluctantly. "Ask David to come in here for a minute, will you, Mac? He'll have to call an undertaker and notify the newspapers. When he's through, come back and I'll show you what I got out of my cup of coffee."

I found David with Linda and Ryker in the long hall, and gave him Jerningham's message. He went grudgingly, obviously hating to leave the other two together. Remembering Nilsson's advice to Ryker, I foresaw that Linda was going to have two cavaliers in unshakable attendance all day, and I withdrew a bit to give her a chance for a word with Ryker if she wanted it.

She wanted it.—And that word struck so straight to the heart of the mystery that I found it impossible to shut my ears as I had honorably intended.

"Do you despise me," she said, "or can you forgive me what I did?"

"There's nothing to forgive," he answered gently. "You simply weren't yourself. But if it's any comfort to you to hear me say it—I shall never blame you for anything. Whatever you did, you had the right to do it."

Her voice shook.

"Oh," she cried, "you're so *good* to me! I don't deserve it."

"You mustn't talk like that," he said. "There can never be any question of deserving between you and me."

They drifted farther down the hall. Presently David reappeared, hurrying to rejoin them, and I went back to Jerningham in the library and told him what I had overheard.

"Remember it, Mac," he said. "Every word, as exactly as you can. It may mean more later than it does just now."

"All right. . . . But Jerningham, when David left the library a moment ago he had the statuette of Kali in his hand. What's the idea?"

"Oh, he asked for it," Jerningham returned absently. "Said he had promised it to Ram Singh."

He strode over and locked the door, then faced me with a triumphant grin.

"Now," he said, "prepare to grovel with me at the memory of how stupid we were last night. We had a fountain pen. We had a sheet of paper that showed Malachi had been exerting strong pressure as he wrote. We had an open ink bottle. And we missed the one obvious, inescapable conclusion!"

I regarded the obvious without enlightenment.

"As far as I'm concerned, we miss it still!" I confessed.

"Well, I'm not in a position to crow over you," he admitted. "But under what circumstances do you bear down hard on your fountain pen?"

"When it's going dry."

"And after you have struggled with it as long as your temper will stand, what do you do with it?"

"You fill it—from an ink bottle," I answered sheepishly. "I suppose the inference is that Malachi filled his pen and continued his writing, so that there was actually more to the will than the first two lines. Only, since he no longer had to bear down, the words no longer printed through and showed on the under sheet of paper."

"Go to the head, sir," Jerningham said with elation. "It only remains to look at Malachi's pen, and verify the guess."

He unscrewed the cap from the pen, drew from a desk drawer two sheets of thin paper, and proceeded to scrawl across the upper one the opening words of Malachi's last will, as Nilsson had read them to us the night before. He wrote rapidly, without pressure, and the words flowed wetly, inkily, from the point of the pen.

"You see!" he said with satisfaction. "When that pen is filled as it is now, you couldn't possibly bear down on it hard enough to print through the paper—without flooding the page with ink. So we know that he wrote the first two lines with his pen nearly empty, filled the pen, and wrote an unknown amount that didn't print through."

"That's interesting," I admitted, "but not very useful so long as we don't know the rest of what he wrote."

"The murderer knows the rest of it." Jerningham commented thoughtfully. "That might prove important. . . . And I rather think we're going to get it too. What does the general look of this page suggest to you?"

"That it needs a blotter," I said, and noticed for the first time the absence of any small blotter on the desk.

"And the look of this desk pad?" Jerningham pursued.

I looked. The pad was covered with a fairly new sheet of fawn colored blotting paper, crossed and recrossed by the traces of many a blotted line. I stood up and started for the door.

"Here! Where are you going?" Jerningham demanded.

"Going to get you the mirror from my shaving kit, so you can read that blotter," I rejoined. "No use losing any more time over it than we have already. We ought to have done it last night, of course."

"We were too clever to do it last night," Jerningham said ironically. "We deduced from that ghost will which Nilsson found, that we knew just how much Malachi had written and just at what point the murderer interrupted him. Anything so obvious as looking at his blotting pad was beneath our dignity."

He broke off to gaze at the marks on the pad, that looked so much like words and yet were so completely illegible in their simple disguise of hind-side-before.

"It's too soon to crow," he said more soberly. "We may find nothing there at all. The murderer may have interrupted Malachi before he had written enough to blot. Or the lines we want may be too mixed up with others to be legible. Go ahead and bring your mirror and we'll find out just how clever we are."

I started with alacrity.

"And oh, Mac," he added. "Don't let anybody see what you're bringing. There may be some advantage in our not having thought of this last night. If we had, David would have known all about it. And so would Ryker, and consequently so would Linda—if he thought the knowledge would do her any good. I haven't any illusions about Ryker's loyalty to us. He's going to do what he thinks best for Linda, without any regard for our plans or our judgment. He isn't a man who can take orders, the way you can."

He paused, with a quizzical glance at me as I stood with a hand on the knob, and laughed a little shamefacedly.

"Oh, go on and get your mirror!" he cried. "Can't you see I'm too keyed up to quit talking? If you wait for me to come to a full stop, you'll stand there all morning. Off with you!"

I made record time up to my room and back. But it was not my speed that made my heart pound as I turned the bit of glass over to Jerningham and stood back to await results. The mirror was small, and he could see reflected in it only a bit of the blotter at a time. He moved it back and forth, up and down, with maddening deliberation, and I could read nothing in his face except the completeness of his concentration on the task.

The suspense began to get on my nerves. It was preposterous that a mere sheet of blotting paper should hold—or withhold—the key to so much. If Jerningham found what he was looking for, we would know who stood to gain or lose by Malachi's death and the will's destruction. We might know how Malachi had proposed to "dispose of Linda." We might,—since mention of the will had waked such fear in Linda's face,—we might even learn the whole secret of the terror Malachi had utilized to break her spirit. Or we might learn that all the things we had imagined were moonshine, and there was nothing in the will except a straight-forward disinheritance of David in favor of Linda or somebody else. My endurance was at the snapping point when Jerningham reached for the sheet on which he had scrawled the first lines of Malachi's will, and began to add a word or two at a time. At last he leaned back with a sigh in which there was no relaxation.

"It's here," he said. "It's all here. And it's a lot worse even than I thought."

"What does it say?" I demanded.

He frowned into space for a tantalizing moment, then answered my question with another.

"Mac," he asked, "are you willing to tackle an awful job?"

"What sort of a job?"

"Will you stay on guard here for the rest of the day, and read over all the papers in Malachi's desk and *not* look to see what's on the blotter?"

"Not unless you give me a whale of a reason why!"

"The reason I want you to stay on guard is that I'll have to go and follow up this lead, and it may take all day. The reason I don't want you to look———"

He broke off to study my crestfallen countenance.

"You're too honest, Mac. Too open and above-board. You show too much in your face. If you know what Malachi wrote—At the crucial moment you'll play your cards too far from your vest, and we'll lose a trick. And we aren't going to have any tricks to spare."

"You talk as though you knew the adversary and could see how the game is coming out," I said.

He shook his head.

"I only know that the adversary will be desperate and the game will be close. Be a sport, Mac, and play it my way."

"You mean be dummy, and let you play the hand," I retorted. "All right. Don't blame me, though, if I make mistakes in my ignorance. What do you want me to do while you're gone, other than go through Malachi's papers?"

"Hang around the library here and see that nobody molests things. I'll leave you the key and you can lock the place when you aren't here, but that's not much use, for we know that the person who's most inter-est has some sort of duplicate or skeleton key. . . . And Mac, I don't know how long this expedition will take, but if Nilsson gets back first, don't let him do anything till I come."

I promised. But I had misgivings. And those misgivings deep-ened as I stood at the big bay window and watched Jerningham's tall, lean figure, in corduroys and high boots and leather jacket, stride off into the drizzling rain, climb into David's roadster where it stood parked a score of yards from the house, and drive off down the wind-ing road on an unknown errand beyond reach of recall. Nilsson gone, Jerningham gone, and Cairnstone House, with its murdered master, on my hands! I need not have worried. Cairnstone House stood silent in the rain, awaiting their return.

That was a strange day. I stayed in the library till noon, going though Malachi's papers, (which shed no light whatever upon his death,) and after that browsing with a divided mind among Malachi's innumerable books. They ranged all the way from the most ancient classics to the most recent detective fiction. But on all these shelves, there seemed to be nothing that could compete with the unfinished drama in the midst of which I moved, and I dipped restlessly into one volume after another. The one that held me longest was an old trea-tise on witchcraft, which caught my imagination, I suppose, because it was so easy to believe that Mrs. Ketchem had stepped out from between its pages.

Lunch threatened to be a silent meal. Ryker and David glowered at each other, and I judged that they had long since exhausted their resources of conversation. Neither could talk with any ease to Linda in the other's presence, and the girl's presence forbade the things that they would have liked to say to each other. I floundered a while for a topic that would avoid the events of the last twenty-four hours and yet not be too far removed from Linda's hopelessly narrow experience, and finally I mentioned Malachi's books.

The result was amazing. The child had devoured Malachi's library with the appetite of a born bookworm. She had bolted the bitter with the sweet, the suitable with the unsuitable. She had a keenly critical opinion of Schopenhauer, and a lively taste for S. S. Van Dine. She had an original and unorthodox set of judgments upon the great folk of history and fiction, depending mainly upon the quality of the courage with which they had faced the problems of their lives. She had the teachings of the Greek philosophers on the tip of her tongue. She was equally at home in Chaucer's fourteenth century England, Dumas' seventeenth century France, Kipling's India, Beach's Alaska, Hergesheimer's New England, and Anita Loos' New York. And she spoke of the things she knew and the thing she thought with childlike candor.

Long before the meal was over, however, I stopped regarding her as a child. I had prejudged her as childish and unsophisticated because she was four years short of voting age and had had none of the usual experience and contacts of a normal girlhood. But she had spent eight or ten years with no outlet for her eager young interests except Malachi's books, and everything they had to give her she had taken with both hands. A girl who judges Mlle. de Maupin and Madame Bovary on the basis of their courage rather than their virtue, a girl who has gone to school to Dumas and Kipling in the matter of intrigue and daring, may lack practical experience, but she is neither unsophisticated nor a child.

That afternoon in the library, I pondered my altered conception of Linda. By the time Nilsson and Jerningham returned, my interest in the girl surpassed my interest in the mystery, and my curiosity as to whether my friends had progressed in its solution was equaled by my curiosity as to what Linda would do if they had. I was not left long in doubt on either count.

It was beginning to be dusk, and I had lit the lamps in the library and half drawn the heavy black velour curtains, when Jerningham arrived. He was damp from the rain, troubled as to countenance, and strangely silent. In the fifteen minutes between his arrival and Nilsson's I learned nothing except that he had accomplished the object of his trip.

Nilsson, when he came, was a different man from the Nilsson who had gone away that morning. In place of corduroys and leather jacket, he had donned his usual "plain clothes" business suit,—and with it the very business-like manner that characterized his attitude toward his work on the Homicide Squad.

"Saw David's partner before the news of Malachi's death was in the papers, and got everything he knew." He reported. "Which puts us in the strongest available position for dealing with David. But it's none too strong."

He hesitated for a moment, frowning.

"In fact," he admitted, "if David were the type that can sit tight and say nothing, we'd stand mighty little show. Luckily he's red-headed. And we ought to be able to get his red-headed goat."

He set off to find his quarry, Jerningham and I following him down the long hall toward the billiard room. The click of balls informed us the two men had abandoned the pretense of conversation and were getting what satisfaction they could out of the only form of battle available. David, it proved, was being badly beaten. He hadn't the temperament for billiards. I doubt if any weapon short of a battle-axe would have suited his mood. Linda wasn't watching the game. She sat curled up on one of the great chairs at the far end of the room, staring out of the window at the dreary drizzle that was bringing the dusk too soon. As we entered, she rose quickly to her feet. It was a graceful, courteous gesture, but it held a suggestion of readiness for flight—or battle.

Nilsson addressed himself bluntly to David.

"I've been to New York," he said. "Talked with a number of people. Learned a lot. I'd like to see you in the library and hear what you have to say for yourself."

Linda's hand went to her throat and touched the locket hanging there, in the unconscious gesture I had grown to look for.

"May I come too?" she asked, in a low voice. "I've heard all about what happened last night, and I—want to know everything."

"I'd rather you didn't," Nilsson answered, his voice losing some of its brusqueness. "This business lies between us and David Trent."

She hesitated, then bent her head in acquiescence and slipped quietly from the room.

David walked over to the cue rack and replaced his cue with conspicuous deliberation.

"I don't know that I care to say anything for myself," he remarked.

"You're going to listen, at least," Nilsson said grimly. "Then, if you've nothing to say, we'll know what to assume."

"Well, I've no objection to listening," David declared, with exaggerated carelessness. "And if you consider it important to confront me with the scene of the crime——"

He shrugged his shoulders, and without looking to see if we followed, he strolled from the room and down the halls to the library, where he took his station on the hearth, his back to the fireplace. Whether by accident or design, he had chosen the spot farthest removed from the place where we had found Malachi Trent's body the night before.

Nilsson planted himself squarely in the middle of the room. I dropped into Malachi's desk chair. Jerningham paused for a moment outside the door, suggesting to Ryker with veiled authority that the latter should keep Linda company while we questioned David. Ryker acquiesced and went off to find her. Jerningham came in, locked the door behind him, and draped himself carelessly over one corner of the big desk.

"Well,—shoot," said David.

"Last Thursday," Nilsson began, in hard, even tones, "Malachi Trent cornered the stock of Galera Copper, caught a lot of people who were short of it, and made them pay through the nose for the shares they had to have to fulfil their contracts."

"Right," David said dryly.

"Last Wednesday," Nilsson continued methodically, "you started the false report that Galera Copper was going to skip its dividend. You deliberately persuaded your customers to sell short,—so they'd be caught next day."

"Wrong," David answered coolly.

"I heard it from a dozen different men," Nilsson assured him.

"All wrong," David repeated. "The report came from my office, and I've been held responsible. But I wasn't even in New York on Wednesday. My partner Dolliver was the man who started it. If you had talked with him, he'd have told you so."

"You mean," Nilsson answered, scornfully, "your partner obligingly did the dirty work."

"There wasn't any dirty work—on our part," David declared, rather less coolly. "Dolliver acted in absolute good faith. The tip came straight from Malachi Trent. And Dolliver was so sure it was good that he sold five thousand shares of Galera short in his name and mine!"

"Well! Well!" Nilsson exclaimed in mock sympathy. "What an expensive mistake! Five thousand shares short! Let's see—Malachi ran the price up fifty points before he would sell a share. Dolliver's little error must have cost the two of you a cool quarter million. . . . But of course Malachi took pity on your blundering and let you off easy!"

"Like hell he did! He held us up for the full quarter million— every cent we had in the world and then some!"

"Pity you didn't confide in Dolliver and wise him up that the tip was a fake!"

The last of David's coolness went up in blue smoke.

"Damn it! I tell you I didn't know a thing about it! I was in Chicago. I was called there Tuesday night, and I didn't get back till Thursday. The first I heard of it was when Dolliver confessed he had sold Galera short on a tip from my grandfather and the corner had wiped us out."

"The first you heard?" Nilsson repeated skeptically. "Is your partner in the habit of plunging on tips without at least calling you up?"

"He couldn't reach me. The telegram that called me to Chicago said not to tell even my partner where I was going."

"That's a new one," Nilsson commented, with relish. "Who wired you and what did he want?"

David flushed.

"A banker's name was signed to the telegram. When I got there, he denied having sent it."

"Really?" Nilsson mocked. "Then what?"

"I called him a liar and came back home."

"*You* called *him* a liar?" Nilsson marveled.

"Oh! Go jump in the lake!" David exploded. "If you can't recognize the plain truth when you hear it, and keep a civil tongue in your head,—you're a disgrace even to the Philadelphia police!"

Nilsson's face hardened, but he was not to be diverted.

"If you'll try stating the plain truth," he suggested, politely, "we'll see whether I can recognize it or not."

"All right!" David fired back. "The truth is that Malachi Trent sent that telegram himself, to get me out of the way. He gave Dolliver the false tip about Galera, knowing he'd act on it exactly as he did. And he engineered the whole corner in Galera on purpose to smash me and wreck my reputation in the Street."

"He did?" Nilsson said, more politely still. "And what, if I may ask, had you done to him?"

"Nothing!" David growled. "He sent for me last week and offered me a little squirt of a job in his employ. I told him I'd rather paddle my own canoe. He said he'd smash the canoe. I told him to go ahead and try."

Nilsson turned to us with sardonic amusement.

"Inspiring, isn't it?" he observed. "Noble young hero—clean hands—pure heart—lily-white conscience—and he tries to dodge off to South America like an absconding bank clerk!"

"That's a lie!" David snapped. "I wasn't dodging anything! I was taking my medicine. I didn't know, Friday, who it was that had cornered Galera. So I settled,—on the terms that were offered me. Paid over my last cent. Signed notes for the rest of it,—which put me over my ears in debt. And chose the quickest way of climbing out."

"Clearing out, you mean, don't you?" Nilsson suggested.

David glared.

"I signed up for a five year job in South America," he went on grimly. "One of those God-forsaken places with twice the salary and ten times the death rate you'd get in civilization. The death rate had just disposed of the last incumbent, and there wasn't any competition for his job. I told 'em I wanted it. And they asked me to sail at once."

"Oh, I see!" Nilsson cut in sarcastically. "That accounts for your presence here. Cairnstone House is on your way to South America!"

"Shut up, and I'll tell you," David said bitterly. "I came to say goodbye to Linda—for five years."

"But that was on Saturday. Sunday you came again—to say goodbye to the cat?"

"I came again Sunday because I'd learned the truth," David answered hoarsely. "The Saturday noon editions said it was Malachi Trent who had cornered Galera. Men who had trusted me cut me dead, believing I'd betrayed them into his hands. And when I realized it was he who had robbed me of everything I cared about—my business and my reputation and my girl——"

He stopped,—and in the silence that fell I could have sworn—I could have sworn in court that I heard a little sobbing breath somewhere in the empty space behind me, a quick little sudden breath drawn hard upon those words of his—"my girl!"

Nobody else heard it. The silence lengthened, and nobody moved. David standing silent on the hearth, his young face drawn with emotion. Nilsson towering immobile in the center of the room, watching, waiting, his eyes never leaving David's face. Jerningham moveless in his lazy perch upon the corner of the desk. I stole a look over my shoulder.

There was nothing behind me—nothing but the long window seat across the front of the room. The window seat with its half-drawn velour draperies, and behind them in the shadow something that might have been a fold of Linda's billowing, ruffled skirt. I hesitated, but only for a moment. If I spoke or moved now, I should destroy a crucial moment that might not come again.

I turned my back, and left the matter on the knees of the gods. If Linda really crouched there behind the curtains, she had heard a deal already. She should hear the rest.

Nilsson was speaking again.

"Your girl!" he said, scathingly. "You can talk about losing your business and your reputation, but lay off that 'girl' stuff. You're no lover! You're a—a—a——"

He groped for an epithet.

"A night-watchman! All you're good for is to sit and watch a door so you can prove nobody came out—so you can swear it was your girl who killed the man you hated—the man you were too cowardly to face yourself!"

David's eyes were blazing in his white face.

"No! Damn you! I came to have it out with him—and I did!"

"Shook your finger at him, eh?" Nilsson scoffed.

"I gave him his chance——" David cried.

"His chance to kick you out again?"

"His chance to clear my name—his chance to make good to the men who trusted my firm. He said he'd see me in hell first. He laughed, and started to write something on a sheet of paper. Said he'd keep me a beggar while he lived, and that paper would keep me a beggar when he died. He laughed in my face. I——"

"You made an after dinner speech to him!"

"No!" David said thickly. "I killed him with the first thing that came to hand!"

Nilsson resumed his usual courteous demeanor.

"You're more of a man than I thought," he said briefly. "I'm glad you owned up."

He turned to Jerningham and me with grave satisfaction.

"That lets Linda out," he said.

"Quite," Jerningham agreed. "There are just one or two points I'd like to verify."

"Ask what you like," David said quietly, the fury gone out of him.

"What was the idea of the broken lock on the door?"

"I didn't know that Linda was there, of course," David answered. "I thought that an accident in a locked room would never be questioned. So I pulled the socket off. I was going to pretend to break in the door."

"I see," Jerningham answered. "But in that case, why didn't you turn the key in the other door?"

If David hesitated, it was only for a second.

"I ought to have done it," he acknowledged. "I meant to. And then in my excitement I forgot. When I remembered it was too late."

He smiled at us, a rueful, curiously crooked smile.

"If I had locked that other door," he said, "you would still be hunting far and wide for your murderer. For then I'd never have made the mistake I did. I wouldn't have told you that tale about watching the library door and being sure nobody came out. And then you couldn't have narrowed suspicion down to Linda and me. And then you couldn't have goaded me into confessing. Oh, well!"

Jerningham nodded.

"So you simply forgot to lock it. Plausible enough!" he said. "You know it was just that one point that made me doubt your guilt last night. By the way, what did you do with the paper Malachi was writing?"

"Burned it in the fireplace."

"Did you read it first?"

"How much had he written when you—interrupted him?"

"Just a couple of lines."

"What did they say?"

"Said it was his will, and he bequeathed all his property. It didn't say to whom."

"How did you manage not to leave any finger prints?"

"I wore my gloves."

"And what did you use to dust with?"

"A handkerchief."

"Where is the handkerchief now?"

"I burned it in the fireplace too."

Jerningham reached into his pocket, brought out his beloved pipe, and filled it carefully. With his hand cupped about the bowl to light it, he spoke again.

"Did you ever consider abandoning Wall Street for Broadway? I think you would succeed."

David stared at him in silence.

"For one thing, you're a 'quick study'," Jerningham went on calmly, between puffs. "This was a brand new role, and you had only one night in which to get it letter perfect. A fine piece of work!"

"What are you talking about?" David demanded.

"Your very convincing impersonation of a murderer confessing his crime. For a man without any experience, it was quite the finest bit of acting I ever saw!"

There was a stunned silence in the room. Jerningham watched a smoke ring dissolve, and through the wreck of it his eyes met mine.

"So fine, indeed," he added, "That if my morning cup of coffee hadn't cleared my wits, I should never have known you were playing a part at all."

PART
3

9
JERNINGHAM
CROSS-EXAMINES

I t is evidence of Nilsson's essential bigness that in that moment, when the confession he had so skillfully wrung from David was challenged by Jerningham's cryptic disbelief, his reaction was pure astonishment, untinged by irritation.

"What's the trouble, Jerningham?" he demanded, eyeing his friend with a puzzled frown. "Are you crazy, or are you holding something out on me?"

"I'm not crazy—yet," Jerningham answered, "though I may be before we're through."

"Then what's this nonsense about a cup of coffee?"

"This morning at breakfast," Jerningham explained, "an idea jumped up out of my coffee cup and hit me. I've been following it around all day, and I know a bit more now that I did when you went away before breakfast this morning. At least I know enough to prove it wasn't David who killed Malachi."

"Prove it then," Nilsson took him up promptly. "Or rather, disprove what David has just confessed."

Jerningham looked quizzically across at the young man on the hearth.

"Disprove it, by all means," David challenged, "I must admit I'm interested in seeing you acquit me."

"All right," Jerningham agreed. "To begin with, the crime lies between you and Linda. Your own original story narrowed it to you two, as you pointed out just now. Also, if you knew of any fact which tended to clear yourself and Linda and incriminate a third party, you'd have trotted it out before now."

"You're darn shouting I would," David agreed, wryly.

"It's between you and Linda, then," Jerningham pursued. "Ryker and Nilsson to the contrary notwithstanding, I never thought you wanted to shove the blame on her. Your confession sufficiently disproves that. There remain, however, two possibilities. You may have killed Malachi. Or you may be lying to protect Linda."

"I've told you the truth," David declared earnestly.

"To some extent," Jerningham conceded. "But I know one part of your story to be a lie."

"Which part?" asked David instantly.

Jerningham shook his head.

"If I tell you that, you'll invent some plausible excuse, and we'll be exactly where we were before."

"You'll be exactly there anyway," David shrugged. "You can't get anywhere calling me a liar unless you point out the lie."

"Can't I? Suppose I challenge *you* to point it out—if you want the rest of your story to be believed?"

"I don't follow you," David said, but I thought he seemed a bit troubled. "If you contend I'm lying, it's up to you to prove it."

"By the rules of evidence, perhaps it is," Jerningham admitted, "but we're trying this case by rules of our own. What I propose is a very simple test for the truth. I know you made one statement that isn't so. If all the rest of your story is true, you can easily enough point out the single lie."

David said nothing. Nilsson's eyes were narrowing. "Sounds like a fair enough test," he commented. "Out with it, David, if you want us to believe your tale. What was the lie? . . . Or don't you know?"

David still stood silent, dismay written on his face.

"He doesn't know," Jerningham said. "His whole story of the murder is made up. He doesn't know even as much as we do about what really happened last night."

There was desperation on David's countenance, but his voice was steady.

"You can't bluff me out that way," he said. "I've told you what happened. I stand on that."

"Is that your last word?" Jerningham asked quietly. "You're going to let your whole confession fall if I can prove the one lie?"

"I am," said David. "You're bluffing and I call the bluff."

Jerningham turned inquiringly to Nilsson.

"Satisfied with the conditions of the test?"

"Yes," Nilsson answered slowly. "If he killed Malachi he would tell the straight story. If he hasn't told a straight story it's because he can't."

"Exactly," Jerningham agreed. "Well—he said Malachi wrote only a couple of lines of the will. We discovered this morning that he finished it, and we have the text of the whole."

Nilsson whistled. "How did you find out?"

"Tell you later," Jerningham promised. "But there's no doubt about it."

"Then I guess that's conclusive," Nilsson said. He looked curiously at David. "So you were putting your neck in the noose for Linda. And I played right into your hands,—tried to force a confession which you meant all along to make!"

David said nothing. He only bent his head and stared at the dead ashes on the hearth.

"Don't take it so hard," Jerningham said kindly. "It was a generous thing you tried to do, but not very wise. You'd have put Linda under an intolerable obligation if you'd succeeded. In fact, she never would have let you succeed. She couldn't have accepted such a sacrifice. It would simply have forced a confession from her."

"I'm not quite such a fool as you think," David said sullenly. "If you had just kept out, Linda would have believed me and Nilsson would have believed me, and that would have been the end of it."

"Linda would have believed you?" Jerningham asked sharply. "How could she?"

It was David's turn to be scornful.

"You saw her last night. You talked with her this morning. She's scared to death about something, but if you think she's got a guilty conscience, you're a worse blunderer than I am!"

"You think she didn't kill Malachi?" Jerningham demanded. "Then why were you confessing?"

David hesitated, then suddenly decided on candor.

"I think she doesn't *know* she killed Malachi," he declared. "Her memory is a blank from the time she lost consciousness there on the window seat, till she came to herself standing over Malachi's body. I don't know whether it was a brainstorm, or what. But she doesn't remember a thing about the murder or about camouflaging the murder. She has no reason to suspect herself. And she'll never know that anyone else has suspected her—if I can help it."

"How do you think you can help it?" Nilsson asked, with genuine interest.

David gave him a rueful grin.

"I've already tried what I thought was the surest method," he answered. "Lay awake half the night figuring out my story and trying to foresee every question you might ask. And then this fellow with his cup of coffee balls me all up!"

He looked ruefully from one to another of us,—far more like a school boy caught playing hookey, than like a man just prevented from sending himself to the chair.

"I suppose the next best bet," he said with a sigh, "is to convince you three of the obvious fact that Malachi deserved what he got. And that if you try to convict Linda of a murder she can't even remember, you're fighting on the devil's side."

"In other words, persuade us to go away and mind our own business?" Jerningham said quizzically. "That's a much neater solution. Pleasanter, too!"

"You'll save everybody a lot of trouble if you'll just use your heads," David urged. "Suppose she did kill him. It was too good for him! All she has to do is stand up and tell how she's been treated and say she doesn't remember what happened, and any jury in the country would acquit her on the first ballot. You know that as well as I do."

"Better," Nilsson amended dryly. (He has never forgiven the "great American jury" for the acquittal of Mrs. Rosier.) "They'd call it temporary insanity and let her go with their blessing. I've seen it happen often enough."

"Well, then," David was quick to press his advantage, "why not bow to the inevitable before it knocks you over the head? You know you couldn't convict her in a hundred years. You don't even want to convict her. What's the use of subjecting her to all the horrors of a lurid trial and all the burden of lifelong notoriety, just because she did a thing that any one of us would have done in her place?"

He had me converted, heart and soul. I was ready to thumb my nose at the laws of the Commonwealth, compound a felony, and swear that Malachi Trent had come to his death by accident while alone in a locked room. But Nilsson is made of less impressionable stuff.

"That sounds all right," he said slowly, "but it's not. We all know it's the fashion nowadays to disregard the laws that inconvenience you. 'Personal liberty,' and all that stuff! You're asking us to disregard a law that will inconvenience Linda. I can't do it. If she was justified in what she did, it can be proved in her defense, and the law will set her free."

He stood like a colossus in the center of the floor, towering above the rest of us, his great voice rumbling as he declared his allegiance to the law he served.

"You admit, yourself, that the law will set her free," he went on. "You're not afraid of a miscarriage of justice. You know that if there's any error it will be in her favor. But you don't want her to have to submit to the law."

He turned to Jerningham.

"You've heard me rail against juries for years," he said, "because I've seen them time and again setting aside the law out of maudlin sympathy for the accused. If I covered up the truth now, as David asks, I'd be guilty of exactly the same thing,—putting sentiment ahead of the law. I can't do it."

He had spoken thoughtfully, not like a man justifying himself, but rather as one who digs down among his deepest convictions, that his decision may be built upon the rock. At the end he turned to David, with a finality in his manner that was beyond question or argument.

"I'm sorry for you," he said. "And sorry for Linda. But if she killed Malachi Trent, she will have to stand trial."

David took it quietly, but there was a reckless light in his eyes.

"That's about what I expected from you," he said. "That's why I tried to convince you I did it myself. Well—you force me to use the only weapon I have left."

His voice had a finality that matched Nilsson's.

"Either you give me your word to let Linda alone, or else I go over your head and confess to the District Attorney—and the newspapers. That'll clinch it. The papers will have me all tried and convicted over night, and the District Attorney won't care to be far behind." He shrugged. "You see, the law can have a victim if you insist,—but it won't be Linda."

I could see Jerningham and Nilsson, each after his own fashion, calculating David's chances of success. He read their thoughts.

"Oh, I can get away with it," he assured them. "You won't be able to ring in your trick rules of evidence on me this time. The case will be out of your hands. And you haven't any official standing in this county. The District Attorney won't give much weight to the stuff you've suspected and guessed and deduced,—not when it conflicts with my sworn confession. And you haven't a scrap of evidence against Linda, except my original story, which I'll deny under oath. You'll only make yourselves ridiculous if you try to drag Linda into it. You couldn't even get her arrested!"

He paused, watching us keenly to judge the effect of that last challenge. Neither Nilsson nor Jerningham disputed the statement. It was entirely probable.

David grinned with a sort of wry triumph.

"You see, that's checkmate," he said. "Owing to my shocking disregard for the truth where Linda is concerned. . . . *Now* will you promise to leave her alone, or must I throw away my life and liberty, such as they are, to satisfy your fanatical reverence for the law?"

"Nilsson's face hardened. He is not a good man to drive.

"I'll make you no promises whatever," he said brusquely. "If you want to commit suicide, that's your own affair."

David's face grew set.

"All right," he said grimly. "It'll be my suicide, but it'll be at your door. I wish you pleasant dreams!"

Jerningham was drawing vainly at his pipe. It had gone out. He looked at it with mild surprise, lit it deliberately, and promptly forgot it again.

"Wait a minute, David," he said. "You called it checkmate. It isn't. It's stalemate—a drawn game—no good to anyone. Nilsson loses his case; you lose your life or your liberty; Linda loses her self-respect as soon as she finds out. And it's irrevocable. Once you've made that confession, the whole thing is out of our hands."

"That's the argument I used to you last night," David retorted, "when I tried to persuade you not to make a murder scandal out of Malachi's accident! I don't notice that it stopped you."

"Don't you?" Jerningham said. "We haven't made any scandal yet. We agreed to do nothing irrevocable until we had the truth. You ought to be willing to meet us halfway. Suppose you postpone your confession to the District Attorney for twenty-four hours, and we'll take no action against Linda in that time. Nilsson won't be court-martialed for a few hours' delay."

"Armistice, eh?" David asked impatiently. "What's the good of that?"

"Impossible to say in advance," Jerningham returned calmly. "But we haven't half got to the bottom of this business yet. By this time tomorrow we may all have changed our minds."

"Not I," Nilsson said bluntly.

"Nor I," said David.

"Am I the only open-minded man among you?" Jerningham mourned. "Even so, give me the twenty-four hours."

"Oh, have it your own way," David acquiesced. "If you agree to make no move against Linda in the meantime."

"We agree," Jerningham said.

"And you won't so much as drop a hint to her that she's under suspicion," David insisted.

"We won't," Jerningham agreed.

"Very well," David said. "Twenty-four hours truce. But tomorrow evening," he glanced at his watch, "tomorrow evening at six o'clock, if you haven't agreed to let Linda go scot free, I take my confession to the District Attorney."

"All right," Jerningham said. "Let's leave it at that, and talk of something else. Have you seen the paper today? Malachi's death isn't the only story on the first page."

He went and fetched an afternoon paper which he had left on the hall table. It carried the news that the Vestris was sinking and her people had taken to the boats. We talked of how long it would be before the nearest rescuers could reach them. Presently Ryker drifted in through the open door,—a freshly delivered paper under his arm.

"Where's Linda?" David demanded, seeing that Ryker had come alone.

"Couldn't find her," Ryker answered. "Pretty bad about the Vestris, isn't it, Jerningham?"

I scarcely heard him. Where was Linda, indeed? Recollection swept over me in a sickening wave. I had lightly decided that, if she was really in hiding behind the curtains, she might as well hear the remainder of David's confession. I realized now, too late, how much else she must have heard. Jerningham breaking down that confession,—David pleading that Linda be protected from the knowledge of what she had done—I groaned inwardly, and cursed myself for a thoughtless, blundering fool.

There was just one saving possibility. Linda might not have been behind the curtains after all. It was easy enough to find out. I had only to stroll over to the window seat and look. To save my life I couldn't do it!

Ram Singh's announcement that dinner was served put an end to my opportunity. The others filed out, Jerningham and I bringing up the rear. As he stopped to remove the key from the inside of the door, I took a sudden resolution. If Linda was there, she mustn't be locked in. I laid a hand on Jerningham's arm.

"Don't lock it," I begged beneath my breath.

"I wasn't going to," he murmured. "How did you know she was there?"

Relief flooded over me. The responsibility was not mine after all.

"I heard her," I said. "Was that how you knew?"

"No, I knew from the start she'd be there," he answered softly. "When Nilsson refused her permission and she walked out of the billiard-room, there was only the one thing for her to do."

We joined the others, as they stood waiting in the great hall outside the dining room. And presently Linda was there, pale and composed, and we all went in to dinner.

The talk ran still on peril at sea. Nilsson and Jerningham recalled nights on the transports in 1917. Ryker spoke of a hurricane he had seen in the Paumotus.

Linda did not talk. She sat at the head of the table, and attended graciously to our needs. And ate nothing at all.

10
THE WRATH
OF KALI

I do not remember whether it was Jerningham or Nilsson who first recalled the existence of the ruby. We had all repaired to the library after dinner,—all, that is, except Linda, who had slipped away upstairs. And a silence had fallen upon us, a silence which somebody broke with a sudden question.

"By the way, if Malachi still had that ruby,—what did you call it, the 'Wrath of Kali'?—where did he keep it? Safe deposit box?"

"No," Ryker answered reflectively. "I used to tell him he ought to, but he never would. Said a safe deposit box was all right for securities, but he wanted the Wrath of Kali where he could enjoy it."

"You don't mean he kept it here?" Nilsson protested.

"Right in the safe over there," Ryker motioned toward the bulky cabinet on which had stood the statuette of Kali. "When he wasn't carrying it around in his vest pocket!"

Jerningham got to his feet with lively interest.

"So that's a safe. I thought it was just a rather heavy cabinet. Let's have a look."

He opened the walnut doors and they revealed the very business-like front of a small steel safe, around which the cabinet had evidently been designed. It was quite ordinary, except that the dial bore letters instead of the more usual set of figures. Jerningham was greatly interested.

"I'd give a lot to see the inside of this thing," he said. "Does anybody have the combination?"

"I doubt it," Ryker replied. "His lawyer might, but more likely Malachi kept it to himself. He didn't even approve of writing it down."

"That's good sense," Nilsson grunted. "A man who can't carry a combination in his head shouldn't be entrusted with one."

Ryker nodded. "I suppose that's one reason he got this type of safe. You see, the combination is a four-letter word, or the first four letters of a longer word, instead of a string of figures. Much easier to remember. On this particular model, too, it's quite simple to change the combination, and Malachi used to keep switching around from one pass-word to another, trusting to his memory to supply him with the current word, whatever it happened to be."

"Then how are we going to get in?" Jerningham asked.

"We might telephone Malachi's lawyer," Ryker said dubiously. "But if he hasn't the combination, I expect we'll have to wait till morning and get an expert out to look at the safe, or listen to it, or whatever they do."

At Jerningham's insistence, David called up the residence of Malachi's lawyer and routed him out of a dinner party,—only to tell us that he knew nothing whatever about the combination.

"Ask him if he has a will in his keeping," Jerningham suggested.

David complied.

The tiny far away voice from the receiver crackled so distinctly that we all could hear.

"No, Mr. Trent," it said. "So far as my knowledge goes, your grand-father never made a will."

"It's no use trying to get an expert at this hour," David said, as he hung up the receiver. "Wonder if Ram Singh knows anything about it."

He called the Hindu, who listened impassively to David's explanation, and disclaimed all knowledge.

Last of all, he sent Ram Singh to summon Linda, and when she came, put the same question to her. She did not seem to find the inquiry strange.

"I'm afraid I don't know anything that would help," she said. "Except—I happened to be in the room here once when he was changing the combination, and I noticed that he glanced at the calendar first. You might get a lead from that."

Jerningham regarded her with extreme interest.

"What would you suggest?" he asked.

"Why," she answered diffidently, "I just wondered if perhaps he chose a day of the week or month for his combination. You could try all the days and see if any of them work. S-U-N-D and M-O-N-D and so forth. Or F-I-R-S and S-E-C-O and so on."

"Good girl," cried Jerningham, and was down on his knees before the safe in a twinkling to put her advice to the test.

For several minutes he spun the dial patiently this way and that, without result. I watched over his shoulder and the others, including Ram Singh, awaited with silent interest the outcome of his efforts. He used up the days of the week and started on the numerals. It was not till he came to E-I-G-H that the tumblers clicked into place and the safe door swung open in answer to his hand upon the knob.

There was a little sigh of relief from the waiting audience. But before Jerningham could more than glance inside, Nilsson caught his arm.

"Just a minute," he said. "Before you touch anything, I want to take a look. Hold the lamp for me, will you? With the light slanting, like that."

With practiced eyes he examined the interior of the safe for fingerprints. The only clear prints that he found were some old ones on the black japanned document boxes in the bottom of the safe, and a fresh one, that made him exclaim with satisfaction, on the outer face of one of the two small drawers the safe contained. The document boxes and the little drawer he removed from the safe with great care.

"Probably all these prints are Malachi's," he declared, "but just the same I want to verify them. All right, Jerningham, now you can go ahead."

But Jerningham was maddeningly slow to set down the lamp and proceed. I was more eager than I cared to admit for a sight of the great ruby, and I had been studying the contents of the safe with a speculative eye while Nilsson conducted his investigation. One object in particular whetted my interest.

"What did he keep the Wrath of Kali in?" I asked Ryker hopefully.

"A black velvet case," Ryker said. "I've seen it a number of times."

Exactly! The object that had caught my eye was a chunky little black plush case about four inches wide, wedged snugly into one of the pigeon holes. So when Nilsson gave permission and Jerningham was so slow to take advantage of it, I dropped to one knee before the safe and thrust my right hand into the pigeon hole to draw the treasure forth.

A stabbing, stinging pain in the heel of my hand halted me. Startled, I drew back, looked at my palm, stared in unbelief. An arrow head— a bamboo arrowhead—had half buried itself in the flesh at the base of my thumb.

I stood staring at it stupidly enough. But my sharp exclamation had brought the others crowding round me. And one glance at my hand was enough for Linda.

"Oh! *Oh!*" she cried, with a quick gasp of horror. "Pull it out— *quickly!* It's one of the poisoned arrows!"

And then, in a voice of urgent command,

"*Ram Singh!*"

My memory of what came next is blurred. Jerningham plucking the razor-sharp bit of bamboo from its deep bed in my palm. Linda gripping my wrist in a vise-like clasp that numbed my hand even before I had time to wonder at its strength. Ram Singh's white-robed figure looming beside me. The girl's impatient order.

"Hurry!"

The laconic answer.

"Hold fast, Miss Sahib."

The flash of steel in lean brown fingers. The searing pain of a knife slash across the width of my hand. Blood running across my palm and dripping between my fingers. Ram Singh's impassive voice.

"Let it bleed, sahib. And come quickly."

Jerningham's arm around me, guiding me down the long hall. And after that, the healing sting of cold water, gallons of it, floods of it, running from the tap into the wound and out again dyed with red, until the sight of the steady crimson stream made my head swim.

"It is enough," Ram Singh said at length, and his brown fingers closed around my wrist with a grip that stopped the bleeding as by magic. "Bandages now, and rest, and a doctor to make stitches,—and there will be no great evil to come of it."

"How did you know what to do?" I asked curiously, my head clearing.

"It is *bish*," he answered briefly. "*Singyia-bis* they call it in Hindustani. All the hill people of Assam use it, and there is no remedy but much washing—and much swiftness. In the forest, for a man alone, the end comes quickly. But there will be no great harm from this."

In that he spoke the truth. I felt a great weakness, some headache, and an odd trouble with my breath, but these things passed. And even at their worst, they were not so burdensome as to distract my fascinated attention from the procession of events.

Indeed, when Jerningham presently left me in Linda's hands to be bandaged while he telephoned Dr. Lampton, I was well enough to feel a childish pang of disappointment at the thought that he and the others would open the case and have their first glimpse of the Wrath of Kali in my absence. But though it was some minutes before I returned, a trifle unsteadily, to the library, I found the black velvet case still in the safe, untouched.

"We waited for you," Jerningham explained. "Seeing that you suffered the jab destined for the fellow who went after the case, we thought you'd earn the right to open it."

"We've been figuring out how it happened," Nilsson added. "Pleasant little device of Malachi's, wasn't it?"

He showed me the vicious little bamboo arrowhead, swallow-tailed in shape, grooved to hold the poison more generously, and so fitted to its shaft as to pull loose immediately upon striking and stay imbedded in the wound. The shaft itself had remained in the pigeon hole till they gingerly fished it out.

The trap that Malachi had set was simplicity itself. The pigeon hole ran back for twelve or fifteen inches, and the case that held the Wrath of Kali was shoved in just so far that none of it projected to afford a grip. Anyone removing it, therefore, had to do exactly as I had done,—stick his hand into the pigeonhole and hook his fingers behind the case to draw it out. The poisoned arrow, its shaft broken off to the proper length, had been braced against the back of the pigeon hole, and the case itself had served to hold up the point of the arrow in the most effective and deadly slant.

But I was more interested in Malachi's treasure than in the device he had used to guard it. Jerningham drew out the black velvet case and set it before me on the desk, and they all crowded around my chair while I fumbled awkwardly at the catch with my left hand. I mastered it at last and raised the lid.

The case was empty!

My reaction was pure disappointment. But Jerningham's face was alight with interest. So was Nilsson's.

"It looks," said Nilsson dryly, "as though there might be something to be learned from those finger prints after all. We'll stop right here and find out."

"Haven't the equipment for taking finger prints, have you?" Jerningham asked.

"Enough for this purpose," Nilsson said. "Ordinary thin tumblers will do. Bring us five, Ram Singh,—*clean* ones,—and a fresh towel, and tell Mrs. Ketchem we want her here."

It was just as Ram Singh was starting on this errand that Dr. Lampton arrived. The plump, gray-haired little doctor was as kindly and sympathetic over my injury as he had been over Malachi's death, but we did not entrust him with very much of the truth. We told him I had cut myself by accident on a poisoned arrow which had been sticking over the edge of the mantel shelf. And we described Ram Singh's emergency treatment, which he thoroughly approved.

"But I don't recommend poisoned arrows as household ornaments," he observed in mild censure, as he put the necessary stitches in my palm.

"I've always regarded them as dangerous," Ryker agreed. "Though I never expected anything exactly like this to happen!"

"I didn't mean to imply," Dr. Lampton added rather hastily, "that Mr. Trent was wilfully careless of his guests' safety——"

"Oh no, not in the least," Ryker concurred dryly.

"And if Mr. Trent had lived," Dr. Lampton observed, as he fastened the last of my bandages, "he would, no doubt, have seen to it that no one should leave any of the arrows lying where they could inflict such an injury."

"No doubt!" I agreed.

We heard in the hall outside a pleasantly convivial sound, the light chink of glass against glass, as Ram Singh appeared in the doorway with a tray. Dr. Lampton looked up expectantly. His mouth remained slightly open at the sight of the tray's contents. Five water glasses, polished and gleaming—and empty. Ram Singh set down the tray. None of us took any notice of the glasses. After a moment of puzzled silence, the little doctor rose to go. He was still friendly, but there was a cloud of bewilderment upon his open countenance.

As soon as he had gone, Nilsson took command. David, following his instructions, implanted a full set of finger and thumb prints on a freshly polished glass, which Nilsson marked by wedging flat in the bottom of it a folded sheet of paper bearing David's name. Linda, Ram Singh, and Mrs. Ketchem, in turn, contributed their finger prints and saw them similarly marked. At the end there was one glass left. Nilsson picked it up and left the room. He came back in a few moments, marked it, and set it with the others.

"Malachi's," he said briefly, and for no reason at all a chill went down my spine.

"Now comes the tedious part," Nilsson proceeded. "Mac, you'd better lie down over there on the davenport till we finish. You're looking a bit dragged out. Jerningham, you help me on this. You compare the thumb print on that drawer with each set of prints in turn, and I'll do the same for some of the prints on this document box. Then we'll verify each other's findings before we look at the names at all."

I followed Nilsson's advice and lay down, while the two men pored over their tasks, and the others waited in silence.

"Got it," Jerningham said at last.

"So have I," Nilsson answered. "Check me up."

They exchanged places, and each confirmed the other. I sat up and looked. Three of the glasses stood in a row, rejected. The fourth stood by the document box, the fifth by the little drawer from the safe. Nilsson drew out the sheet of paper from the fourth glass.

"The prints on the document box," he said, "were made my Malachi."

We waited, breathless. Nilsson drew out the paper from the fifth glass.

"And the print on the drawer—by Linda."

I looked at Linda She was standing very straight, a hectic spot of color in each cheek.

"Yes," she said, "you'll get the truth in the end. You might as well have it now."

She drew a long breath.

"I took the Wrath of Kali," she said. "And I killed Mr. Trent."

Silence. Then David's anguished voice.

"Don't say it! Don't say it! Oh, Linda, Linda!"

11
THE WINE OF DISASTER

She turned to David with an odd exultation.

"Oh, but I've got to say it," she cried. "I can't keep still any longer. I've got to—talk."

"But whatever you say," David protested wretchedly, "they'll use against you. Nilsson's from the Philadelphia police. He thinks it's his duty."

"I don't care," she answered recklessly.

I marveled at the change in her. She was no longer the pale, controlled girl we had known. The bright color burning in her cheeks, the quick impulsive movements of her hands, the restless energy that surged in her slight body, all spoke of resolution taken, of restraint discarded, of inhibition tossed to the winds. It was impossible to think that she had ever been afraid.

There flashed across my mind a fragment of the little verse from the locket that hung about her neck. "The wine of disaster strengthens the brave." She had drunk so desperately deep of that bitter cup, that she had drawn from it not only strength but a subtle intoxication. She had drained the dregs of disaster, and found in them a final release from fear.

I looked at Jerningham. There was sharp anxiety in the little frown between his brows. He glanced around the room, from one tense face to another.

"You shall talk all you like," he told her gently. "But there are too many of us here for you to talk to all at once. Will you say what you want to say, just to Nilsson and Mac and me?"

"Yes," she said, "you three."

Jerningham swept the others from the room. Ram Singh and Mrs. Ketchem went at once, Ryker under worried protest, David belligerently adjuring Linda not to talk. Jerningham shut the door decisively behind them. Then he put Linda into the most comfortable of the great chairs. Nilsson, following, took another. Jerningham, with a lazy grace, dropped down at my side into the depths of the davenport.

"Mind if we smoke?" he asked. "We can listen better."

She shook her head.

"You smoke, and I'll sit on my feet," she answered gravely. "We'll all be comfortable."

She curled up with her ruffled skirt billowing about her, leaned both elbows on one arm of the big chair, and watched Jerningham while he groped in my pocket for my pipe, filled and lit it for me, then duplicated the process with his own.

"Now!" he said.

She met his eyes with a searching gaze.

"I suppose you know," she said abruptly, "why I want to talk."

"I think so," he answered.

"I listened this afternoon," she went on, "behind the curtains in the library."

My heart warmed to her frankness. For all she knew, she needn't have told us that.

"And I can't let David confess to something I did myself."

"Quite right," Jerningham assented.

"So, I'd like to tell you all about it."

"We'd like to hear," he agreed, between puffs.

"And when I get through," she prophesied, "you'll ask me to prove my story by telling you what was in that will."

"Right," he said.

"So I propose to tell you now and have it over with."

Jerningham stopped smoking and leaned forward.

"He left all his property," she said slowly, "to a private hospital for the hopelessly insane, on condition——"

She drew a long shivering breath.

"On condition that they should keep me in custody for the rest of my life."

For a moment I did not grasp it. Then the sheer horror of the thing smote me.

"Wasn't that it?" she challenged, her voice unsteady. "Tell them!"

"That was it," Jerningham answered beneath his breath. "The gift was conditional upon their continuing to take care of you in the asylum."

I found the silence intolerable.

"But I don't understand," I cried. "An institution can't just reach out and take custody of a person! It's preposterous."

Linda shivered again.

"They can reach out and take *me*," she said, "anytime, anywhere. Because———"

She stopped for an instant, her eyes dark with some nameless memory.

"Because I've been there once before. I'm only out on 'leave of absence,' and the superintendent can order me back at any time. All they need—all they need is a motive,—and I'll spend the rest of my life between their walls."

"I can't believe it!" I cried, in futile protest against the unendurable.

"It's true, though," Jerningham said quietly. "I found that out too this afternoon."

"But why—why were you———" I couldn't say it.

"Why was I committed in the first place?" Linda asked bitterly. "Because he thought it would break me—and it did. I was fifteen, and I was there for six months while he was in India. I would have killed myself, but he had told them I had a suicidal mania, and they gave me no chance."

She fell silent, her eyes brooding.

"I hope there is a hell," she said, simply.

I sat still, trying to swallow the lump in my throat.

"When he came back," she said at last, "he got me paroled in his custody. He said that the first time I disobeyed him, he would send me back for good. For two years I've had to heel at his lightest word like a whipped dog."

Her eyes grew stormy, her voice passionate.

"You don't know—you can't imagine what that meant. When he discovered how abject I was, he amused himself inventing ways to torture me, thinking up things to make me do,—humiliating things, impossible things. Once he filled two suitcases with books and ordered me to carry the pair of them upstairs. I couldn't. I couldn't even lift them both at once. He said I was disobedient and he would send me back. I was sure he was simply looking for an excuse, and I tried till I dropped. If it hadn't been for Ram Singh—that would have been the end. He got me out of it somehow. I think he has saved me more than once."

"And you didn't run away?" I marveled.

"I told you I used to—as a child," she answered, and her face was suddenly wistful. "I used to do all sorts of valiant, foolish things. I knew from the start that he wanted to break my courage,—because my mother had flouted him, I suppose. And I was so afraid of being afraid that I had to keep proving I wasn't. Can you understand that?"

"I've been there myself," said Jerningham shortly. "Belleau Wood, 1918."

"Ah, but you could fight," she said. "And there wasn't anything real that I could do. Just useless little gestures of defiance. Like refusing to apologize when I wasn't in the wrong. And telling him the truth about himself, when he demanded what I was thinking. And running away,—when I hadn't a penny and didn't know a soul and my queer clothes marked me wherever I went. I was always caught inside the first five miles. And every time I tried it, it made things worse."

She looked up wonderingly.

"Wouldn't you think, since he hated me so, he'd have been glad to be rid of me? But it didn't work that way. I seemed to be one of his chief interests in life. When he was going to India, he tried to make me swear I wouldn't run away in his absence. I swore instead that I'd get free some day, if I died in the attempt. So he put me in the 'hospital'. 'Hospital!' " her voice shook on the word. "It was blasphemy to name it so!"

She shifted restlessly in the great chair.

"I never ran away after that. I never dared. I stayed, and obeyed him, and prayed for his death every night on my knees. Though sometimes I wondered whether even his death would set me free. He took an uncanny pleasure in talking about what would happen when he died, and the power a man could wield over other people's lives by the kind of will he left. He thought about it a lot. Once he asked me how I'd like to be his heir. I knew it was a trap, and didn't answer, and he laughed."

Jerningham's eyes narrowed.

"Did he say anything else about that?" he asked. "Can you remember? Give us the exact words if you can."

She gave us more than the words.

Her face drew into a gaunt grimace. And her voice, grown suddenly rusty, sneering, evil with malice, set the old man all too vividly before us.

" 'Overcome with gratitude, are you? You needn't be. There will be a condition—a very—clever—condition. You'll pay for all you get—for as long as you have it!' "

She shivered.

"That was all," she said. "He never explained, and I never knew whether he made such a will or not. But I used to lie awake at night and remember the way he laughed, and resolve that I'd never take a penny of his, no matter how innocent the conditions of his will might seem."

"How long ago was that?" Jerningham asked.

"Some time last spring—about six months ago."

She fell silent, as though the urge to talk had spent itself. Jerningham waited a few moments, then prompted her gently.

"Go on and tell us the rest of it. What happened last night?"

"It didn't start last night. It started Saturday afternoon. I—disobeyed him. He shut me in my room, and I thought the end had come. But later in the afternoon he told me Mr. Ryker had interceded for me, and I was to have two days to reconsider, under lock and key. I didn't sleep that night. I couldn't give in. And I couldn't go back to the 'hospital'. And I couldn't escape, except by walking the ledge to

Mrs. Ketchem's windows. That ledge is only three inches wide and there aren't any hand-holds—and every time I looked at it I went cold all over.

"So one of my days of grace dragged by. Then Sunday afternoon, just before supper, he came up to my room in his blackest mood. He wasn't going to wait any longer. Would I obey him or wouldn't I? I wouldn't. So he said he'd telephone the 'hospital' to send for me at once. And he would write a new will that would keep them from ever letting me out again."

"That settled it. The minute he was gone, I climbed out of the window and walked the ledge. And I made it, though by the time I crawled in Mrs. Ketchem's window I was limp as a kitten. I figured I had about half an hour to myself, before supper would be over. It wasn't just a question of getting out of the house. I had to have money, too, and the only hope of that was to open the safe. He usually kept gold pieces in there to pay Ram Singh."

She smiled a rueful little smile.

"You know what sort of job the safe was. I took a minute to fish my locket out of the ashes on the hearth, and then I tackled the dial. I had to work out the combination just as you did this evening, by trial and error, and it took a fatally long time. And when I got it open there wasn't any money there at all."

Her voice went flat with the memory of that disappointment.

"In desperation I took the Wrath of Kali,—and then I heard footsteps, and hid because there wasn't time to get away. There wasn't even time to take the revolver from the desk drawer, as I had planned."

Jerningham's fingers tightened about his pipe.

"So you had decided—then—to kill him if you had to?"

She shook her head.

"No, I had only decided that I wouldn't—be sent to that place—alive."

She fell silent again, brooding, and Jerningham had to rouse her.

"So you hid behind the curtains on the window seat at the side of the room?"

"Yes, and for a while I was scared, but he didn't seem to suspect anything so I settled down to wait till he should go away. And then——"

She stopped, with a little troubled frown.

"And then you fainted?" he asked.

"I don't know whether it was a faint," she answered, hesitantly. "I sat there for a long time, fighting to keep hold of my senses. One minute my head would be clear enough, and the next, things would begin to get blurred and I would be thinking solemnly about the wildest absurdities,—like the importance of exploding three toy balloons at exactly nine o'clock, especially the one named Lady Hamilton."

There was no humor in her voice. Instead I caught a note of appeal that puzzled me.

"I could wrench myself out of it," she went on, "but in another minute the blur would come again. Finally I failed to get out in time, and things went blank completely. I don't know whether that's fainting. Is it?"

Jerningham's reply was conspicuously matter-of-fact.

"Doesn't sound like it to me," he said. "I think you were fighting sleep—and lost. The same thing has happened to me when I've worked all night rewriting a scene for the next day's rehearsal."

A look of passionate relief flashed across her face.

"I suppose it might have been sleep," she admitted. "I hadn't slept at all the night before."

He was studying her intently.

"All right," he said. "You slept for a while, and woke. What happened when you woke?"

She forced herself to go on.

"I saw him standing over me," she said, dully, "laughing in that horrible silent way of his. I was still dazed. I couldn't think of anything to say or do. He said that I had come very opportunely, that he would like me to hear the will which he had just finished. He went back to his desk and read the will aloud, and showed me what it would mean. And still I couldn't think of anything to do."

Her hands, on the arm of the great chair, clenched themselves till the knuckles showed white. She drew a deep breath.

"Then he reached for the telephone book to call the 'hospital'.

And I hadn't any way to defend myself. I couldn't stand that. I started blindly for the door. And then I saw the little statue of Kali. I picked it up and held it upside down, and it balanced in my hand like a hammer."

The last vestige of color had left her face.

"Then I thought of something to do. I killed him."

Somehow that simple statement shook me to the bottom of my heart. We know the fact already, but to hear it so, from her lips, in that lifeless, colorless little voice——

"After that I thought of lots of things to do," she went on. "Almost as though somebody else were standing there telling me what to do next. I could see that the blow might just as well have been from a fall, so I arranged the fall. And I burned the will and dusted the things that I thought might betray me and burned the handkerchief I dusted them with. And then I tipped over the clock and stood back and screamed. And David broke down the door. Poor David!"

She fell silent, brooding, her head down-bent.

"Poor David," Jerningham agreed gently. "He wanted so much to spare you."

Her mouth softened.

"He was too kind," she said. "But it wouldn't have spared me anything to have somebody else suffer for my—crime."

"He thought you need never know it was yours," Jerningham reminded her. "He thought you couldn't remember—that the shock had wiped out your memory of it."

She looked up in startled dismay.

"But of course I remember."

"Of course," he assented. "Tell me about the Wrath of Kali. What did you do with it?"

"I took it along with me when Mr. Ryker sent me up to bed in Mrs. Ketchem's care."

"Where is it now?"

"Hidden," she said laconically. The color was coming back into her cheeks.

"You ought to bring it back at once, of course," he commented.

"She sat up a little straighter.

"I don't know," she said, calmly. "Whose ruby is it now?"

"David's unless we find a will."

"Then I'll let it stay hidden," she declared. "Ram Singh says it's accursed, that it brings evil to whoever holds it. After what David tried to do for me, I'm not going to turn any bad luck over to him, even if it's legally his."

Jerningham eyed her thoughtfully.

"Do you know," he said, "that sounds to me as though you couldn't remember what you did with it."

She caught her breath.

"Very well," she said quietly, after a moment. "I'll bring it down. But it really is accursed, even though you don't believe it, so I wish you wouldn't give it to David. Keep it yourself, if you must have it!"

She went swiftly and returned swiftly, and before we knew it she had dropped the stone that was worth a king's ransom casually into the palm of Jerningham's hand. It was a breath-taking thing, a huge stone that glowed and flamed as though it were itself a living source of light, glorious with the richest tints of the hearts' blood that had been spilled for its possession. But it moved in me no slightest impulse of covetousness. It was too incredibly beautiful, too priceless, too unholy. The wound in my hand throbbed with the memory and the premonition of evil.

"Put it back, Jerningham," I said, suddenly. "The thing *is* accursed. Put it away."

I could see in his grave face that he shared my feeling. He rose without a word, restored the Wrath of Kali to its empty case and the case in turn to its pigeon hole in the safe.

"I'll have to change this combination," he said. "Everybody in the house knows the old one now. Nilsson, come over here and give me the benefit of your professional experience with safes!"

The two men bent over the task together for a few minutes, examining, arguing, experimenting, till they could agree as to how the thing was done. From that point, Jerningham elected to proceed alone.

"Let me pick my new combination and set it up myself," he urged Nilsson. "I have an unreasonable desire to be the only one who knows how to get into this safe. And I shan't pick anything so simple as a day of the month, either."

Nilsson complied. Jerningham worked for a couple of minutes longer, then closed the safe, twiddled the dial and announced himself satisfied.

"By the way," he asked Linda, as he came back to his seat beside me on the davenport and relit his pipe for the third time, "when you took the Wrath of Kali out of the safe, did you see anything of any poisoned arrow?"

"There wasn't any," Linda said positively. "If there had been, it would have kept the case from sliding back in when I replaced it."

"Then Malachi must have put the arrow there while you were hiding on the window seat," Jerningham mused. "That was his only chance. Did you see him at the safe?"

"No, but most of the time I wasn't watching."

"Have you any theory as to why he did it at just that time?"

"Not unless I left the door of the safe ajar, so that it aroused his suspicions. But no! In that case, he'd have looked to see if the Wrath of Kali were still there. I give it up!"

Her tone had become completely natural. And Jerningham's manner had been so casual in the last interchange, that I too had relaxed, and I was utterly unprepared for his next move.

"Tell me," he said to her. "Do you happen to have a skeleton key?"

"A skeleton key?" she repeated, wonderingly. "No. Why?"

He puffed furiously at his pipe for a moment.

"I just wondered," he said at last, "whether that was the way you managed to open the locked door of the library."

She was still puzzled.

"The door of the library?" she said. "When do you mean?"

He put aside his pipe and leaned forward.

"Between two and three o'clock this morning," he said.

She made no answer. Slowly the blood drained from her face, leaving a deathly pallor. Her eyes widened with horror. She pressed the back of her hand against her mouth, as though to steady her lips.

I watched her, not understanding, but sick at heart. I thought she had told us all her tale, and dreadful as it was, pitiful as it was, it had been bearable because her courage made it so. But what now looked out of her eyes was stark terror.

"I didn't! I didn't! I didn't!" she whispered. "I never left my room."

"Then I must have been mistaken," he said quietly.

She drew an unsteady breath, and the fear gradually left her face.

"I'm sorry my question startled you," Jerningham apologized gravely.

She managed a smile.

"It's just that I'm jumpy," she said. "This hasn't been—exactly easy, but I had to go through with it."

She searched our faces.

"Before I leave you," she said, "will you tell me—what you're going to do?"

We both looked at Nilsson. He met her eyes squarely.

"I'm sorry," he said. "When I said, this afternoon, that you'd have to stand trial, I meant it. I can't go back on that. Only—you don't need to be afraid. With a history like yours, and the testimony you can truthfully give about your confused state just before the murder, any jury in the country would acquit you."

She had gone white again.

"Just what are you suggesting?" she asked steadily.

Nilsson flushed. It was a strange role for him.

"A plea of 'Not guilty'," he said bluntly, "with an insanity defense."

She came to her feet in one lovely flashing movement.

"Not in a thousand years," she told him, with a sort of fierce steadiness. "If I have to go to trial, there'll be no defense except provocation."

She checked his half-uttered protest with an imperious gesture.

"It lies in your hands," she said, straight-lipped, "whether I go to trial or not. But while you decide, remember this one thing."

Her voice rang with passionate resolve.

"I'll die in the chair for murder," she said, "before I'll plead insanity in defense."

She waited for an answer. There was no answer.

"Good night," she said.

And she was gone.

N ilsson took out a handkerchief and wiped his brow.

"Whew!" he signed. "I'm glad that's over."

Jerningham regarded him somberly.

"What makes you think it's over?" he inquired.

"What makes you think it isn't?" Nilsson retorted. "I never saw a more complete case. Motive enough to make a murderer out of a saint. And a full confession which fits all your independent deductions. What more do you want?"

"Nothing," Jerningham answered ruefully. "I'd be happier if I had a whole lot less."

"So would I," Nilsson admitted with some reluctance. "I don't like the idea of that child pleading guilty to first degree murder."

"So you recommended that she plead insanity," Jerningham mused. "Does that mean you think she's insane?"

"It does not," Nilsson snapped. "She's as sane as I am,—and a whole lot smarter."

"I know," Jerningham nodded. "It's a completely rational crime, and it came within an ace of fooling us all. In fact, it was so clever and reasonable that it might defeat the insanity plea on that very account."

"No danger," Nilsson said. "Folks are too used to hearing about the fiendish cunning of the insane."

For some reason the statement did not seem to add to Jerningham's peace of mind. Restlessly he got to his feet and began to pace the room. Finally he halted at one end of the davenport and eyed me thoughtfully.

"Mac," he said, "you're a solid, sensible sort of person. Are *you* satisfied?"

"With what?"

"Satisfied that we have the whole truth."

"Well," I answered, "she hasn't told us in what way she disobeyed Malachi on Saturday, but I don't know that that matters."

"Anything else?"

I hesitated to put my impression into words.

"One thing bothered me," I finally confessed. "When you spoke of her entering the library at three o'clock this morning she looked scared to death. And considering that she had just confessed murder, I didn't see what there was left for her to be afraid of."

"Anything else?"

"No."

Jerningham looked disappointed.

"You haven't hit the thing that worries me."

"What's that?" I asked curiously.

"Malachi's motive in placing the poisoned arrow," he answered. "I can't see why he took time off to do it, while he was so busy being angry at Linda."

"What difference does it make why he did it?" Nilsson inquired.

"Oh, I've just got a hunch," Jerningham replied, with one of his rare touches of irritation. "A hunch—and no chance of proving whether there's anything in it or not."

He eyed us despondently, then suddenly his face kindled with eagerness.

"Do you know, Mac," he cried, "there *is* a chance of proving it, if your old memory is on the job. Lean back and make yourself comfortable and shut your eyes, and don't open them till I tell you to."

In complete mystification, I obeyed. If I could serve Jerningham's purposes better blind, blind I would be as long as he liked.

"Now," he begged, "if you ever remembered anything for me, do it this time! When did you first look at those poisoned arrows over the fireplace?"

That was an easy one.

"Last night," I said. "Just before Dr. Lampton arrived to verify

Malachi's death. We were talking about the dust on things, and I gave the room a sort of general survey."

"So did I," he said, "and much good it does me in the present emergency. Think hard, Mac. It's desperately important. Tell me how many arrows there were last night!"

I called up before my mind's eye a picture of the chimney piece. A mantel of dark polished wood. Above it, hung on the wall like a tapestry, a large piece of bark cloth of crude native manufacture, its edges uneven and raggedy. And fastened invisibly to the cloth, the poisoned arrows. My heart sank. Try as I would, I couldn't recall the pattern which the arrows made.

"I don't know how many there were," I confessed with keen regret. "Not less than six or seven. Not more than nine or ten. I didn't count 'em and I don't remember the pattern definitely enough to count 'em from memory."

Silence. With eyes still closed, I waited for Jerningham to voice his disappointment.

"The pattern?" he said at last, and he sounded not half so disappointed as I had feared. "Was it a symmetrical pattern,—the same number of arrows on the right side as on the left?"

"Oh yes. Perfectly symmetrical. But what good does that do you?"

"Plenty," he answered elatedly. "Because it's not the number of arrows that matters. It's whether they're still all there, or whether one has been removed since last night."

"Removed?" Nilsson's big voice broke in. "Where to?"

"To the inside of the safe," Jerningham answered. "To the pigeon hole with the Wrath of Kali."

"What if it has?" Nilsson objected impatiently. "What do we care what Malachi did with his arrows?"

"We don't care a whoop," said Jerningham bluntly, "what Malachi did—*if Malachi did it!*"

"Huh!" grunted Nilsson, as though the exclamation were jolted out of him.

"So that's what you're after!" I cried. "If Malachi didn't, someone else did? And they must have done it since yesterday evening. And in that case there'd be an arrow missing from the pattern now."

"That's what I figured," Jerningham answered. "We know already that there was someone in here in the night."

"You do!" Nilsson grunted. "That's news to me! No wonder I couldn't make head or tail of your three-in-the-morning remark to Linda."

"That was only a shot in the dark," Jerningham admitted. "We don't know anything about the early morning prowler except that he took a diary of Malachi's and burned it in the furnace. And other people beside Linda may have wanted Malachi's diary burned."

"Jerningham," I interrupted in despair, "either come back to the point and tell me about those arrows, or let me open my eyes and look for myself. Is there an arrow missing or is there not?"

"Apparently not," he answered. "The pattern is still symmetrical,—four arrows on each side."

"Then Malachi did it," Nilsson declared, his voice betraying his satisfaction at having the simpler answer turn out to be the right one.

"I suppose he did," Jerningham agreed, "and yet—I'm afraid to believe it, against so strong a hunch."

I heard the quick intake of his breath.

"Mac," he said urgently, "look at that pattern in your memory again. What was in the middle? Anything at all?"

Suddenly what had been vague came sharply into focus.

"Why, yes!" I exclaimed. "There was one vertical arrow, projecting above all the rest. I remember thinking it stuck up like a lightning rod."

"Sure?" Jerningham demanded.

"Dead sure."

"Then that settles it," he said gravely. "Open your eyes and look."

I looked. There were the arrows, four on each side, but in the middle where the vertical arrow had been—nothing.

I glanced at Jerningham. He had jammed his hands into his coat pockets, and was frowning gloomily at the bare spot on the bark cloth, where the center arrow should have been.

"If you hadn't remembered that one thing, Mac," he said soberly, "that one little, little thing,—we'd have walked straight ahead into tragedy, unwarned."

"What do you mean?" Nilsson challenged. "We've had all the tragedy I care for already."

"No," Jerningham answered. "What we've had, or thought we had, is a story of cruelty and courage under cruelty, which ended with the killing of Malachi. We thought we had come in at the end of the last act. But now——"

He paused so long that I wondered if he had forgotten our existence.

"Now we know that the play's not over," he went on at last. "If Malachi had placed that arrow in the safe, it would have been nothing more than a medieval device to guard the Wrath of Kali. But since someone else placed it there, someone who doubtless knew that the Wrath of Kali was gone,—the act means murder."

I looked at my bandaged hand.

"Attempted murder," I corrected with a shiver.

"Attempted murder," Jerningham repeated after me, "and a warning of murder yet to come."

Nilsson shifted his position impatiently in the big chair.

"I don't get this at all," he declared with the irritation which a logical man always feels for an illogical state of facts. "I don't see why the play shouldn't be over, now that Malachi is dead. Why should there be any more murder? Why should anybody try to murder Mac, of all people? The whole arrow incident doesn't make sense."

"Of course it doesn't make sense," Jerningham agreed. "It's wildly inconsistent with the facts as we know them. There's some deadly element in the situation which we've missed entirely."

His frown grew deeper.

"The trouble is," he declared, "we came into this play in the wrong place. Not at the end, as we thought, when everything was over. Nor at the start, when we'd have had a chance to watch the action develop from its beginnings. But right spang in the middle of the second act!"

He sighed heavily.

"With a third act ahead of us," he finished. "A third act in which we'll have to play our parts without knowing the plot, or the ending, or anything except that there's murder yet to come."

"I don't know even that much," Nilsson growled.

"It's written on the wall," Jerningham said. "*Tekel upharsin*. Somebody in this house, some very clever and ingenious person, is trying to kill somebody else, and there's nothing to prevent. We don't know who. And we don't know why. But we do know he's so determined to do it that he was willing to risk killing any one of half a dozen other people who might reach into that pigeon hole instead of the intended victim. Which gives us a pleasant notion of the value he sets upon the lives of the rest of us."

"Well," I said, "at least I'm glad if that arrow wasn't intended for me personally."

Nilsson was reluctantly yielding to conviction.

"But see here," he said, "even if your reasoning about the arrow is all straight, that doesn't necessarily mean there'll be another attempt. This arrow stunt was the one chance in a lifetime to kill a man and have the blame for the deed rest upon the dead. Your would-be murderer won't find many more opportunities such as that."

"He's clever enough to make his own opportunities," Jerningham answered soberly. "The murder of Malachi looked so much like an accident that it nearly fooled us. The arrow in the safe looked so much like a protective device that it fooled us for a while. And the devil only knows what the next attempt will look like."

"Wait a minute," demanded Nilsson, now thoroughly troubled. "You're speaking as though the murder of Malachi and the arrow in the safe were the work of the same person. But it was Linda who killed Malachi. You can't possibly think that she put the poisoned arrow in the safe!"

"I don't know what to think," Jerningham answered.

"But you've just pointed out what an atrociously cold-blooded stunt it was," Nilsson argued, "risking half a dozen people's lives in the hope of getting a particular one. Is it reasonable that Linda could have done a thing like that?"

Jerningham was silent. Nilsson eyed him with growing consternation.

"You think she *could* have done it?" he asked at last.

Jerningham turned a harassed face to his friend.

"This is a horrible business," he said. "Do you really want to know what I think?"

"Of course," Nilsson answered shortly.

"All right. I think it very likely that she did."

"It isn't possible," Nilsson muttered.

"Oh yes, it is," Jerningham contradicted somberly. "There are two possibilities, each one worse than the other. The first is that she had some perfectly rational motive unknown to us, which she considered sufficient to justify such a deed."

Nilsson shook his head.

"That's out," he said. "There couldn't be a sufficient reason. What's the alternative?"

"That she had no reason at all."

"What do you mean?" asked Nilsson. "Everybody has some reason for what they do."

"Everybody," Jerningham assented briefly, "except the insane."

A deadly silence fell between the three of us. I fought back a rising impulse to cry out my protest, my dismay, my unbelief, at the thing Jerningham had voiced. Protest and dismay would not serve. What Jerningham believed could not be dismissed on the simple ground that my soul revolted against it.

Nilsson sat like a block of granite, pondering the matter with a grimness that showed how deep an impress Jerningham's words had made upon his unwilling mind.

"Are you taking seriously her commitment to that 'hospital'?" he asked at last.

"Not as evidence," Jerningham replied. "She *might* really have been sent there for treatment. But it's not a very reputable institution, and the probabilities are that Malachi put her there to break her, as she says. Most likely of all, she went there sane, and came away with her mental balance destroyed, whether Malachi knew it or not. A mind as keenly imaginative and sensitive as hers, won't stand more than about so much mishandling. Six months of despair, and the overwhelming power of suggestion in a place like that, might unhinge anybody's reason."

Nilsson's face was dark with pity.

"I know," he said. "I admit she's had plenty to drive her insane. But I shan't believe it till it's proved."

Jerningham dropped wearily into the depths of the davenport.

"I couldn't prove that she's insane, even if I wanted to," he said. "The thing that convinces me is that she thinks she is, herself."

The quiet words carried a dreadful conviction. Nilsson's face grew more and more overcast.

"She thinks she is?" he repeated, with reluctance in his voice. "How do you know what she thinks?"

"She betrayed it half a dozen times," Jerningham replied. "Why was she so desperately unwilling, in the beginning, to tell us what threat Malachi had been holding over her head? If she'd been sure of her own sanity, she needn't have cared whether we knew or not. Why should she fanatically refuse to take advantage of the insanity defense? Unless she feels that the stubborn assertion of her sanity is her last barrier against despair. Why was she so pitifully relieved when I told her it was sleepiness that had blurred her senses and filled her mind with absurdities about toy balloons? Unless her own thoughts had given her an ominous interpretation of the same facts."

He paused, reflecting.

"And why," he went on more slowly," was she dismayed when I quoted David's belief that she couldn't remember killing Malachi? She turned quite white. Why should that theory distress her unless it struck home to the truth?"

"Just a minute," Nilsson interposed. "Are you contending that David was right? That she really doesn't remember? That she made up her story of the murder?"

Jerningham shook his head.

"I think most of her story is absolutely true," he answered. "But I do believe there's a gap in her memory as to some part of it, and that she filled in the gap by a guess as to what she must have done."

He lapsed into frowning meditation, which I reluctantly interrupted.

"She really is subject to lapses of memory," I said. "That is, if one can believe anything Mrs. Ketchem says. The old witch came in to dust the library while I was alone here this afternoon, and made my refusal to let her do it the occasion for half an hour's malicious gossip. Most of what she said I didn't credit, but she did mention having heard Malachi order Linda to carry a couple of heavy suitcases up the stairs, which Linda failed to do."

"That checks with the incident Linda spoke of," Nilsson remarked approvingly.

"Yes, but Mrs. Ketchem went on to say that a few minutes afterwards she saw Linda carry those two suitcases up the stairs as straight and steady as you please, except that she looked a little queer,—'blank in the face,' Mrs. Ketchem put it. She didn't answer when Mrs. Ketchem spoke to her, and later, on being questioned as to how she managed to carry the suitcases after her original failure, she flatly denied having carried them at all. Mrs. Ketchem told the tale as proving Linda's deceitfulness. But it looks to me like another case of lapse of memory."

Jerningham had listened with rapt attention.

"Something more than lapse of memory," he commented at the end. "Else why was she finally able to carry them up?"

He hesitated.

"There's sometimes an extraordinary strength in the insane," he said.

He fell again into frowning meditation.

"Were you watching her," he asked us at last, "when I spoke of her being in the library at three o'clock this morning?"

"Yes," Nilsson answered, with a puzzled air. "First she looked as though she couldn't believe it—and then she looked scared to death."

"Exactly," Jerningham rejoined. "She couldn't remember being there, but the implication that she *had* been there was enough to set her trembling. . . . There's only one solution I can find for that."

He leaned forward.

"She believed—*she had reason to believe*—that she might have gone down to the library on an unknown errand, without intending it, without knowing it, without remembering it. And the belief that she had done so made her tremble, because it was fresh proof that she wasn't sane. Or perhaps——"

Jerningham's voice was growing more and more somber.

"Perhaps she trembled because she glimpsed the nature of that unknown errand. Perhaps half her terror is the dread of what her other self may do."

There fell another silence, which I, for one, did not care to break. I was too busy mastering the lump which rose in my throat at the thought of a slender, golden girl, summoning the last reserves of her courage to fight the fear of madness, which is so much blacker than the fear of death.

It was Nilsson who spoke first.

"You've said a lot, Jerningham, and hinted a great deal more," he said. "I'd like to be clear as to what you really believe. You think that Linda is insane at times, and knows it?"

"Yes," Jerningham answered.

"And that in one such fit of insanity she put the poisoned arrow in the safe with intent to kill?"

A pause.

"Yes," Jerningham said.

"And you think that shows such an insane determination to kill someone, that we must look for another attempt—that may not fail?"

A longer pause.

"Yes," Jerningham said at last.

He got restlessly to his feet, and began patrolling the hearth rug again, his head bent, his eyes unseeing.

"You make me the devil's advocate," he said. "I may be all wrong. Lord knows, I hope I am. But what I've told you is my best guess at the truth. I had to make the guess. If Linda is mad, she's capable of anything, and there are four people in this house besides ourselves whose lives may be at stake."

He stopped in the middle of the rug.

"But we can't do anything about it on pure guess-work. Whether I'm right or whether I'm wrong, I hope we find some proof before it is too late."

Nilsson was sitting buried in thought. Jerningham shrugged his shoulders as though to release them from a burden, and turned to me.

"Mac, you must be nearly dead," he said, with sudden concern. "You'd better go on up to bed, and get some sleep to make up for last night. I'll just give Nilsson a report on the things he missed,—how we found the diary in the furnace, and how we got the rest of Malachi's will—and then I'll come up too."

Realizing, as he spoke, how desperately tired I was, I acquiesced willingly, and rose to go.

"And Mac," he said. "Go to bed in my room instead of yours. If you have any trouble in the night with your hand—or anything else— I'd like to be there."

I said good night to Nilsson and went out. Passing through the hall, I noticed that the front door stood half open, and paused beside it for a breath of coolness. The weather had cleared. The stars were out. The air was fresh and sweet.

And then I heard Linda's voice, speaking from the shadows of the porch, but not to me,—speaking with a richness of feeling that I had not heard before. The voice was young. The words were very old.

"Neither death nor life," she was saying slowly, "nor angels, nor principalities, nor powers——"

My mind raced on to the end of that immortal sentence,—something about never being separated from the love of God. Was Linda turning to Heaven for comfort? I had never heard such ardor in a prayer.

"Nor things present, nor things to come," the rich young voice went on, "nor height, nor depth, nor any other creature, shall be able to separate us from the love of—one another. My dear—my dear——"

Then a man's voice, murmuring indistinguishable things.

I turned away from the open door, and went very softly up the stairs. There was a stinging in my eyes. Remembering Jerningham's somber prophecy of the future, I wondered whether Ryker's love, or any man's, could be steadfast enough to comfort Linda should the things that we feared prove true.

My last thought as I stretched out in the great bed in Jerningham's room and closed my eyes, was the hope that proof or disproof of his theory might come soon.

It did.

PART
4

13
KNOWLEDGE
AT A PRICE

I did not hear Jerningham come to bed, from which I judge he took great pains not to disturb me. For my sleep was not heavy. A slight sound would have waked me. And somewhere in the little hours, a slight sound did. All of a sudden I was broad awake.

I raised myself on my elbow and listened. The room was very still. There was no movement from Jerningham. His deep, even breathing continued undisturbed. I was just deciding that only the pain in my hand had roused me, when the sound was repeated. It was a stealthy knock upon the door.

This time Jerningham heard it too, and his response was instantaneous. I could see nothing of his movements in the dark, but all in the same moment I felt and heard the soft flop of covers flung violently aside, the creak of bed springs suddenly relieved of weight, and the clink of a gun barrel against bedstead as Jerningham groped for his weapon in the dark. Then his whisper reached my ears.

"Mac?"

"Yes?"

"There's a flashlight under my pillow. Hold it at arm's length to one side of you and point it at the doorway."

I did so. As the yellow circle of light came to rest upon the door, Jerningham spoke aloud.

"Who's there?"

The answer came in a low voice, deadened by its passage through the closed door.

"Nilsson."

I had my doubts. So apparently did Jerningham. For although he promptly unlocked the door, he stepped back out of the circle of light before he called, "Come in."

The door swung open. The man outside was Nilsson, right enough. He blinked a little at the flashlight, then stepped into the room. But no sooner had we switched on the light than it struck me that there was something strange about him,—something wrong.

At first I could put my finger on nothing definite. Then I saw that the strangeness was in his expression—or rather his lack of expression. The alertness, the determination, the driving force, that were characteristic of his face, had vanished. What remained was blank passivity. The effect was uncanny. The man before us was no more Nilsson than a tenantless, unfurnished house is home.

I glanced at Jerningham. He was studying his friend's face with an intent and puzzled frown. Then Nilsson spoke, and I realized that it was not the intervening door, alone, which had made his voice sound dead. There was no warmth, no life, no feeling in it.

"I want the key to the library," he said.

Jerningham looked a bit startled.

"All right," he said. "But why, old man?"

"I want it," Nilsson repeated, without inflection.

Jerningham's left eyebrow went up and the right one down. Without further comment he walked to where his clothes hung, fished the key out of a trouser pocket, and handed it over.

"And what's the combination of the safe?" Nilsson asked, still in the same lifeless tone.

Jerningham hesitated, then laid a hand on Nilsson's shoulder.

"Won't you take my advice and let it go till morning?" he urged. "I'd a lot rather tell you in the morning."

"What's the combination?" Nilsson repeated mechanically.

Jerningham dropped his hand from the other's shoulder.

"*Bish*," he answered, so low we could scarcely hear. "It's the name of that arrow poison."

"B-I-S-H?" Nilsson asked, his voice dropping too.

"Yes."

Without thanks, without a word, without a look, Nilsson turned on his heel and walked from the room, leaving the door open behind him. We watched him silently till his own room, at the far end of the long hall, swallowed him up. Then Jerningham shut the door and his eyes met mine.

"What's got into the man?" I demanded, in bewilderment. "Do you think he's drunk?"

Jerningham's frown was one of pure concern.

"No-o," he replied thoughtfully. "He was steady enough, and his eyes were clear. Besides, he never touches the stuff. He looked a little like a sleepwalker, but he wasn't. Sleepwalkers don't hold reasonable conversations or spell out combinations to be sure of getting them right."

He reached for his dressing gown.

"Are you going after him?" I asked curiously.

He shook his head.

"No use. I can't do anything with him so long as he stays in that state, whatever it is."

"Then what can you do?" I pressed him, reluctant to see him start off on any errand whatsoever.

"I'm going down to the library," he answered, tying the cord of his dressing gown. "Nilsson has the combination, and he's not himself. If he makes any use of it tonight, I want to be on hand."

"You gave him the key too," I reminded him. "How will you open the door?"

"Skeleton key," he answered briefly, fishing something out of another pocket. "I bought it yesterday while I was in town. Didn't expect to have to use it tonight, though."

By this time I was half way into my dressing gown.

"Hold on!" he cried, when he noticed. "What do you think you're doing?"

"I'm going along."

"No, you're not!" he retorted. "You're going right back to bed. There's not the slightest need for two of us. And besides——"

He grinned at me wickedly.

"You can sleep a lot more comfortably up here."

I suppose I flushed, for his face changed.

"Don't be an idiot," he said hastily. "You know I'd take you along if I needed help. But I'd rather you slept. You had a nasty shock, and you lost a lot of blood, and you'll be a rag tomorrow if you don't get some rest."

He switched out the light.

"If nothing happens, I'll be down there the rest of the night," he said. "So don't stay awake waiting for me. It won't pay."

None the less, I stayed awake. Not of choice, but because my thoughts were too busy for sleep. The throbbing pain in my hand was a relentless reminder of the death that lay in wait for someone between the walls of Cairnstone House. For someone—for whom? What deadly purpose lurked in the shadows of Linda's darkened brain? What force, what happening, could have changed Nilsson as we had seen him changed?

Thus I lay and thought. And before I had even begun to listen for Jerningham's return, I heard his familiar knock upon the door. I stumbled over my own feet in my eagerness to let him in.

"Are you all right?" he demanded, before the door was fairly shut. "Anybody been here?"

"Not a soul," I answered. "Has something happened?"

He nodded, his eyes blazing with excitement.

"Did Nilsson come down?"

He shook his head.

"Then what?"

"Plenty—only it wasn't Nilsson who did it," he answered. "Somebody else walked in and opened the safe, and took the Wrath of Kali."

"Who?" I demanded.

"It was—No! Darned if I tell you, Mac! I want your attention on the abstract problem instead of the flesh and blood thief."

I groaned.

"Then tell me at least what you've done with the flesh and blood thief!"

He looked surprised.

"Nothing," he answered. "He never knew I was there."

"But—but——" I was stammering in my amazement.

He was amazed too.

"You think I should have caught him?" he asked curiously.

"It would seem the natural thing to do, considering that he was walking off with the Wrath of Kali."

"But Mac!" he protested. "I don't care two straws about the Wrath of Kali. What I want is to settle our doubts about Linda."

He chuckled suddenly.

"Don't you remember how your algebra teacher used to tell you that the way to turn a minus quantity into a plus one is to multiply it by another minus quantity?"

"Yes," I admitted, "but what has that to do with Linda?"

"Our knowledge of Linda's sanity is a minus quantity—very minus—which we're trying to change to plus. And when I stumbled over a brand new minus quantity which may solve the problem for us, you want me to upset everything for the sake of a piece of red stone! Mac! Mac! Why, a bit of knowledge that would give us the truth about Linda would be worth all the crown jewels of England!"

I crawled meekly back into bed and drew the covers up protectively under my chin.

"All right! All right! I'm convinced!" I said. "Go ahead and tell me what knowledge you arrive at through multiplying one mystery by another."

He perched himself sideways on the footboard of the bed, one knee drawn up so that he could embrace it, the other long leg dangling.

"It isn't knowledge yet, till we work it out," he admitted. "But here's the starting point. The thief opened the safe without any uncertainty or any false starts. He knew the combination. How did he know?"

"He didn't overhear it," I said, "because you spoke too low. You know you didn't give it to him. I know I didn't. He must have got it from Nilsson!"

"Check so far," Jerningham agreed. "But how did he get it from Nilsson—within ten minutes after Nilsson got it from me?"

"Perhaps Nilsson wrote it down, and the thief found the slip."

Jerningham shook his head decisively.

"Nilsson never would have written it down. Didn't you hear what he said last night about folks who couldn't carry combinations in their heads?"

"Yes, but if you're arguing that Nilsson just up and *told* the thief what the combination was,—that's not so plausible either."

Jerningham was frowning.

"Not unless he had to," he said slowly.

I flung back the covers and started to my feet.

"You mean the thief compelled him? Jerningham! He may be——"

Jerningham didn't move from his perch on the foot of the bed.

"He's all right," he said reassuringly. "I went to see—the minute I came upstairs. I knocked, and I spoke softly through the door, and he didn't answer. I was getting right worried. Then I heard him snore,— his own, particular, characteristic snore, that nobody could fake. So I stopped worrying."

I settled back again

"That's a relief," I observed. "But it's a weird business. Nilsson is the last man on earth I'd care to try to coerce into betraying a trust. And the last man on earth to play crooked. And yet he gave up the combination to the thief within ten minutes or less of getting it from you, and all without a fight or an outcry or even the sound of an argument."

Jerningham's left eyebrow went up in a twisted frown.

"I know," he answered. "And there was something awfully queer about his look and manner when he came in here. I'm wondering——"

His voice trailed off into exasperating silence.

"Wondering what?" I prompted, when I saw he had forgotten my existence.

He came back with a start.

"Wondering whether the mischief wasn't already done before he ever got the combination. Whether he hadn't already been fixed before he knocked on our door."

"You're not suggesting," I said, horrified, "that he asked for it on purpose to give it to the thief?"

His mouth twisted.

"Sounds impossible, doesn't it?" he commented somberly. "I'd

swear it was impossible, except—I'm beginning to believe that anything can happen in this house."

He fell silent, and my mind ran over and around the things he
had said.

"If you're right," I said at last, "your new scrap of knowledge boils
down to this:—Somebody in this house has a method of coercion
powerful enough to make a man like Nilsson come and ask the secret
of the safe from you and hand it over—without raising any alarm."

Jerningham repressed a shiver.

"You're cold," I said. "Come on back to bed."

Jerningham shook his head.

"I'm not cold," he answered. "I was just thinking—that the man
who could do that, could make anybody do anything! Anything he
wanted done!"

This time his shiver was undeniable.

"A thought like that is enough to make you cold," I said. "Stop
thinking and come to bed. You can't get any further with this till you
see Nilsson in the morning."

Jerningham looked at me for a thoughtful instant, then swung
himself down from his perch on the foot of the bed.

"All right," he said "I suppose I can't."

He switched off the light, and I felt the bed springs shift and creak
with his weight.

"There's one thing, though," I said. "I'm a patient man,
Jerningham, but I don't propose to lie awake and suffer with curiosity
while you sleep. Who was the thief?"

Silence in the dark. Then I heard his head shift on the pillow.

"Ram Singh," he said.

I slept—but a tall dark man with a white turban stalked through
my dreams. It was with distinct relief that I awoke to find the morning
sun shining in my face.

14
A METHOD OF COERCION

Jerningham and I dressed hurriedly that Tuesday morning, and even so were some ten minutes late to breakfast. Nilsson was later than we, and the fact caused me a few minutes of uneasiness. But when he at last appeared, he was his alert and competent self, with no trace upon him of any untoward occurrence. I began to wonder if the events of the night before had really happened,—or had happened in quite the way that I recalled.

Breakfast, of course, with six people making forced and desultory conversation, offered no chance for discussion of the matter upper-most in my mind, but no sooner was the meal over than Nilsson steered us apart from the others.

"Jerningham," he said seriously, "I want to talk to you about this business of the Wrath of Kali."

The words brought a tell-tale look of relief to Jerningham's face. If there had been any delusions about the night before, at least Jerningham had shared them.

"You see," Nilsson went on, as we sauntered down the long hall to the library, "the responsibility for the thing's safety has began to worry me a little."

Jerningham shot him a startled glance.

"What do you suggest?" he inquired, as we stopped in front of the locked door to the library.

"Why, I think," Nilsson answered calmly, "that you'd better take it out of the safe and put it in a safety deposit box somewhere in town."

Jerningham and I stared at him in stupefaction.

"You think *I'd* better take it out of the safe?" Jerningham repeated. Nilsson looked puzzled.

"Why not?" he asked. "Anyhow, hurry up and unlock this door. We don't want to stand here all day."

Jerningham turned upon him squarely.

"Unlock it? Where do you think the key is, anyway?" he demanded.

"You have it, haven't you?" Nilsson returned. "How should I know?"

"You ought to know," Jerningham retorted. "Seeing that you came to my room in the middle of the night and made me give it to you!"

The two men stared at each other, unguarded amazement on each face. Something made me turn and look over my shoulder. Mrs. Ketchem was coming noiselessly down the hall, and watching us as she came. I jogged Jerningham's elbow.

"Use the skeleton key," I urged, in an undertone, "and let's get inside before we talk."

He acted on the suggestion, and we went in, followed by such a malicious bright glance from the old crone that I closed the door and shut her out creepily, as a child does the dark. But the others were not thinking about Mrs. Ketchem.

"Now!" Nilsson demanded. "What do you say I did in the middle of the night?"

"Don't you remember—at all?" Jerningham asked.

"Remember what?"

Jerningham whistled.

"You knocked on our door," he informed Nilsson succinctly, "and then asked for the key to the library, and got it. And you asked for the combination, and got it. And I asked for your reason—and didn't get it. Then you went back to your room."

Nilsson was listening with frowning concentration.

"That all there is to it?" he asked grimly, as Jerningham paused.

"No," Jerningham answered bluntly. "Ten minutes later Ram Singh had the key and the combination, and used them—both."

"Took the ruby?"

"Yes."

"Got away with it?"

"Yes."

"Sure?"

"Yes."

Nilsson's face looked suddenly gaunt.

"And I can't remember a damned thing about it!" he said.

He dropped heavily into one of the great chairs beside the fireplace, and stared at us.

"Rather knocks me out," he said, after a bit. "I'm not given to sleep walking—and I've always assumed I was of reasonably sound mind."

He dropped his great head into his hands with the gesture of a man who tries to push away a headache with his fingers. When he looked up again his face was drawn and tired.

"I wouldn't believe it on anybody's word but yours, Jerningham," he said heavily. "Ram Singh! Why Ram Singh? What do you make of it? I haven't anything to go on."

"Well, for one thing, I don't make such a calamity of it as you do," Jerningham answered with brusque sympathy. "You don't need to feel so down! The theft of the ruby is more my responsibility than yours, because I could have stopped it—and I didn't."

Nilsson's face did not lighten.

"It's not the ruby," he answered slowly. "It's realizing that— that I can't depend on myself, that there's no knowing what worse thing I'll do next time. Brrhh!"

"There isn't likely to be a 'next time'," Jerningham consoled him. "There wouldn't have been a 'this time,' if Ram Singh hadn't wanted something he could only get through you."

Nilsson straightened in the great chair.

"You mean Ram Singh *made* me go and get the combination for him?" he demanded incredulously.

"I haven't a doubt of it," Jerningham returned crisply. "You were obviously not yourself. Since it wasn't drink that put you in that state, nor drugs,—it must have been either sleep walking or something Ram Singh did. I'm betting it was Ram Singh."

"But see here, Jerningham!" Nilsson was leaning forward now. "I locked my door when I went to bed last night, and it was still locked when I woke up this morning."

"No doubt," Jerningham conceded. "But—whose windows are over yours?"

"Ram Singh's!" Nilsson answered, and stopped short.

After a moment he nodded.

"Yes," he admitted. "Ram Singh could have come in through the window—easily. And out again!"

Anger rumbled in his voice.

"Jerningham," he declared, "that's an intolerable thing! That a thief in the night should be able to steal a man's wits, and send him on an errand without his consent,—without even his knowledge at the time or his memory of it afterward——"

And then suddenly I saw the anger wiped from his face.

"By jingo!" he cried, "I've got something!"

Jerningham leaned forward, his eyes snapping with eagerness.

"What have you got?"

"Proof of Linda's sanity!" the big man answered. "Told you she was sane! Told you all along!"

He laughed in our astonished faces.

"Don't you see it?" He turned to Jerningham. "Last night you had me just about convinced that she isn't sane. And your proof was that she doubts her own sanity. But the reason she doubts it is that occasionally she does something without knowing it, or intending it, or remembering it! Exactly the way I did last night!"

He laughed again in sheer excitement.

"That girl's as sane as I am!"

Jerningham's face was alight.

"By George!" he exclaimed. "You *have* got it! Nilsson, I take off my hat to you!"

Nilsson shook his head.

"That's only half of it," he demurred. "Linda and I are in the same boat. We're not crazy,—not by a long shot! But when we lose our memories and start doing crazy things,—what's the answer?"

A preposterous thought rose in my mind, gained strength, and escaped into speech.

"If this were the sixteenth century," I said, "I could give you the answer in a word. You were bewitched!"

I saw an odd light in Jerningham's eye.

"Go on," he said. "Pretend it's the sixteenth century, and go on."

"If it were the sixteenth century, I wouldn't need to go on," I retorted. "You'd know, without telling, whom to suspect—and it wouldn't be Ram Singh. Who in this house has the Evil Eye? Who is it that talks of devils with every breath she draws? Who is it that has sold her soul to the Arch-Fiend, so that she has no feeling but malice for her fellow men?"

I stopped, half-ashamed.

"I know it's all moonshine," I admitted, "but three or four hundred years ago I'd have been in the fore-front of those who dragged her to the stake to be burnt as a witch."

Jerningham relit his pipe.

"No doubt you would," he said dryly. "It's always a temptation to dispose of the things we can't understand by calling them supernatural. It saves such a lot of hard thinking! And I admit Mrs. Ketchem is enough to make Cotton Mather turn in his grave."

He slouched lower in the depths of the davenport, and blew three careful smoke rings.

"But nevertheless and notwithstanding," he finished meditatively, "we needn't resort to the supernatural this time. The twentieth century can solve Nilsson's puzzle in one word, too."

Nilsson leaned forward in his chair.

"What is it, then?"

"Hypnosis," said Jerningham, matter-of-factly.

Nilsson shook his head, unbelieving.

"There's no such thing," he scoffed. "Not outside of a magician's act in vaudeville."

"Oh yes, there is," Jerningham returned calmly. "Ask any of the biggest psychiatrists,—Freud, or Jung, or Adler. Hypnosis is as common place a tool in their work as a typewriter is in mine."

He chuckled.

"You mustn't let the vaudeville fakers prejudice your judgment with their monkey business," he added. "They do use bogus hypnotism, of course. They also pick coins out of the air. Does that prove that there's no such thing as the Mind?"

"No," Nilsson admitted. "But you can go up to Sixteenth and Spring Garden any day and see the Mint. That's different!"

"Not a bit," Jerningham contradicted. "You can go to an expert psychiatrist and see the real thing in hypnosis."

"I don't admit that," Nilsson said. "But in any case, I wasn't hypnotized last night. I didn't see or talk with a soul."

"You were hypnotized just the same, though. While you slept," Jerningham declared calmly. "It's the only logical explanation."

"But it's not possible, is it?" I protested. "When the subject is asleep?"

"It's easier than when he's awake," Jerningham answered. "Bramwell cites a dozen authorities who have observed that natural sleep makes a person more susceptible to hypnosis, and who recommend the use of hypnosis during sleep for especially stubborn and resistant subjects."

He grinned at Nilsson.

"Like yourself," he added.

Nilsson was unmoved.

"You always call me stubborn when you can't prove your case," he observed dryly. "But I'd just as soon listen to the details of your theory even if they aren't proved. They might come in handy some time, if I should suddenly be converted to your views in an emergency. How much do you really know about hypnotism?"

"Only the fundamentals," Jerningham answered. "I've read a book or two on the subject, but most of what I know, I've picked up in talking with Esdaile. He uses it right along in psycho-analyzing his most difficult mental cases."

"All right," Nilsson said. "What's this about resistant subjects being handled easier during sleep? You mean that Ram Singh couldn't have hypnotized me if I'd been awake?"

"Not if you'd opposed him," Jerningham answered.

"Well, that's one bit of solid comfort," Nilsson remarked, wryly. "So long as I see him coming, I'm all right!"

"Of course," Jerningham went on, "a man may be hypnotized

without wanting to be, or expecting to be, or knowing what's happening to him, if he follows the hypnotist's instructions about fixing his eyes steadily on something—provided he leaves his mind open for suggestion. But if he actively resists, there's nothing doing."

Nilsson considered.

"Then the point of that," he said, "is—if Ram Singh asks you to look hard at anything, don't! But suppose he does succeed in hypnotizing you, then you lose your power of choice entirely? You have to do anything and everything that you're told?"

"Pretty nearly," Jerningham answered.

"For instance, if Ram Singh had told me to come in here and shoot you two, I'd have done that?"

"Nobody knows," Jerningham returned. "Personally, I don't think you would. Hypnotized people will do ridiculous things, or dangerous things, but there seems to be usually a strong resistance against obeying commands that offend the subject's moral sense—providing he has any."

It was Nilsson's turn to grin.

"Then if I hadn't any moral scruples against shooting you, but had merely refrained hitherto from motives of prudence, I'd have obeyed such an order?"

"Probably," Jerningham answered. "And if Ram Singh had removed your scruples by some deceit, such as telling you that the men you would find in our room were burglars, you would have believed him and carried out the order despite the evidence of your eyes."

"But then your moral sense is no protection at all against really skillful deceit," I protested. "You could be made to turn against your nearest and dearest."

"Perhaps you could," Jerningham answered. "At least, that's what the hypnotic experiments seem to show. Naturally, nobody has cared to experiment with actual homicide."

Nilsson shrugged his big shoulders.

"Then perhaps we're going to establish a new precedent," he said dryly. "The person we're dealing with now doesn't seem to be hampered by any objections to homicide! That is,—if the same person who made me betray the combination, made Linda kill Malachi. I suppose you think he did!"

Jerningham nodded thoughtful assent.

"That's my guess," he answered. "If we had nothing to explain except the murder and your experience last night, I'd think that the two events might be quite independent of each other. It could, of course, be pure coincidence that Linda's killing of Malachi and Ram Singh's theft of the ruby occurred so near together. But when we add the incident of the poisoned arrow, which doesn't seem to fit with anything else, we strain coincidence too far. I can't believe in three unrelated crimes occurring in the same house within thirty-six hours. It's more reasonable to think that there's a hidden pattern which relates them all."

"Now you're talking sense," Nilsson agreed. "And the designer of the pattern must be Ram Singh."

"Hold on," I objected. "It might just as well be Mrs. Ketchem, and she's shown malice enough to account for half a dozen murders. She could have done the hypnotizing, and simply have given the combination and key to Ram Singh so that he could take the ruby for himself,—perhaps to buy his silence about something. Or perhaps she hypnotized Ram Singh too, and sent him to bring her the Ruby from the safe. Don't you think that's a possibility, Jerningham?"

With sudden decision, Jerningham rose to his feet.

"I think there are entirely too many possibilities," he said. "We need some expert assistance—quick. I'm going to make Esdaile drop whatever he's doing and come down."

He strode over to the desk, picked up the phone, and called Esdaile's office in New York. Listening in silence, we heard him arguing, appealing, bullying, in an effort to persuade Esdaile to take the next train. When he hung up the receiver there was a frown of dissatisfaction on his brow.

"When is he coming?" I asked.

"What do you expect him to do for us?" asked Nilsson.

Jerningham's frown grew deeper.

"He says he can't be here till eight o'clock tonight," he answered.

"And as for what he can do—he may prevent a murder or two, if he just gets here in time."

15

JERNINGHAM
STICKS BY HIS GUNS

Nilsson rose from his chair like a big bear heaving himself out of his den.

"Why wait for Esdaile?" he growled. "Why can't we prevent a murder or two ourselves?"

"We don't know what murders to prevent or how!" Jerningham demurred, rumpling his hair with a gesture of half humorous despair. "We don't even know as much as we did last night. When I predicted that the poisoned arrow meant another murder coming, I honestly thought it was Linda and her insanity which we had to fear. Now that you've demolished the insanity theory, we don't know whom to fear. And Linda's in as much danger as the rest of us,—perhaps more."

"All the more reason for action," Nilsson declared.

He thrust his hands deep into his pockets, and planted himself solidly on the hearth rug.

"Whatever else we do," he went on, "this hypnotism stuff must be stopped."

"What do you suggest?" Jerningham asked.

"Lock up Ram Singh for the theft of the Wrath of Kali. I doubt if he can hypnotize his way out of jail."

Jerningham's eyebrows twisted slantwise in his characteristic frown of perplexity.

"I was afraid you'd want to do that," he confessed.

"It's the logical, sensible course, and I haven't an argument against it. But on my soul I think it would be a mistake!"

"But why?" Nilsson protested. "When you've got the goods on a criminal, you'd better nab him before he can do any more mischief!"

"Not if nabbing him spoils your chances of proving anything." Jerningham replied. "If Malachi was killed by Linda while she was under hypnosis, it's going to be next to impossible to prove the real murderer's guilt. If Ram Singh is the real murderer, arresting him now for theft will put him on guard, and we'll never be able to convict him of the murder. If he's not the real criminal, arresting him will deprive us of our best lead in getting at the truth."

"But we won't get at the truth by just sitting around and waiting for the next crime," Nilsson objected. "What's your plan of action?"

Jerningham shook his head.

"Nothing definite yet. When Esdaile comes, I'm confident he can unlock the closed doors in Linda's memory, and tell us what they hide. In her normal state, she'll never remember what happened while she was under hypnosis. But once she's hypnotized again, she'll remember everything that has happened to her, sleeping or waking. We can find out from her then who hypnotized her, and what she was ordered to do. With that knowledge, we ought to be able to devise a way to make the criminal convict himself, whoever he may be. Always supposing we haven't upset the apple cart by betraying our suspicions too soon."

"I don't like it," Nilsson growled. "You're proposing to give him a free hand till you're ready to strike. That's taking a crazy risk—when we know already who he is."

"We don't," I protested sharply. "You can't seem to think of anyone but Ram Singh. There's just as much reason to believe the real culprit is Mrs. Ketchem, and she used Ram Singh exactly the way she used you. In that case he isn't even guilty of theft."

Jerningham began nervously to pace the floor. Nilsson stood belligerently on the hearth rug, frowning his disapproval of temporizing and delay. At last Jerningham halted in his tracks.

"We'll never agree on this, Nilsson," he said. "By all the rules, you're right and I'm wrong, and we ought to put Ram Singh into custody. But I don't want to do it. The issue's between your logic and my hunch. Which do we follow?"

Nilsson shrugged his big shoulders.

"Well, if you put it that way, I guess we follow your hunch," he said. "If it weren't for your hunches, we'd never have come even this far. But I still don't like it."

Jerningham grinned.

"Well, anyway, thanks for lumping it," he said. "Of course I may be making a fearful mistake. But it's only till after Esdaile's visit tonight, and not much is likely to happen between then and now. Not in broad daylight."

He strolled over to a window and gazed out. A pleasant sunlight lay warm on the autumn landscape, and though the ground was already carpeted with leaves, the trees were not yet bare. The prospect seemed the fairer by contrast with the sense of oppression that pervaded the house.

"Why don't you two go out?" Jerningham asked suddenly. "Take a look around the place and see what you can see. I want a friendly talk with Ram Singh, if I can get it, and another with Mrs. Ketchem, and I'll probably do better if I see them alone."

We went gladly. If the day had to be spent in inaction, it was far pleasanter to spend it out of doors. There was not a great deal to see, but we studied the lay-out with some care, looking for any possible way a stranger could enter the premises, though we agreed that the murder of Malachi Trent was all too clearly an "inside job." The grounds, neglected as they were, had a wild charm of their own, and Cairnstone House itself, seen in the sunshine, with the English ivy mantling its warm brick walls, gave no hint of the terror and tragedy it had harbored,—and harbored still.

The spread of its wings gave it somewhat of a rambling look, and dwarfed the height of its three stories. I looked with interest at the mansard roof, with its narrow ledge which, from the ground, seemed hardly to offer footing for a cat. It took a real effort of the imagination, in the midst of the placid, sunny morning, to picture the desperation which had hounded Linda along that perilous way in the dark, two days before.

But one thing which I noticed in my casual survey, was to come back to me later. The ledge, as Linda had said, ran all round the house,—with one important exception. There was no ledge across the front of the projecting central section of the building. Above the entrance door the wall ran up sheer into the broad gable of the roof, and the ledge came to an abrupt unguarded end at either corner. That architectural detail I noticed with idle interest. A few hours later I had occasion to remember it with despair.

It was nearly noon when we completed our investigation and re-entered the house. We found Jerningham in the library, alone.

"About time you came back," he greeted us with mock indignation. "David and Linda and Ryker have all been in here, one at a time, hounding me for news of our decision. I hadn't realized it, but of course they haven't an inkling of what we've been doing or thinking since Linda's confession last night. The suspense has got their collective and individual goats, and I had a sweet time standing them off."

His left eyebrow went up in a humorous twist, as he hummed a snatch from a current tune, in rueful parody.

"They all want to know what we're going to do, and I don't know what we're going to do,—and that's my weakness now!"

"All your own fault," Nilsson informed him unfeelingly. "What did you tell 'em?"

"Nothing much. But I did tell David and Ryker that there was a chance that by tomorrow we could clear Linda from responsibility for Malachi's death. And I suggested that she might be in some danger and they'd better act in the meantime as a body guard for her protection. I figured that would tend to keep them all together during the day, which is the best protection I can devise, off-hand, against danger that may threaten any of them."

"What did you tell Linda?" Nilsson asked, with some concern.

"Nothing about danger. I said we hoped to prove she wasn't responsible for the murder. And she repeated 'Not responsible?' and went white, and I knew what she was thinking. So I told her point blank that she was just as sane as we were, and we'd prove it to her satisfaction presently."

"Glad you did," Nilsson said gruffly. "How did she take it?"

"She looked at me for a minute as though I were St. George with my foot on the dragon's neck," Jerningham answered. "And then she turned her face away suddenly and made for the door, and—and fumbled the knob as though she couldn't see it."

Jerningham cleared his throat.

"And now," he said, with forced lightness, "if I don't make good I shall have to go jump in the lake."

I looked hastily around the room in search for a change of subject.

"Did you get any new light from the interviews you wanted?" I inquired.

"Nothing at all from Mrs. Ketchem, except one lead which I plan to follow up after lunch. She happened to mention that Malachi's funeral ceremony this afternoon is to be performed by a minister of the wrong denomination, because—mind you—Malachi quarreled with his own minister, here in this house, last Saturday afternoon."

"Hm?" Nilsson commented. "Just about the same time he had the row with Linda."

"Exactly," Jerningham agreed. "Mrs. Ketchem couldn't say what it was about, and I have a violent desire to know. Anybody care to go with me to the parsonage this afternoon, and investigate?"

"I do," I said promptly.

"Then you two go," Nilsson said. "I'll stay here in case something turns up. Have your talk with Ram Singh?"

"Yes, and much good it did me!" Jerningham returned, with mingled relish and chagrin. "I thought I'd get a line on what sort he is, but I swear I don't know what to make of him. I started out by asking a few respectful questions about Kali, and he gave me an account of her cult and worship that was amazing. He spoke as one having both knowledge and authority,—and a remarkable mind. So I began asking him about himself. He grew more reticent then, but he admitted he's a Brahman, of the highest priestly caste."

"He is?" I exclaimed incredulously, and then, remembering the clean-cut ascetic features, "Well, he does look the part. But if he's high caste, it's perfectly preposterous for him to be here as a servant!"

"I know," Jerningham agreed. "I asked him bluntly how he could possibly have chosen to take service with Malachi, and he said it was necessary that every man should expiate his misdeeds, in one life or another. He spoke as though that were a complete explanation of his presence here. Perhaps it is,—but I'd like to know whether he meant he was expiating his own misdeeds, or helping Malachi to expiate the theft of Kali's ruby! It makes considerable difference!"

"Considerable!" Nilsson agreed grimly. "But there's not much doubt which he meant. If he were merely doing penance for sins of his own, he could just as well have stayed in India. I think at last we're on the right track."

He thrust both hands deep into his pockets and planted himself in the middle of the room in his favorite attitude,—legs spread wide apart, elbows out, big shoulders slightly hunched. His eyes were narrowed with concentration.

"Did he say what kind of priest he is?" he asked.

"He didn't say he was a priest at all," Jerningham corrected. "He only said he belonged to that caste."

Nilsson shrugged the distinction aside.

"Plenty of reason for his being indefinite," he declared with conviction. "He's a priest of Kali. We ought to have seen that before. He hired himself to Malachi because Malachi stole the Wrath of Kali. And now he's got it back."

"I believe you're right," Jerningham admitted thoughtfully. "He certainly showed a phenomenal knowledge of Kali-worship."

"And Malachi picked him up in the vicinity of Kali's temple, right after the theft of the ruby," Nilsson went on, methodically. "And that entry you showed me, from the burned diary, said he was extremely anxious to accompany Malachi to this country. It all hangs together."

"It certainly does," Jerningham assented. "But in building up the motive, you've knocked the crime itself to pieces. It looks as though Ram Singh were merely recovering stolen goods instead of committing grand larceny. Perhaps we haven't anything on him after all!"

"We've got a lot more on him than grand larceny," Nilsson answered impatiently. "We've got murder. Remember what he said when we found Malachi dead? He called it the vengeance of Kali. I thought then it was nothing but a superstitious explanation of an accident. But it wasn't an accident and it wasn't superstition. He knew blamed well it was vengeance, because he had tended to it himself."

Jerningham nodded slowly.

"Yes, that fits in too. Vengeance for the sacrilege, and recovery of the sacred ruby. The picture looks complete. But the poisoned arrow is still unaccounted for, and that may be part of a larger design."

Nilsson thrust his hands deeper in his pockets.

"Or part of the vengeance," he said, grimly.

Jerningham looked up quickly.

"But Malachi was already dead," he objected.

Nilsson jerked his head toward the corner where the statue of Kali had stood.

"Have you taken a good look at *her?*" he asked, dryly. "She's got a necklace of human skulls around her throat, and a sword in one hand and a human head in another. Her tastes apparently run to violence. Suppose she doesn't consider the death of Malachi alone sufficient vengeance for the insult he offered her?"

"What more would you say she wanted?" Jerningham asked.

Nilsson shrugged.

"If I were Ram Singh," he said slowly, "and believed in Kali, and had the job of satisfying her,—I'd make a clean sweep of the house of Trent."

Jerningham whistled.

"No piker, are you?" he said, but his eyes were very grave.

"Neither is Ram Singh," Nilsson returned grimly.

The two men regarded each other for a silent minute.

"Ryker was along on that expedition," Jerningham said presently.

"That's right," Nilsson acknowledged. "Ryker too!"

Jerningham drew a long breath.

"Linda and David and Ryker!" he said. "Then the placing of the poisoned arrow wasn't so reckless after all. He had three chances of getting a victim he wanted. And even if he missed them all, he'd get one of the interlopers who were meddling with his affairs."

Nilsson grunted.

"Under the circumstances," he said, "I wonder the man doesn't poison the soup and dispose of us all at once!"

Jerningham shook his head.

"He won't do anything so obvious," he said.

"He won't do anything more at all, if you'll listen to reason,"

Nilsson said sharply. "Knowing what we know now, it's perfect folly not to lock him up."

"Is it?" Jerningham said dryly. "Then a fool I must be."

"You're worse than that!" Nilsson retorted in despair.

"All right," Jerningham answered stubbornly. "Call me what you like, but I stick by my guns. The supremely important thing is to find out the truth about Malachi's murder—and prove it. That can't be done by ordinary methods. We haven't so far a single scrap of evidence that would stand in court. We haven't any case at all—unless we lead Ram Singh somehow to betray himself. And we can never do that if we arrest him now."

"Very nice and logical," Nilsson said doggedly. "Only while you're proving the original murder, you give him the chance to commit three new ones."

"I'm not so sure we can prevent him from committing the new ones," Jerningham answered with deadly seriousness. "Certainly not by an arrest. He could appeal to the British embassy, invoke the wealth and influence of his temple, and prove that he was simply retrieving stolen goods, recovering Kali's property for her. And the minute he was free, he'd go on about his business—and hers—and carry out the rest of the program. There's no use blinking the facts. The people for whom that poisoned arrow was intended, will meet death in some form sooner or later—arrest or no arrest—unless we can make Ram Singh hang himself with the rope we give him."

Nilsson looked a bit stunned by the overthrow of his plan of action. But he knew logic when he met it.

"You may be right," he admitted, reluctantly. "But—I draw the line at sitting around waiting for the next murder. It's too ghastly. We've got to do something to stop this fanatic."

Jerningham's mouth twisted.

"Well," he said, "there are two ways to stop him—and only two. Take your choice. We can catch him in the act. Or we can prove he murdered Malachi—if he did!"

Nilsson stared at the last words.

"You don't doubt it, do you?" he demanded.

"No, I don't doubt it," Jerningham said wearily. "But you may remember that twice before———"

There was a slow, even knock on the door. Jerningham stopped short. I went to open the door.

Outside stood the tall, turbaned figure of Ram Singh, his dark face impassive, his eyes inscrutable. He looked us up and down before he spoke.

"Luncheon is served," he said at last with elaborate dignity, and turned away.

Jerningham watched him out of sight with an odd expression.

"I don't doubt he killed Malachi," he repeated mechanically. "But you may remember going to bed Sunday night with the comfortable conviction that David was the murderer. And Monday night we slept on the far less comfortable theory that Linda killed Malachi in a fit of insanity. And what theory we'll sleep on tonight, after Esdaile's call, the devil only knows!"

As it turned out, the last was a needless speculation. Tuesday night we did not sleep at all.

16
CONSEQUENCES

I remember almost nothing of luncheon that day, nor of the conversation that accompanied the meal. I was watching Linda's face, and marveling at the change wrought in her by Jerningham's assurance of her sanity. She said very little, but there was a clear bright flame of happiness burning within her, and the light of it shone through every look and word. She had been lovely before. But now her beauty was a thing to lift the heart.

The memory of it stayed with me as Jerningham and I drove off to find the minister who had quarreled with Malachi. I was not so interested in this mission as I had been earlier. I could see no way in which a quarrel between Malachi and his spiritual adviser might bear upon the problem of convicting Ram Singh, and if Jerningham saw any possible connection he kept it to himself. It was a silent ride.

We found the parsonage without difficulty, but Dr. Dinwiddie was not at home. Jerningham, however, was stubbornly determined on the interview. Accordingly, we waited. We waited on the porch of that small, pleasantly shabby house for nearly two hours, before we saw the tall, awkward figure of the minister coming up the walk beneath the flaming maples.

He was a middle-aged Scotsman, gray-eyed and sandy-haired, with big-boned hands and wrists that stuck too far out of the sleeves of his black coat. I judged him kind, in spite of his long face and his dry and cautious manner.

Jerningham introduced himself and me as friends of Linda Marshall of Cairnstone House. Dr. Dinwiddie seemed to weigh the introduction before he answered.

"She has friends, then," he said finally, with the slightest trace of a burr in his voice.

"She has friends, now," Jerningham said gravely. "But I'm afraid it's rather a new experience for her. Have you known her long?"

"I would not say so," Dr. Dinwiddie answered. "I met her only the once."

"That was on Saturday?" Jerningham hazarded.

"On Saturday last."

"Would you mind telling us the circumstances of your visit that day?" Jerningham asked, most persuasively.

Dr. Dinwiddie hesitated.

"Could not Miss Marshall tell you what you wish to know?" he countered. "It would be more fitting."

Jerningham's eye met mine with a gleam of triumph. Evidently Linda came into this somewhere.

"She could," he said. "But it is important for her sake that we should have the account from you."

Dr. Dinwiddie nodded assent.

"Aye," he said. "I can see it might be."

But he stopped there, and Jerningham had to try again.

"Was it a regular pastoral visit?" he asked.

"I would not say so," the minister answered. "I was sent for."

"By Mr. Trent?"

"Aye."

"Did Mr. Trent give his reason for wanting you?"

"Aye." Dr. Dinwiddie hesitated. "He said there was to be a wedding."

I did my utmost to imitate Jerningham's composure, as he put the next question.

"And was there a wedding?"

"I would not say so," Dr. Dinwiddie answered.

"Why not?"

Dr. Dinwiddie seemed to ponder his reply.

"As to the ultimate cause, I cannot say," he answered at last judicially. "The immediate cause was that Miss Marshall responded by saying 'No!' at a point in the ceremony where it is customary to say 'I do!' With that irregularity, the ceremony could proceed no further."

Jerningham sent me a look that demanded silence.

"And then what happened?" he asked.

"There followed," Dr. Dinwiddie admitted, "certain protests and recriminations of a more or less violent nature."

"From the bridegroom?"

"No. Mr.—ah—Ryker, as I believe he was called seemed to exercise great restraint in spite of his quite perceptible dismay. His conduct exhibited a marked contrast to that of Mr. Trent."

Jerningham nodded.

"I shouldn't wonder. What explanation did Miss Marshall offer?"

"None."

"Didn't she say anything at all?"

Dr. Dinwiddie paused to consider.

"No. She seemed, if I may presume to say it, too absent-minded, too—ah—preoccupied with her thoughts, to discuss the matter."

Jerningham looked loath to leave that field of inquiry, but went on without comment.

"What was the nature of Mr. Trent's remarks?" he asked.

Dr. Dinwiddie frowned.

"It would not be overstatement," he declared, "to call them blasphemous."

"But aside from blasphemy?"

"I would say that his discourse was apportioned with approximate impartiality between announcements that Miss Marshall's conduct was unpleasing to him, and reminders of past warnings as to the consequences of causing him displeasure."

"And Miss Marshall merely listened without reply?"

"I could not say she listened. She remained in a passive attitude until Mr. Trent noted that she was fingering some trinket that hung about her neck. The sight seemed so to augment his disapprobation, that he snatched the bauble from her and flung it in the fire. Whereupon she roused from her abstraction sufficiently to walk from the room."

"Did you see her again?"

"No,"

"What happened after she left?"

"Mr. Ryker and the servant who was the second witness to the ceremony both attempted to mitigate Mr. Trent's displeasure."

"The servant was a woman?"

"No, a man. A native of India, or some such place, I believe."

Jerningham's look grew more intent.

"And was it Mr. Ryker or the servant," he asked slowly, "who seemed to have the greater influence on Mr. Trent?"

"I should say—the servant."

"Do you remember anything that was said?"

"I believe Mr. Ryker urged that if Miss Marshall were left in peace she would feel differently another day."

"And the servant?"

Dr. Dinwiddie paused to reflect.

"I remember one speech with, I think, approximate accuracy," he answered at last, "because it struck me oddly at the moment of utterance."

"Can you quote it?"

"It ran in this fashion: 'Leave her to me, Sahib. In a little time I will change her mind—as I have done before.' "

Jerningham drew a quick breath.

"Did he mention how he expected to change her mind?"

"No. That seemed to be understood by Mr. Trent without explanation."

"And how did Mr. Trent take the proposition?"

"It appeared to strike him as an eminently satisfactory solution to the problem. He stated that he would allow forty-eight hours for this change of mind to be effected, and that at the end of that period the interrupted ceremony must be resumed."

A faint flush appeared upon Dr. Dinwiddie's countenance. For once he continued without urging.

"At this point I stated, with what may, I fear, have been ungodly emphasis, that I would have not part in a resumption of any such ceremony. Whereupon Mr. Trent intimated that my usefulness to him was at an end."

The deepening of the flush on Dr. Dinwiddie's face betrayed something of the actual fact behind that masterpiece of understatement. His big-boned hands were clenched with a quite ungodly vigor.

"So I came away from that house," he finished. "And I rejoice that it does not fall to my lot to return to it to preach the funeral sermon for its master. I fear I could hold out little assurance of his present welfare."

Jerningham released his stern control of his features and frankly grinned.

"That would be perfectly all right with me," he averred. "Is there anything else, no matter how trivial, you could tell us about your visit?"

Dr. Dinwiddie was himself again.

"I recall nothing further," he asserted, more distantly.

"About what time were you there?"

"In the neighborhood of two o'clock."

"Did you happen to see David Trent, either in going or coming?"

"Is he a young man with red hair?" Dr. Dinwiddie asked.

"Very."

"Then it was probably he whom I saw in the front hall as I entered."

"What was he doing?"

"He appeared to be bidding farewell to Miss Marshall."

"Did you hear anything that she said?"

"She said nothing in my hearing."

"Did she seem, at that moment, to be—preoccupied?"

"I could not say."

"And there is nothing else you can tell us?"

"No."

Jerningham rose to go.

"We're very much in your debt," he said, "for the information you've given us, and—I'm sorry you're not going to conduct Mr. Trent's funeral. I can imagine no one better qualified."

As we climbed into the car again, Jerningham chuckled aloud.

"I'd give up an opening night," he said, "to hear that chap

indulging in 'ungodly emphasis'. But his story was startling enough
without it. Whew!"

"But what do you make of it?" I queried. "To find that the row
that started the whole business was over Linda's refusal to marry Ryker,
simply turns things upside down!"

Jerningham made no answer till he had pointed the car again in
the direction of Cairnstone House.

"The crux of the whole matter," he said, "is why she refused. We
can't get very far with deductions or inferences until we learn that.
And the simplest plan is to ask her."

"Yes, but you have a theory," I insisted. "You always have. Out
with it!"

"I have two theories this time," Jerningham acknowledged with a
chuckle. "And neither of 'em any good!"

"What if they aren't? Trot 'em out—quick, before we get back."

"Well, the obvious one is that something happened which suddenly changed her mind about marrying Ryker,—a quarrel, for
instance, or even a proposal from David! But we know by the testimony of three people that David's errand Saturday was to say
goodbye—for five years. And there are no traces of any quarrel between
Linda and Ryker. Perhaps——"

For a moment he gave all his attention to passing a milk truck that
was bottling up traffic on our side of the pike.

"Perhaps?" I prompted when we were past.

"Perhaps she refused on conscientious grounds, because she
doubted her sanity."

"But you don't think so," I said. "What's the other theory?"

He turned off the pike into the walled grounds of Cairnstone
House. At once, the bustle of traffic died away behind us, and the
world became a still and lonely place.

"The other theory," he said, "is that Ram Singh used his power
over her to prevent the marriage."

"But why? It was no business of his!"

"Wasn't it?" Jerningham argued, frowning at the leaf-strewn drive
that stretched before us. "Marriage with Ryker would have meant

Linda's escape from this place—and perhaps from the vengeance of Kali."

I felt a sudden coldness in the November afternoon. Had Ram Singh been able to pluck her back from the very threshold of safety? Was there no limit to what he could do? I turned the matter over in my mind.

"If Ram Singh didn't want Linda to marry Ryker," I objected, "why did he offer a guarantee that she would do so on a subsequent occasion?"

"He never meant to carry out the guarantee. He gave it simply to appease Trent and keep Linda from being sent off to that 'hospital,' where she'd have been even farther out of reach of his vengeance."

It sounded all too plausible.

"I refuse to believe it," I said. "If Linda broke off that ceremony because she'd been hypnotized and ordered to break it off, somebody would have noticed something—surely!"

"Dr. Dimwiddie did. At least he said she seemed 'absent-minded,' and he says only about one fifth of what he means."

"But Ryker would have noticed!"

"He did notice something," Jerningham returned. "Remember that conversation you overheard? What was it Ryker said?"

"She asked him to forgive her, and he said there was nothing to forgive,—that she simply wasn't herself. What do you think he meant?"

"Temporary insanity, probably. It must have seemed like that to him. And he carefully suppressed all mention of the incident in the account he gave to us. I suppose he feared we wouldn't help in her rescue, if we knew she'd thrown away one chance of escape!"

There was a distinct tinge of admiration in Jerningham's voice.

"Single-minded chap, isn't he? There aren't many men devoted enough to run the risk of marrying insanity under circumstances like these."

He glanced at his watch.

"Almost the hour for the funeral," he said. "There's just time to ask Linda a question or two. And if she doesn't remember jilting Ryker at the altar, we can chalk up one more misdeed to Ram Singh's account."

Jerningham spoke casually enough, but I was not so calm. No doubt this last misdeed of Ram Singh's was a lesser crime than making Linda the instrument of his murder of Malachi. But somehow when I considered how close Linda had come to happiness and peace and shelter, only to be forced to refuse them by her own act, the irony of it stirred me to impotent wrath.

If Jerningham shared my feelings, he did not betray the fact. He brought the car to a leisurely stop outside the entrance to Cairnstone House, remarked that the modest car already parked there must belong to the clergyman who was to conduct the funeral, and strolled casually up the front steps at my side.

As we entered the hall, we heard voices from the drawing room on our right.

"Now," Jerningham said, "if Linda's there, we'll soon find out whether she jilted Ryker of her own accord."

She was there. So was Ryker. They were standing by the front windows, with their backs toward us,—standing very still, very close together, in the late afternoon sunshine, facing the minister who had come to bury Malachi. The voice we had heard was the minister's, repeating familiar words.

"Will you obey him, serve him, love, honor and keep him, in sickness and in health, so long as ye both shall live?"

And Linda's answer, barely audible.

"I will."

A feeling of peace stole over me. For the moment, all was right with the world. I glanced about the room. At its rear stood Malachi's casket, closed. There were some flowers upon it of the undertaker's providing,—no others. And the shadows were beginning to gather about it. But where Linda stood, the late sunshine flooded around her. Its slanting gold was a benediction on her slender figure, as she listened with bent head to the minister's words.

The only witnesses to the ceremony were Nilsson and Ram Singh. There was a vigilant look in Nilsson's eye. Ram Singh's dark face was inscrutable. I looked curiously for some indication of defeat, but found none.

The minister's voice was intoning the closing words.

"Whom God hath joined, let no man put asunder."

Ryker's arm went round Linda's shoulder and he kissed her with grave gentleness. Then they turned in our direction, and I saw,—and a coldness closed about my heart.

Linda's face was blank as death.

The revulsion of feeling which seized me was so strong that I would have cried out in dismay, but the words caught in my throat. No wonder Ram Singh had watched that ceremony with an unmoved face. He could afford to. He had permitted it,—ordered it,—because in some way it now suited his plans to allow the marriage which it had formerly pleased him to prevent.

But why—why——? One grim possibility raised its head above the rest,—that he planned to strike at Ryker through the marriage. Or had he struck already, so that now he need only wait and watch the thrust go home? Was that the truth? There was no answer to be had from Linda. Though she stood sheltered in the circle of her husband's arms, she was a thousand miles beyond our reach.

A deep sense of foreboding filled me. Behind the mask of that still little face, what alien purpose of Ram Singh's ruled her? What thing had she been told to do, that she must do before she woke? And would the man who loved her be the victim of his faith?

I heard Jerningham's murmur in my ear, as we stood together in the doorway. It was hardly more than a despairing whisper.

"And I thought nothing would happen in broad daylight. Oh Mac, what a fool I was! What a fool I was!"

17

"FORGIVE ME – LINDA"

I do not know how long Linda stood there, motionless, before she stepped from Ryker's side and moved toward Jerningham and me in the doorway. I watched her with a sort of fascination. The expressionless calm of her face, the unseeing stare of her wide eyes, sent shivers up my spine. Not until she was within arm's length could I realize that she didn't know I was there. Then I followed Jerningham's example, stepped back into the hall, and let her pass unhindered to the stairway. Jerningham laid his hand on my arm and drew me after her up the stairs.

"You surprised us very much," he remarked cheerfully to Linda's unhearing ears, his tone loud enough to carry easily to those in the drawing room below. "We'd have come back earlier if we'd known."

The contrast between the heartiness of his voice and the anxiety in his face was grotesque. But once in the upper hall he laid pretense aside.

"Listen, Mac," he told me in an urgent undertone. "I don't dare leave Linda alone a minute. You go on down to the funeral and make my excuses. Tell 'em I never go to funerals. Tell 'em whatever you like. And pretend you didn't notice anything wrong. But get word privately to Nilsson not to let Ram Singh out of his sight, even if he has to arrest him formally. And as soon as you're back from the cemetery, come up with Ryker, and find me. I'll be with Linda, wherever she is. Poor Ryker! He's in for a jolt,—unless he's already begun to understand."

I went back to the drawing room and did my best to follow instructions. There was no talk of the wedding beyond my brief congratulations. Presently David appeared from somewhere, and last of all Mrs. Ketchem. Whereupon the minister, a well-fed unimaginative young man with his black hair parted in the middle, proceeded with the second ceremony as calmly as though such combinations of events were his daily lot.

He might not have been so calm had he realized the weird nature of the wedding he had just solemnized, or had he guessed that among us sat the murderer of the man for whom he read the funeral service,—or had he known that at every mention of death, Nilsson and I at least were thinking, not of the death that had stricken Malachi Trent, but of that other death which waited, hovering, and had yet to strike.

By the time we returned from the cemetery, the early dark had fallen, and Cairnstone House lay as lightless and somber as when I saw it for the first time. Ryker acceded readily to my suggestion that we look for Jerningham, and we went upstairs, turning on the lights as we went. I confessed to a sense of relief each time a light flashed on and showed us nothing changed. Ryker was very grave, but I could not guess what he was thinking.

We found Jerningham pacing up and down the long hall on the third floor.

"Where's Linda?" I asked.

He nodded toward her room. There was a light burning within it, which we had not seen as we approached the house, because her room was on the rear corner of the east wing. The open door afforded a view of Linda, lying fully dressed upon her bed, apparently fathoms deep in sleep.

"She's been lying like that ever since she came up to her room," Jerningham explained. "She's so sound asleep she doesn't rouse at all when you speak to her. It worries me a bit."

That, I could see, was as flagrant an understatement as any of Dr. Dinwiddie's. But Ryker didn't know Jerningham as I did.

"I think she's only feeling a reaction," he said, "from the strain of the past days. You can't keep your nerves on the stretch forever. She came up for a nap after lunch, and I guess she slept all afternoon, until Ram Singh woke her just before the minister arrived. She seemed still a bit dazed with sleep when we came down for the ceremony."

"Had you planned ahead to take advantage of the minister's presence?" Jerningham asked with sympathetic interest. "Or was it a sudden inspiration?"

"Inspiration," Ryker answered. "Ram Singh asked if we were going to be married this afternoon, and it struck me as a good idea. So I proposed it to Linda at the last moment, and she acquiesced."

"I think she was wise," Jerningham assured him, and added experimentally. "A lot wiser than she was last Saturday."

"So you know about Saturday." Ryker commented, with a rueful but impenitent smile. "It wasn't quite fair not to tell you. But I was afraid your enthusiasm for rescue might weaken if you knew how my previous attempt at deliverance had flivvered."

"I'm not blaming you," Jerningham declared. "But how do you account for Saturday's failure?"

Ryker's face darkened.

"I hate to account for it," he said reluctantly, "but I suppose you ought to know. I told you in the beginning, you remember, that terror was driving Linda over the edge of sanity. I didn't want to admit that she's already subject to states of—a sort of blank depression, during which she is not herself. One of those moods came upon her Saturday. There was nothing to do but wait for it to pass. But *now*——"

His voice warmed with relief.

"Now that I have the right to take care of her, things are going to be different," he finished. "You said this morning that you'd decided she wasn't morally responsible for Malachi's death. Are you sufficiently satisfied of that, so you'll stop investigating her and let me take her away to rest?"

"Almost," Jerningham answered with a smile that only half covered the anxiety in his face. "We need a bit more proof, but there's a chap coming tonight, a psychiatrist named Esdaile, who can help us out. And after that—I hope you take her where she'll never hear of Cairnstone House again."

There came to us the faint ringing of the telephone far below us in the library, and in a minute or two the sound of Nilsson's steps ascending the stairs.

"Telegram for you, Jerningham," he said. "Esdaile's taxi had a collision on the way to his train, and he's too battered up to come. Sent you a list of three or four men in Philadelphia who might serve."

Jerningham looked stunned.

"All the breaks against us!" he muttered. "I'd counted—absolutely—on having Esdaile tonight. Probably none of these other men will even come."

There was a little silence. Nilsson and I knew, as Ryker did not, how indispensable Esdaile was to Jerningham's plans. But it was Ryker who stepped into the breach.

"You think it's important to have a psychiatrist—tonight—for Linda?" he asked, with sudden anxiety.

"I know it is," Jerningham said.

"All right! I'll get you one," Ryker promised grimly. "Give me the list."

Five minutes later we heard his roadster start off down the drive. And still Linda slept like one of the dead, heedless of who left her or who stayed.

The moment Ryker was gone, Nilsson turned to Jerningham.

"I told David to keep an eye on Ram Singh till I came down again," he said. "Ready now to have me take him to the lock-up at Media?"

Jerningham shook his head, frowning.

"No. Ready to have you arrest him on suspicion—suspicion only— of stealing the Wrath of Kali, and lock him in his room with a guard outside."

Nilsson looked disappointed.

"That's better than letting him run around loose," he said grudgingly, "but why not jail?"

"We've got to keep him in our hands," Jerningham said. "He has Linda in such a deep hypnosis that I can't rouse her at all. Ryker believes she's merely sleeping heavily, and I thought it better not to undeceive him, but I'm afraid it may take a psychiatrist's help to bring her to herself."

"We could make Ram Singh bring her out," Nilsson suggested, with a grim set to his jaw.

"As a last resort, we could,—perhaps," Jerningham conceded, slowly. "Though I doubt if Ram Singh is easy to coerce, even by the fear of death. . . . But unless it becomes absolutely necessary, I don't want his influence to touch her again. We don't know what orders he has given her already. But at least he shan't have the chance to give her any more."

"Then the sooner we lock him up, the better," Nilsson declared, and departed with considerable satisfaction upon that errand.

If he expected Ram Singh to show dismay at being arrested, however, he was disappointed. When the Hindu passed us presently in the third floor hall on his way to his room in the west wing, he appeared completely oblivious of Nilsson striding along behind him. His bearing was that of a prince withdrawing from the cares and annoyances of court life, to the privacy of a favorite retreat. Which did not in the least deter Nilsson from locking him in and pocketing the key.

"Now what?" the big man asked, as he rejoined us.

Jerningham pulled himself out of the abstraction that enveloped him.

"Now," he answered, "if you will guard Ram Singh, and keep an eye on Linda, Mac and I will go downstairs and see if either David or Mrs. Ketchem can add anything to our knowledge of what happened this afternoon. If Linda stirs, shout down to us and we'll hear."

We found David in the billiard room, moodily practicing carom shots. He looked up eagerly as we entered. Then his face fell.

"What's happened to Linda?" he asked.

"A great deal," Jerningham answered gravely. "Did you see her at all just before the wedding?"

David's cue clattered to the floor, but I do not think he heard it. He was staring at us in petrified amazement, the color going from his thin face till it was chalk-white beneath the red thatch of his hair.

"Wedding?" he repeated haltingly at last. "Who—whose?"

"Linda's—and Ryker's," Jerningham answered. "Before the funeral this afternoon."

David's hand clenched on the edge of the billiard table.

"That's a damn lie," he choked. "She never married him. She wouldn't? She couldn't!"

"She did," Jerningham returned coolly.

David's voice rose uncontrollably.

"I tell you she couldn't!" he cried. "She—She—Damn you, man, she's in love with me!"

Jerningham's eyes narrowed.

"Careful," he warned. "She's been engaged to Ryker since—let me see—since a week ago Monday morning."

David stared.

"A week ago Monday morning," he muttered. "And I met her that afternoon—for the first time."

"Then you see," Jerningham pointed out reasonably, "she was engaged to Ryker before ever she knew you. Besides, she's not a girl who'd marry one man if she loved another."

"But she *couldn't* have married him," David insisted desperately. "She promised me nothing should ever come between us,—not life or death, or anything that had happened or might happen,——"

His voice broke.

"Nor angels, nor principalities, nor powers," I quoted softly.

He looked up, startled.

"How did you know that she said that?" he asked huskily.

"I heard," I said. "Only of course I thought it was Ryker to whom she spoke. Jerningham, he's telling the truth."

"Of course I am!" David blazed.

"I believe you are," Jerningham told him gravely. "But so was I, when I said she married Ryker. There's only one explanation—she married Ryker without knowing what she did."

"You don't mean—she's—insane," David said jerkily.

"Not insane. Hypnotized—by Ram Singh. She was under hypnosis at the time of the ceremony, and she is yet, and how much longer she'll be in that state, nobody knows."

"But can't you *do* anything about it?" David demanded. "Can't you bring her back to herself?"

Jerningham's face grew somber.

"I tried. But I couldn't do a thing. She's too far under. I couldn't reach her at all."

He turned to me and his brow twisted in a rueful frown as he went on.

"I had great hopes when she first came upstairs after the wedding. I thought that since she was already under hypnosis I could ask her the things I needed to know, and get the answers without waiting for Esdaile. But it didn't work. The hypnosis is too deep. Instead of answering any questions, she went off into this trance-like sleep. And now all I want is to get her out of it, answers or no answers. I'm—worried."

David's white face grew desperate.

"You're afraid she—won't wake up—at all?" he asked hoarsely.

For the moment Jerningham abandoned restraint.

"I'm afraid she won't, and I'm afraid of what will happen when she does," he answered. "I'm afraid of the whole damned business. It's incalculable. The old rules are off—and we don't know the new ones. If Linda is no longer following her own will and her own judgment—she may do *anything!*"

He pulled himself up sharply.

"It's not quite that bad, of course," he said, in a more normal tone. "She isn't mad. There'll be a perfectly sound reason for anything she does,—only it will be Ram Singh's reason, not hers. That's the basis we must go on. What has Ram Singh told her to do? What would I have told her to do, if I'd been in his place?"

He shook his head in discouragement at the riddle.

"Afraid we'll have to wait and see," he said. "In the meantime we'd better find out whether Mrs. Ketchem knows anything that may help."

"Do whatever you can think of," said David, unhappily, "I—I'm going up to stay with Linda."

We found Mrs. Ketchem in the kitchen, preparing dinner single-handed, in high dudgeon at the loss of Ram Singh's assistance. She was in no mood to be helpful, but Jerningham disregarded her mood.

"When did you last see Linda, Mrs. Ketchem?" he inquired.

"Not at the funeral, where she should have been!" the old crone snapped.

"When *did* you see her?"

"At lunch. And what good does that do you?"

"Very little," Jerningham admitted. "I hoped you might know something about her doings in the last half hour before the funeral."

I caught a malicious gleam in the old woman's eye.

"Why didn't you say that in the first place?" she inquired acidly.

"I amend the question," Jerningham replied pleasantly. "What do you know about her doings?"

She permitted herself a brief cackle.

"More than she thinks—the hussy! I know she had a man in her room—with the door shut."

Jerningham's eyebrows went up in polite astonishment.

"Indeed! And how did you know—with the door shut?"

She cackled again.

"I heard him! They didn't know I was in my room. But I was! Oh, yes, I was!"

"And what did you hear?"

"He talked too low," she admitted reluctantly. "I only caught one thing he said. But that was enough for me!"

"And what was that?"

The wicked old eyes sparkled.

"The same thing over and over," she said. " 'Forgive me, Linda! Forgive me, Linda! Forgive me, Linda!' "

She shrugged her crooked shoulders.

"Now what," she inquired with malice, "do you suppose there could have been for her to forgive?"

"I can't imagine," Jerningham replied blandly. "Did she make any answer?"

She shook her gray, untidy head, and turned back to her pots and pans.

"Did you recognize the man's voice?"

She shook her head again.

"Or see him when he left her room?"

"No. he sneaked away, and I didn't hear him go."

"And about what time was this?"

"Half an hour before the funeral, perhaps."

She emptied the contents of a saucepan into a serving dish with unnecessary vigor.

"Now I'll ask a question," she said tartly. "Where's Ram Singh?"

"We've confined him to his room," Jerningham informed her.

She filled a plate with great care, and placed it on the kitchen table for herself. Then she pointed a skinny finger at the dishes of food in the warming oven.

"There's your dinner," she croaked. "If you want to keep your butler locked up, you can serve it yourselves. I'm nobody's butler, and I won't be put upon."

"I assure you solemnly," Jerningham responded, with a quirk in a corner of his mouth, "that I know better than to attempt any infringement of your rights."

As we carried the food into the dining room, his brow was clearer than I had seen it for hours. But he soon fell back into his abstracted reverie, made no comment on Mrs. Ketchem's queer story, and barely went through the motions of eating. After five minutes or so, he filled another plate, and got to his feet.

"I'm going to take this up to Ram Singh," he said, "and relieve Nilsson so that he and David can come down and eat."

For a few minutes I was alone with our self-served meal. Then Nilsson joined me.

"Isn't David coming down?" I inquired.

"Says he's not hungry," Nilsson replied, as he attacked the food before him. "What did you learn from David and Mrs. Ketchem? Jerningham said you'd tell me all about it."

I began with the housekeeper's tale. In the midst of it, the old crone stalked ostentatiously through the room, remarking that she was going upstairs and we could clear the table ourselves when we were through. But before we had finished either the meal or the discussion of the interviews, Jerningham rejoined us, his eyes blazing with excitement.

Nilsson looked startled to see him, and half rose, asking, "What about Ram Singh?"

"Oh, David's on guard," Jerningham assured him. "But see here! I want you to look at this! I found it in Linda's desk."

He tossed a sheet of paper on the table between us. We bent forward to read the contents. There were hardly a dozen words.

> *"Dear—I'm going to end it.*
> *I can't face the future.*
> *Forgive me—Linda."*

Nilsson looked up, aghast.

"A suicide note!" he exclaimed. "But she's not that sort."

"No," Jerningham agreed, quietly. "She's not."

"Then she didn't write it," Nilsson declared.

"Oh yes, she wrote it," Jerningham contradicted. "But—look again at the last three words!"

We did, and the words stared up at us from the white page.

> *"Forgive me—Linda!"*

Our eyes met Jerningham's

"You see!" he said. "It was dictated. While she was under hypnosis. And that's what Mrs. Ketchem heard!"

Nilsson pushed back his chair, and stood.

"A suicide note—dictated!" he said slowly. "That means only one thing."

Jerningham nodded.

"Yes. We've had crimes that looked like accidents. The next one is going to look like suicide."

Involuntarily I held my breath and listened. There was a dreadful silence in the house.

"But now—" Nilsson said, brusquely, "now that we're forewarned——"

He stopped. The silence in the house was broken by the sound of footsteps—descending the long stairway on the run. In another instant David stood breathless in the doorway of the dining room. "She's coming to herself," he told us hurriedly. "She's beginning to stir ——"

Jerningham's voice cut across the words like the lash of a whip.

"And you left her—alone!"

Before David could open his mouth in defense, Jerningham plunged for the door, and up the hall to the stairs. We followed at full speed, close upon his heels. But we were not quick enough. Even as we topped the first flight of steps we heard a sound that confirmed our darkest fear.

It came down to us from the upper floor,—piercing, desperate, terror-stricken,—the sound of a woman's scream!

PART
5

18

THE SCREAM IN THE NIGHT

With the sound of the scream ringing in our ears, we managed somehow to annihilate the second flight of stairs and the length of hallway that separated us from Linda's room. Her door was open. Bracing ourselves for what we should find, we looked inside. The room was empty!

We could see the depression on pillow and counterpane that showed where she had lain. We could see the curtains fluttering peacefully at her window in the cool evening breeze. But of Linda herself, there was no sign.

There was a sound, though,—the first sound we had heard since that scream had shuddered away into silence. There was a low moaning from the room next door, from Mrs. Ketchem's room. That door was closed. We did not wait to knock before we entered.

Linda was not there. The moaning proceeded from Mrs. Ketchem. With her apron flung over her head, she was rocking herself to and from in a little ladderback chair, huddling herself together into the smallest possible compass, and wringing her hands. She seemed unhurt. She was unhurt. But she was in an ecstasy of terror.

Jerningham snatched the apron from off her head and caught her wrists in a compelling grip.

"Did you scream?" he demanded. "Was it you?"

She shivered in his grasp.

"Oh—oh——" she moaned. "It was a ghost—her ghost— oh——"

"Answer me!" Jerningham ordered. "Did you scream because you thought you saw a ghost?"

"Yes!" she wailed, on a note of hysteria. "I did see a ghost. It was Linda's ghost, I tell you—floating in the air——"

He was almost shaking her.

"Where? Where did you see it?"

She pointed a skinny, shaking finger toward her three windows in turn.

"There—and there—and there——" she shuddered. "It looked in them all—all——"

I heard Jerningham's quick-drawn breath as he turned and flung open the window she pointed to last. I was at his shoulder as he thrust his head out into the night.

At first I could see nothing. But as my eyes became accustomed to the darkness I could distinguish a dim figure, and I realized with a pang of horror that Mrs. Ketchem had not been so far wrong after all. Only what she had seen—what I now saw—was not one already dead, but one about to die.

Far beyond our reach, on the opposite side of the ell, walking the narrow ledge that skirted the steep mansard roof, went Linda. Her every step was perilous enough, since the ledge was only a few inches wide, and the steep roof offered no handhold. But the road she traveled was the lesser peril. What struck me with cold despair was the goal to which her steps were bent.

"Jerningham," I gasped, "that ledge stops! If she tries to step around the corner, she's doomed."

"And if we startle her awake, she'll fall," Jerningham muttered.

He took a quick breath, and his voice, cool and assured, reached out to her through the darkness like an authoritative hand laid upon her arm.

"Linda, stop!" he called. "The ledge doesn't go any farther! Turn and come back!"

She took another step forward and answered him over her shoulder.

"I can't stop," she explained, gently, absently, as she might have explained a commonplace to a child. "I have to go on. I have to go all the way around the house. It is an order!"

She took another step.

I heard a scuffle at the window on our left. David was half outside it, with some wild notion, I suppose, of walking the thirty feet of narrow ledge that stretched between him and Linda and carrying her back willy-nilly in his arms along the same knife-edged way,—before she could take the last two steps that divided her from death. Nilsson was holding him back by main strength.

"Don't be a fool," the big man adjured him gruffly. "You can't get there! And you couldn't hold her by force on that ledge if you did! She's got to come back of her own accord. Give Jerningham his chance."

"Chance!" I thought despairingly. What chance was there, in the next ten seconds, of dislodging the fatal obsession in Linda's dreaming mind? No chance in the world.

She took another step.

Jerningham's voice reached out to her again, this time in a tone of sharp rebuke.

"You have mistaken the order," he called sternly. "You are going the wrong way!"

She was standing at the very corner now, a slender figure silhouetted against the night sky, poised between heaven and earth. She gave no sign that she had even heard.

"You should have gone in the other direction," Jerningham told her sternly. "You must turn and go round the house the other way!"

She made no move.

Jerningham's shoulder against mine was hard as iron with the tension of muscles straining uselessly to help.

"You were ordered to go the other way!" he repeated inflexibly. "It is an order! It is an order! It is an order!"

It seemed to me that she swayed where she stood. I tried to look away, and could not. And then I saw that she had taken a step— another step. She was coming back.

After that, time stood still. Jerningham warned us beneath his breath against word or movement that might distract her from her uncannily sure progress along the perilous way. And we neither moved nor spoke until at last she passed before the window where Jerningham and I stood, and he stretched out his long arms and gathered her in to safety.

She lay like a child in his arms as he carried her to her own room and set her down on the edge of her own little bed. He was very calm and gentle with her. But the sight of his face shocked me. He looked as though he had aged ten years.

She sat where he had put her, in complete passivity. Ignoring the rest of us, he pulled up a small straight chair and sat before her, taking her hands in his.

"Look at me, Linda," he said.

She obeyed.

"You're in a kind of sleep," he told her, slowly and carefully. "It's what we call a hypnotic sleep. It's a sleep in which you do what you're told. Do you understand?"

"Yes," she said dreamily. "I understand. I do what I'm told."

"And now you're to answer some questions for me."

"Yes," she agreed docilely. "I'm to answer questions."

The room was very still. Here would be the truth at last.

"Who put you to sleep?" Jerningham asked softly.

She answered calmly, without hesitation.

"Ram Singh."

"Has he done it before?"

"Yes."

"Often?"

"Yes."

"Who told you to go through the wedding ceremony with Ryker?"

"Ram Singh."

"Did you want to?"

"No."

"Why did you do it?"

"I had promised Mr. Ryker."

"But you broke that promise Saturday!"

She made no answer to the comment. Jerningham changed it to direct question.

"Why didn't you let it stay broken?"

"Ram Singh said a promise to marry could not be broken."

Jerningham drew a deep breath.

"And did Ram Singh tell you that you must walk on the roof ledge all the way round the house?"

She answered, but we did not hear the answer. For in the same second of time there was a sudden bang behind us. The door of Linda's room had slammed shut.

Nilsson jerked it open again.

"The hall's empty," he said, after one look. "I suppose it was a draft. But I'm going to take a look in Ram Singh's room just the same."

He started off down the hall, and we turned again to Linda. The blankness was gone from her face. She was staring at us, wide-eyed, looking from one to another of our intent faces with astonishment and keen anxiety.

"What have I been doing?" she asked, urgently. "Tell me—quickly. What have I done—this time?"

"What can you remember?" Jerningham asked.

She glanced in dismay at the lights that were lit, at the darkness outside the windows.

"Nothing," she said. "Nothing since coming up here for a nap after lunch."

Jerningham drew a long sigh that was half regret and half relief.

"I'm glad you are yourself again," he said, "gladder than you'll ever know. But—if that door had waited for another five minutes before it slammed, we'd have had the whole solution of Malachi's murder in our hands."

She kept her composure with an effort.

"I don't understand, of course," she said, pleadingly, "but before you talk about anything else, won't you *please* tell me what I've done?"

"Forgive me," Jerningham said contritely. "I didn't mean to keep you in suspense. The first thing you did was to write a note saying you were going to commit suicide."

Her eyes widened and darkened, but she made no comment.

"What else?"

"After that you came downstairs and went through a wedding

ceremony. And then you came up again and insisted on walking around the house on that roof ledge,—including the stretch across the front of the house where there isn't any ledge at all. Which last proceeding—" he added with assumed lightness, "was highly unreasonable of you."

Linda had ceased to listen.

"Whom—did I marry?" she asked with her hand at her throat.

David stood silent, devouring her with his eyes.

"Ryker," Jerningham said.

The color drained from her face, and her eyes sought David's.

"Oh—*no!*" she cried, on a note of anguish.

David was at her side in an instant, with a protective arm around her.

"It'll be all right, honey," he assured her, in clumsy comfort. "We'll *make* it all right. We'll get you unmarried in a jiffy, and if Ryker puts any obstacles in the way," his voice grew savage, "I'll knock his damned head off."

"Oh, but you mustn't blame it on him," she protested miserably. "I—I'd been engaged to him———"

"So they told me," David said, with a hint of grimness. "I didn't believe it."

"It was before I knew you," she said, in wistful defense. "I was a coward, I know. But he was so kind—and it was my only way of escape. I—wish you could understand."

She drew a quick, pitiful breath, her eyes on David's face.

"I accepted his proposal, you see. Then I fell in love with you—and I knew I couldn't marry him. But I was a coward still. I didn't tell him,—nor you. I waited and waited, because I was afraid of Mr. Trent."

"With reason," Jerningham muttered under his breath.

A faint color stained her cheeks.

"I thought—" she faltered, "that if you showed you loved me, I'd pluck up courage to tell you everything, and you might find a way to help me. But you stayed away for three days, and Saturday came. . . . I was to have married him on Saturday. Did they tell you that?"

"No," said David huskily.

"Saturday!" she said. "I watched the clock. The time came for the ceremony, and still I hadn't told him. I was so sure you would come."

She had forgotten our existence.

"And then at the last minute you did come. I thought it was an answer to prayer."

David groaned.

"And I failed you," he muttered bitterly. "Blurted out my goodbye and went away again,—and never knew."

She nodded, speechless.

"I was too stunned to think," she said after a moment. "They took my acquiescence for granted, and went ahead with the ceremony. I couldn't think of anything to say to stop them. Until the minister asked 'Do you take this man to be your husband?'—and I said 'No,'—and waited for the storm to break."

She drew a shaky breath.

"I couldn't explain. I couldn't say I was in love with a man who didn't love me. I didn't say anything. Mr. Ryker was very kind and defended me. He said it was a passing mood and I'd get over it. If I—married him—this afternoon, he must have thought, of course, that I was over it. I can understand his part of it—but—*mine!*"

Her face was tragic.

"Unless——"

She turned pitifully to Jerningham.

"Unless I am insane after all. You said I wasn't. And I took your word. But I don't see how I can believe you now."

"You can believe me now more certainly than ever," Jerningham said gently. "For now we have the proof. Do you know anything about hypnotism?"

"I've only come across it in books," she said, wondering. "I never knew whether it was something real, or merely superstition."

"It's very real," he said. "It's a queer kind of sleep, in which part of your brain stays awake, and you do whatever you're told. And when you wake up, you can't remember anything about it. But the next time you are hypnotized, you can remember what happened the first time."

She was listening with growing hope and wonder in her eyes.

"It isn't a form of insanity?"

"Not in the least. At the hands of a skillful operator it can happen to anyone."

Suddenly he grinned.

"It has even happened to Nilsson since we've been in this house," he said. "So you can see it's no respecter of persons."

She glanced at Nilsson, now back again from his trip to Ram Singh's room, and standing watch in the doorway. There was acute embarrassment in his face. In spite of herself she smiled.

"And that's what—happened to me?"

"It is. You were hypnotized when you married Ryker this afternoon, and wrote your suicide note, and went walking on the ledge of the roof. You did all those things because you had been told to, and you couldn't help yourself. Those things and more. There's not a doubt in the world but that the other gaps in your memory, which have made you doubt your sanity, have been due to the same cause. So you see— you're quite as sane as Nilsson."

Her eyes filled suddenly.

"If Saint Peter ever raises a question about your passport into heaven," she said, with a shaky little laugh, "just tell him what you've done for me!"

"It was Nilsson who proved your sanity," Jerningham said in quick disclaim. "He's the one to thank. The things *I* want to do for you haven't been accomplished yet. I'm worrying about your life and liberty, as well as about your happiness."

He hesitated for a moment, then went on frankly.

"You see, since you were hypnotized, you weren't responsible for these various acts,—but somebody else *was*. Somebody else wanted you to die. And that person, we believe, was the real murderer of Malachi Trent."

She looked up in startled interest.

"I've thought all along," he confided, "that your story of the murder was partly imagination,—that is, partly your guess as to what you must have done, rather than your memory of what you did. Is that the case?"

She nodded.

"Yes. There's no reason why I shouldn't admit it now."

"And the part you guessed at was the actual killing?"

"More than that—the concealment, too. I guessed at the whole thing."

She smiled a rather ironical little smile.

"The very first story I told you was the truth," she said. "I didn't know Mr. Trent had been murdered. I didn't remember a thing between the time that I hid on the window seat and fell asleep, and the moment after the crash when I found Mr. Trent's body lying on the floor."

"Then I was right after all," David gasped. "You *didn't* know you'd killed him. But then—why on earth did you confess to doing it?"

"It's not so strange, is it?" she said. "I knew from what I overheard that you believed I had killed him, and I realized it must be true. I'd been afraid for some time that I was insane. I knew Mr. Jerningham had discovered the contents of the will, and had found out about the 'hospital'. I knew if I said I couldn't remember what I'd done, you'd all be sure I was insane, and send me to an institution. I couldn't stand the thought of that. I'd rather have paid the penalty for murder three times over. So I confessed. I didn't tell you any lies. I only told you my guesses at the truth!"

"You weren't guessing at the contents of the will," Jerningham observed. "You had that straight. How did you know?"

"Mr. Trent told me what he was going to do," she answered simply. "It was part of the last threat he made."

There was a little silence. No one offered a comment on this explanation which she considered so natural. But for my own part, I was paying amazed homage in my mind. Homage to the spirit that could make the choice which she had made. Homage to the resolution that could hold its chosen course so steadily that, except for Jerningham, we had all accepted her "guesses at the truth" as literal and indisputable fact. Homage, above all, to the fine temper of mind and character which, after all she had been through in the last hour, scorned the luxury of emotional reaction, and calmly attacked the problem that confronted us all.

"You said a while back," she reminded Jerningham, "that if some door hadn't slammed, you'd have had the whole solution of Mr. Trent's death. How would you have got it?"

"From you," he answered, ruefully. "You were still under hypnosis, and answering questions as fast as I could ask them. You told us who hypnotized you, and how he made you marry Ryker. But before we reached the murder, or the attempt on your life, the door slammed and waked you up."

She was intent upon the problem.

"Who hypnotized me?

"Ram Singh."

"Strange!" she commented, with a shudder. "Then it was Ram Singh who made me marry Mr. Ryker, and kill Mr. Trent, and try to kill myself?"

"So we believe."

"And I know all about it, you say, only we haven't access to my knowledge. Can't we tap it somehow?"

"Yes, by hypnotizing you again. Ryker is in Philadelphia now, enlisting the services of an expert psychiatrist for that purpose. He's going to bring one out tonight. Then we can proceed against Ram Singh!"

Faint and far below us in the library, shrilled the telephone bell. I hurried down to answer it. Ryker's voice came over the wire.

"I've had the most atrocious luck," he said. "One man is reading a paper tonight before some society, and another is attending his daughter's wedding, and the third is ill. The fourth man is out of town, over in Merchantville and I'm going to drive over there and see if I can't kidnap him by main force. But it's quite likely to be a wild goose chase. If I have to come back empty-handed, it'll be late and I'll sneak in quietly and not disturb you people."

I went back upstairs and reported to Jerningham. He heard the message through without comment. For a long moment he was silent. Then his jaw set.

"If it's fate," he said at last, "I'll accept the omen."

He threw up his head with the gesture of the war horse that smelleth the battle afar off, and saith among the trumpets, "Ha, ha."

"I shan't wait any longer," he said. "I'm going to have it out with Ram Singh—now!

19

THE SERVANT
OF KALI

Good!" boomed Nilsson. "I'm with you!"

Jerningham's brows twisted in his familiar quizzical frown.

"I'd rather have you just outside, within call," he said. "I want to deal with Ram Singh alone."

"Nothing doing," Nilsson declared. "It's not safe. That bird doesn't fight with our weapons. You may think you know just what he can do. I'm not so sure."

"Neither am I," Jerningham admitted. "But that's one reason there should be a reserve force, outside the danger zone, to act as rescue party if necessary."

"That'll have to be David and Mac, then," Nilsson said with decision. "I'm going along."

"So am I," I said. "I'm a casualty already, and I'll be more use as an observer than as reinforcements."

"What you mean," Jerningham declared shrewdly, "is that you don't want to miss anything. However, come along, you two, if you must. But this is *my* duel. Leave the choice of weapons and technique to me."

He cast a somewhat anxious glance at the girl who stood listening.

"I wanted to detail David to guard you," he said. "I don't think you ought to be alone again till this is over. There's such a thing as post-hypnotic suggestion, you know,—orders to be carried out after you wake. It's not nearly so strong, of course——"

"If you don't want me left alone," she suggested quietly, "give me a gun and detail me to the rescue party. I—I'm not exactly neutral, you know."

Jerningham gave her a moment's approving scrutiny.

"Great!" he said. "I never did have any use for the heroine who stands around and wrings her hands during the big fight scene."

"Nor I!" she smiled. "If it comes to fighting, it's as much my fight as yours."

We left it at that. Linda and David, armed with our shotguns, stationed themselves outside Ram Singh's door. Jerningham, Nilsson and I went in together, unarmed, by Jerningham's desire, except for the automatic that Nilsson always carried in his right hip pocket, no matter where he went.

Altogether, the five of us seemed an overwhelming force to be ranged against one man, but I had an uneasy feeling that the shotguns and the automatic were an absurd defense against the enemy we went to meet.

There was nothing of the enemy in Ram Singh's bearing, however, as we came in. He suffered our intrusion impassively, watching us with inscrutable eyes as we took possession of his room. It was a large room, nearly empty of furniture, bare to the point of austerity, scrupulously neat. Apart from its size, it might have been a monastery cell—except for one thing.

Between two windows, on a small table, stood the black marble statuette of Kali, which Ram Singh had begged form David. And her custodian had done her a curious honor. He had placed beneath her what looked like a golden mat. Something about its texture attracted my attention, and I moved closer to look. It was not a mat, but a mosaic of gold pieces, row after row. I remember that Linda had said Ram Singh was always paid in gold. By the look of the little table, the untouched earnings of two years of servitude were spread to make a golden carpet for Kali's feet.

I doubt, however, whether Jerningham even saw that golden tribute. He had eyes for nothing but the tall white-robed figure that stood confronting us with folded arms.

"Ram Singh," he said, crisply, "we've come for an accounting."

The dark face showed no flicker of interest.

"There must in the end be an accounting." Ram Singh assented, "for all deeds, the greatest and the least."

"I'm glad you agree," Jerningham said dryly. "The deed I want accounted for, to begin with, is the theft of the Wrath of Kali."

The dark eyes gleamed.

"It would content the Sahib, would it not," Ram Singh observed calmly, "if the thief were punished and the Wrath of Kali restored whither it belongs?"

"It should," Jerningham admitted.

"Then the Sahib may rest content," Ram Singh returned serenely. "He witnessed with his own eyes the death that overtook the thief. And the Wrath of Kali goes even now with great speed to its own place."

There was unwilling appreciation in Jerningham's face.

"I referred," he explained concisely, "to your theft of the ruby from the safe in the library. You are not dead, nor has the ruby been restored."

"The Sahib speaks from his vast ignorance," Ram Singh replied. "He should listen to the voice of instruction, that wisdom may dwell with him."

"I'm perfectly willing to listen," Jerningham declared with genuine interest, "so long as the voice of instruction sticks to the truth."

"There has been no theft but one," Ram Singh said austerely. "The Wrath of Kali was stolen from the Temple of Kali by Trent Sahib. Not by his hand, but by the hands of two whom he bought with gold to commit the sacrilege. The gold—in coins of this nation—was found upon the two."

He paused for a significant moment. That pause was the only clue we ever had to the fate of the unlucky two, but it was enough.

"It was through my fault,—the fault of permitting myself to meditate when vigilance was needed,—that the sacrilege was successful. It was permitted that I should expiate my fault by repairing the sacrilege. I put myself in Trent Sahib's way when he was in urgent need of guidance. I became his servant. I remained his servant until the vengeance of Kali was accomplished. I restored to Kali the treasure that was hers. The account is cleared."

I gasped at the effrontery of his reference to vengeance. Jerningham passed it by and went off at an apparent tangent.

"The account is overpaid, I think," he said with cool censure. "You've trespassed on the lives of people who never wronged your goddess. You've forced Miss Marshall into a marriage it was not her will to make."

Ram Singh was loftily undisturbed.

"I have acquired merit," he answered, "by saving her from a great sin,—a sin that she would have expiated through many lives. A word of betrothal once given may not be broken. She owes me a debt of thanks that that sin is not upon her soul."

The words struck me as an echo from the Middle Ages. The fanatics of the Inquisition, from Torquemada down, had endeavored to save the souls of their victims with one hand, even while they executed the poor wretches with the other. Here was a fanatic running true to form.

"I suppose," Jerningham was saying ironically, "she also owes you gratitude for the other occasions on which you have hypnotized her?"

Ram Singh could give irony for irony.

"Assuredly," he answered. "As the Sahib may have observed in his wisdom, she is not a free soul. She is a slave to illusion. She believes that it is of importance whether she lives out her life in one place or another. The enlightened are not subject to that illusion."

His glance swept momentarily about the bare room that had been his for the last two years.

"She lived in fear," he went on, "of being sent away. She endeavored in all things to obey Trent Sahib. At times, being wearied of her, he demanded from her that which was impossible to body or spirit. By my aid she has more than once achieved the impossible, and strife has been avoided. Thus have I acquired merit."

Jerningham's face was a study.

"Perhaps you have, on that one score," he conceded. "Was the incident of the suit cases full of books, one of the occasions you refer to?"

Ram Singh nodded.

"And when you had hypnotized her she was able to carry upstairs a load she hadn't been able even to lift?"

"Why not?" Ram Singh answered. "The word of command can release strength hitherto unknown. Also——" was there a note of warning in the level voice? "it can take strength away."

"I stand enlightened," Jerningham said dryly. "And what merit did you acquire by sending Miss Marshall to her death on the ledge of the roof?"

I held my breath. Would the Hindu admit this charge as complacently as he had the rest? Not a muscle moved in the dark face.

"Is she dead?" Ram Singh inquired, simply.

"No," Jerningham answered. "We brought her back from the brink, and while she still slept she answered questions,—concerning you."

A silence grew in the room.

"The Sahib is pleased to speak in riddles," Ram Singh said at last.

"You know the answer to the riddle," Jerningham retorted. "You ordered her to walk on the roof ledge—and to continue to walk where no ledge existed."

Another silence. It seemed to me that the dark eyes began to glow with a baleful light.

"I gave no such order," Ram Singh declared at length.

He paused for a moment, then went on with quiet assurance.

"Nor did she tell you that I gave such an order."

I remembered the slam of the door that had prevented her from telling us. Did Ram Singh know of that? Or had he merely read our faces?

Jerningham ignored the challenge.

"It was a very cleverly planned crime, Ram Singh," he said. "It was almost as clever an idea to make Linda kill herself, as it was to make her kill Malachi Trent."

There was not a flicker in the dark face beneath the turban.

"The Sahib has taken counsel with folly, and has lost his understanding," Ram Singh replied disdainfully. "Of what use to lay the jewel of truth before such an one?"

The line of Jerningham's mouth hardened.

"You might try it!" he suggested.

The shoulders beneath the white robe shrugged slightly.

"For what purpose does the Sahib imagine I took service with the desecrator of Kali's shrine? By what necessity did I follow him to his own land and endure two years of servitude in his house? Had my hand been free to strike, to reach out and recover the Wrath of Kali, there was no need to have set foot outside the gorge of the Brahmaputra. A knife is swift and silent, and the waters of the Brahmaputra tell no tales."

"You pique my curiosity," Jerningham remarked. "Why didn't you use the knife, and make an end?"

"For the only reason that would have held my hand," Ram Singh answered, with more than a touch of scorn. "It was forbidden. Kali is a jealous goddess. No servant of hers may presume to rob her of her vengeance. Twice before in a hundred years, the Wrath of Kali has been stolen. Twice before, a servant of Kali has followed the thief, wherever his fate might lead him, till Kali herself saw fit to strike him down. Twice before, the Wrath of Kali has been restored to its ordained place when her vengeance was accomplished."

He wrapped himself in a dignified silence, but his eyes were watchful.

Jerningham's brow slanted in his characteristic frown.

"So you attribute the murder to Kali herself," he said, deliberately. "That's ingenious,—but not very convincing to my Occidental mind. In fact, my feeble intelligence persists in laying the guilt of the murder upon your head!"

Ram Singh's eyes were contemptuous.

"To enlighten the ignorant is to acquire merit," he said stiffly. "If the Sahib's ignorance is not so stubborn as to resist all proof, I can establish the truth before his eyes."

"Great!" said Jerningham. "Suppose you do!"

"The Sahib has said that questions concerning me were asked of her who slept," Ram Singh declared slowly. "He did not ask enough— or there could now be no doubt as to the truth."

Again that uncanny knowledge of what we had and had not asked of Linda! Jerningham made no answer. He waited intently for Ram Singh to proceed.

"She shall sleep again," the slow significant voice went on, "and the Sahib may ask whatever he will."

"I would not trust her to your hands," Jerningham said.

A shrug of the shoulders beneath the white robe.

"She shall go to sleep in the Sahib's presence," Ram Singh offered, "where no harm can befall her."

I could see, mirrored in Jerningham's face, his struggle to fathom the intent behind that proposal. I remembered that a few hours before, Linda had been in a state of hypnosis so deep that she could not answer questions, so deep that we feared she would never wake. Did Ram Singh plan to trick us in some such fashion? Or was there a deadlier project lurking in his mind?

"To enlighten the ignorant is to acquire merit," Jerningham quoted at last. "Tell me, Ram Singh, might it be that while Miss Marshall falls asleep at your command, another,—a bystander, perhaps,—would also sleep, in obedience to the command that was not meant for him?"

Ram Singh hesitated. I could not judge whether in truth he weighed his answer, or only the advisability of giving it.

"It might be," he admitted slowly.

"Or that several bystanders would sleep—or all the bystanders?" Jerningham pursued.

"It might be," Ram Singh agreed.

So that was it. I listened for Jerningham's scathing rejection of the treacherous proposal. But it was Nilsson who broke out.

"That's what his game is, Jerningham. Don't fall for it."

Jerningham laughed reassuringly.

"Don't worry," he said. "There's no danger of any such wholesale hypnotism. Ram Singh overrates himself. I've no doubt he thinks he can do it,—but it's one thing to hypnotize a young girl who has been terrorized for years, or a man who is asleep and defenseless, and it's quite another proposition to enforce your will on a bunch of men who are wide awake and in their right minds. I think we're quite safe—" he bowed ironically to Ram Singh,— "in accepting the opportunity for enlightenment which Ram Singh offers us."

I was watching the Hindu's face, and I felt a sharp regret that Jerningham had been so reckless in his skepticism. Added to whatever intention Ram Singh might already have nursed, there was now evident in his smoldering eyes a determination to make good his words at any cost.

"Is it in the Sahib's mind," he inquired, pointedly, "to warn those who will stand by? Or is the Sahib's disbelief truly as great as he has said?"

"I shan't warn 'em," Jerningham said, shortly.

He turned to Nilsson and me.

"And neither shall you," he enjoined us. "There's not the slightest need."

There was a distinct gleam of satisfaction in the dark face.

"And when does the Sahib desire to receive his enlightenment?"

"In the morning," Jerningham decided, with the faintest suggestion of a yawn. "Mr. Ryker has a right to be present, and he won't return till very late tonight. In the meantime—" his voice hardened, "I strongly recommend that you suspend your activities till daylight. There will be a guard all night in the hall outside your door."

Ram Singh made no answer. But as we left the room I carried with me an uneasy recollection of the satisfied look I had glimpsed upon his face.

We found David and Linda waiting for us in the hall, and looking as though guard duty had not bored them in the least.

"Did you get what you wanted?" David asked hopefully.

"We got a lot of admissions," Jerningham answered. "But not the ones we need most. We have a good chance of completing the case in the morning, but that chance—" he turned to Linda,—"depends on you."

"What do you want of me?" she asked, with eager interest.

"Something braver than fighting," he said gravely. "I want you to let Ram Singh hypnotize you once more—for the last time."

The color went out of Linda's face.

"She shan't do it," David declared flatly. "Not to catch all the criminals this side of Chicago."

"She'll do it to catch this one criminal," Jerningham explained patiently, "because—there isn't any safety for her till he's caught."

Linda put a hand on David's sleeve, but it was Jerningham to whom she spoke.

"I'll do it if it's necessary," she said steadily. "I don't think you'd ask it if it were not."

"I wouldn't," Jerningham said.

"And you'll be there yourself?"

"Every second," he promised.

"All right," she said, simply. "When?"

"Not till morning."

Her mouth curved.

"I hope you aren't going to recommend that I go to bed and get a good night's rest!"

"No," he conceded, "I think you'd be much wiser not to sleep."

"I'm certainly not sleepy now. I'm starving," she said, and her eyes met David's. "Let's go down and see what we can find in the kitchen."

"You'll find things in a mess, I'm afraid," I said. "The dinner table isn't even cleared. We left very suddenly when we heard Mrs. Ketchem scream and thought it was you."

She linked her arm in David's.

"We'll clear things away," she said. "It'll be a satisfaction to deal with something as prosaic as a dishpan."

We watched them till they passed out of sight on the stairs.

"She takes it lightly," Nilsson said.

"She takes it bravely," Jerningham corrected.

Nilsson turned upon him.

"I kept my mouth shut, but I think you're clean crazy," he said grimly. "You said you were going to give Ram Singh rope enough to hang himself. You've given him rope enough to hang us all."

Jerningham's face was very somber.

"I know," he said. "I did it because I had to."

His brows twisted in a frown of anxiety.

"You and Mac and I," he said, "will have to stand ready to cut the rope—for the sake of all our lives."

20

THROUGH THE CRACK
OF THE DOOR

for the rest of that night, Cairnstone House was an armed garrison, whose members, one after the other, took their turns at guard duty on the third floor, keeping watch over Ram Singh's room at one end of the long hall, guarding the rooms of the two women at the other. I was allowed no turn myself, since the wound in my right hand barred me from effective action in an emergency. And we did not call upon Ryker, who returned alone and unsuccessful from his wild goose chase to Merchantville between two and three in the morning, and went straight to his room. But Jerningham, David and Nilsson, stood watch in turn.

As a matter of fact, Jerningham might as well have stayed on duty continuously. He returned to our room about two o'clock only to resume his pacing with silent, cat-like strides, up an down the border of the rug. Five paces up, five paces down, stepping always mechanically on the same spots, till I thought he would have them worn through to the boards before the dawn.

I did not interrupt his vigil by any protest. Sleep was impossible for either of us. And it was not rest that Jerningham needed. The thing he needed could come only from the depths of his own mind, and I watched him struggle to bring it forth as I had watched him through many lesser crises in the past. But never before had he worn such a haggard, desperate face, and never before had there been such stakes upon the board.

It was shortly after four o'clock that the long silence was broken by one small, significant sound.

A sharp click from the direction of the door.

Jerningham stopped dead between one silent stride and the next. We both stared at the door. There was nothing to see. Nothing—except—the key was not in the key-hole. It was lying on the rug, two feet from the door.

I gazed at it, fascinated. I had used that key myself to lock the door, after letting Jerningham in, two hours before. Used it, and left it in the lock. Could it have been forced out with only that single click which we had heard? Forced out by someone who was even now standing outside the door?

I strained my ears—and caught the stealthy grating of the lock as it yielded to a key from outside.

Jerningham reached noiselessly for his shotgun. As the knob began to turn, he raised the gun to his shoulder.

"Who's there?" he demanded sternly.

There was no response. The door began to swing toward us, slowly, slowly, with the uncanny deliberation of a slow-motion picture.

"Answer, or I'll fire."

He was answered, but not in words. Slantwise through the opening came the blued steel muzzle of a twelve gauge shotgun. We knew of two such guns in the house besides the one that Jerningham now held tensely to his shoulder. There was mine—which I had lent to David for his turn as sentry. And there was Nilsson's. I began to feel a little dizzy. David or Nilsson,—which of them had been overpowered—without a sound?

I braced myself for the roar of Jerningham's gun. It did not come. The door opened wider. That ominous muzzle swung nearer to its mark, and nearer. And still Jerningham held his fire.

Amazed, I turned to look at him. His face was twisted in a very agony of indecision. And suddenly I understood. He dared not fire until he knew who was behind the door. It might be Nilsson. It might be Linda. We were helpless until we knew whether the enemy had brought us death by his own hand, or sent it by the hand of one we loved.

The line of the gun barrel swung closer still to Jerningham. In desperation I moved toward the door. My right hand might be useless, but surely I could deflect the gun barrel and give Jerningham his chance.

Jerningham's voice halted me in my tracks.

"Get back, Mac!" he shouted, with such assurance that I obeyed automatically, thinking he had seen the enemy's face.

But even as I obeyed, I saw what he had seen. Not a face but a hand on the gun barrel, a lean, strong hand, neither large nor small. Neither large nor small! Not Nilsson's! Not Linda's! The roar of Jerningham's gun filled my ears.

Like one in a dream I watched the hand and the gun barrel jerk back, the door go shut. Like one in a dream, I marveled that the charge from Jerningham's gun made no mark upon the door or casing. And then Jerningham's voice shattered the dream,—Jerningham's voice, broken and husky, crying,

"Mac!—Mac!—Are you there?—What happened?"

I turned. He was swaying as he stood, groping for me with his left hand while his right arm hung limp. His face was a dreadful mask of blood. I stepped within reach of that groping hand, and put my arm about his shoulders.

"I'm here," I said, as steadily as I could. "Did it get you in the eyes?"

"I don't—think so," he answered, "Forehead—is where I feel it. But—I can't see."

"No wonder," I muttered shakily.

I fumbled through his pockets and mine, found a couple of fresh handkerchiefs, and thrust one into his fingers.

"Hold that against your forehead," I said, and once the crimson stream was checked, I began with dread in my heart to wipe the blood from his eyes.

"Thank the Lord!" he exclaimed after a moment. "I *can* see,— after all. Whew! That was close!"

For a few seconds I was dizzy with relief. Then I became conscious of voices outside the door, clamoring.

"Jerningham! Mac! Are you all right?"

Jerningham laughed unsteadily.

"In spots," he called back. "Come in!"

They came. David and Ryker first, from their rooms on either side of us. Nilsson, with his gun in hand, close on their heels, having come down on the double quick from the upper hall where he had been standing guard.

Nilsson took one look at Jerningham, and turned to me.

"Who did it?" he demanded grimly, and if ever I heard death in a man's voice, it was in Nilsson's then.

"Don't know," Jerningham answered, the handkerchief against his forehead growing more crimson every minute. "Somebody poked a gun through the doorway at us, and when I fired, the world blew up in my face. But get back on the job, quick! See if Ram Singh's in his room, and look after Linda!"

"Somebody else can look after them," Nilsson returned gruffly. "I'm looking after you."

"I'll go," David volunteered hastily. "Give me your gun."

He grabbed Nilsson's and went back up to the third floor with all speed.

Nilsson turned to Ryker.

"Call Dr. Lampton, will you?" he said. "Tell him to step on it. And keep your eyes open as you go! If you see anything, shout to us!"

Ryker ran downstairs to make the call. Nilsson gave his whole attention to Jerningham's injury. When he had examined it closely and replaced the sodden crimson handkerchief with a fresh one, he drew a breath of relief.

"Raked the bone," was his gruff verdict. "You look worse than you did the day we finished the Prussian Guard, but I don't think it's dangerous. Narrow squeak, though! If that hunk of steel had struck an inch lower, through the eye,——"

"Curtain!" Jerningham finished, laconically, and switched the subject. "Can't you tie this handkerchief in place? My hand's getting cramped holding it."

"Hand pressure's better for stopping the blood," Nilsson advised. "Use your right hand for a change. Or—can't you move your right hand?" he asked sharply.

"Oh yes," Jerningham answered, with a wry smile. "I can move it, but it's not worth what it costs."

Nilsson whistled. Then he laid clumsily gentle hands on Jerningham's right arm and shoulder.

"Collar bone," he said succinctly. "You won't want to lie down with that. Better sit on the bed and lean back here,—" he was chucking the pillows together as he spoke,—"and keep still till Dr. Lampton comes. We won't meddle with the wound. That's a doctor's job."

Jerningham obeyed docilely.

"And now, how'd it happen?" Nilsson demanded.

"Search me," Jerningham returned. "It was my own gun. Something blew out."

Nilsson stooped and lifted the gun from the floor where Jerningham had dropped it.

"Blew up at the breech," he said. "First case I've ever seen. Might have got some obstruction in the muzzle—but then it would only have split the barrel. Blamed queer!"

He frowned at the shattered gun.

"Shell must have been defective," he said finally, "with a heavy overload of powder. But that's blamed queer too!"

"That's not all that's queer," I said. "Where'd the shot go? They didn't touch the door or the casing—or anything else, so far as I can see."

It took Nilsson only a glance to verify that.

"Queerer and queerer," he growled.

"Not queer at all," Jerningham corrected, his quiet argumentative voice coming strangely from the blood streaked mask that was his face. "If the shot went nowhere, there weren't any shot to begin with. So the shell wasn't defective—it was fixed!"

"Fixed—how?"

"Shot taken out, extra powder put in. Sure damage to the man behind the gun. No danger whatever to the man in front. Beautifully simple! And it explains a lot."

He settled back gingerly into the pillows, and winced at the stab of pain from his broken collar bone.

"Explains what?" Nilsson demanded.

"The enemy's queer tactics. He gave me every provocation to fire, without trying to get in a shot himself. That didn't make sense at the time. But it does now. All he wanted was to make me pull the trigger."

"Strange business," Nilsson growled.

"Purposely strange," Jerningham surmised. "If Mac hadn't been here to see what I saw, nobody would believe my tale of a slow-motion assailant who vanished when I fired. They'd think I was half asleep and fired at a nightmare."

Nilsson was going doggedly over the facts.

"Fellow did have a gun, you say. Whose gun?"

"It looked like mine," I answered. "I'd lent it to David. I suppose when he finished his turn of guard duty, he leaned it against the wall outside our door, all handy!"

"Fine kid trick!" Nilsson rumbled, in disgust.

He stalked to the door and looked outside.

"Yeah! Here it is," he commented, and came back, holding the gun in cautious fingers, to look at it under the light.

"And not a decent print on it," he growled.

Jerningham, restless and feverish with pain, was looking from one gun to the other.

"You'd better examine the shell in Mac's gun, too," he remarked suddenly. "It was right here with mine, and nobody tampering with 'em would have known which was which."

Nilsson complied, pried out the disk of cardboard that closed the end of the shell, and whistled at what he saw.

"Right you are," he said soberly. "No shot, and a terrific over-charge of powder. Jerningham, if this is the way your gun was loaded, you're lucky to be alive.!

"We're all lucky to be alive," Jerningham answered. "And I'd give all the royalties of a dozen plays to know whether the luck will hold for the next four hours."

From outside came the sound of a motor car rushing up the drive.

"There's the doctor," Nilsson said, and started for the door. "While he fixes you up, I'm going to hunt some evidence that will hang this atrocity on Ram Singh."

"You won't find any," Jerningham said wearily. "He wouldn't have done it if he hadn't been able to cover his tracks."

Nilsson stopped short in sudden exasperation.

"I'm fed up," he snapped. "I'm going to take that bird to Media—now!"

Jerningham's face, under the blood smears, was ghastly but inflexible.

"The hell you are!" he said. "Shut that door and come back here, Nilsson."

Nilsson came, but there was no yielding in his face. It was a moment or so before Jerningham proceeded. When he did, his voice was low and uneven.

"You've *got* to back me up, Carl," he said, and the rare use of Nilsson's given name startled me by its note of appeal. "We're fighting an extraordinary criminal in the midst of an extraordinary crime. We've got to beat him at his own game. If we don't, he wins hands down."

Jerningham leaned forward, regardless of his broken collar bone.

"We've just one chance to beat him," he went on, "and I'm risking all our lives on that one chance. Because the game is worth the candle."

We heard Dr. Lampton's knock on the door, but not one of us so much as glanced that way.

"I followed you into Belleau Wood ten years ago," Jerningham said. "Follow me now."

There was a silence. Nilsson cleared his throat.

"Damn you," he said huskily. "What else can I do?"

And turning his back upon us, he strode to the door and let the doctor in.

21

THE OPENING OF
THE LAST ACT

T he plump, gray-haired little doctor had his share of human curiosity, but he was a physician first of all. He devoted himself with deft and gentle skill to the dressing of Jerningham's injuries. And he accepted without comment Jerningham's statement that he had been hurt by the explosion of his own gun. That is, he accepted it until he had done all he could for Jerningham's comfort. Then he began to ask questions, sympathetic but searching.

He wondered why Jerningham's gun had exploded. And what he was doing with a gun at four o'clock in the morning. And why all of us were up and fully dressed at such an hour.

It was my unhappy duty to answer him. Jerningham had been instructed to keep still and not talk. Nilsson had left the room. So I floundered unassisted, scarce knowing what I said. And with every clumsy evasion, the friendly little doctor's expression grew more doubtful, and his face became overcast. He went away presently with the hurt conviction that I had not been quite frank!

Meanwhile Nilsson was searching for evidence to connect Ram Singh with the latest "accident." As Jerningham had predicted, he found nothing. Neither David nor Ryker had heard any suspicious sound before the explosion of Jerningham's gun roused them. Nor had they seen anyone in the hall when they emerged from their respective rooms. David's remorseful admission that he had left my shotgun leaning against the wall outside our door, was of little help. Less helpful still was the fact that when he ran up to the third floor immediately after the accident, to reassure Linda and take up the guard duty that Nilsson had laid down, he found Ram Singh apparently sleeping soundly in his bed.

Jerningham took no interest in the investigation. With the doctor's departure he fell into a fit of deep abstraction which I forbore to disturb. Whatever the problem that had troubled him through the earlier watches of the night, it was not yet solved, and his face grew more haggard as the hours passed.

When the first streaks of dawn showed through the window, he rose painfully to his feet.

"Zero hour!" he said, and stalked over to his dresser. He started involuntarily at sight of his own gaunt features in the glass, and made a left-handed try at subduing the wild rebellion of the hair that stood erect above his bandages.

"I look like a gory pirate!" he commented with grim humor. "An unprejudiced observer would pick me for the murderer without any hesitation. Not much I can do about it, either. . . . Well, see you downstairs presently, Mac. I'm going up to have a word with Nilsson, first."

It could hardly have been more than a word, for when I got down I found Jerningham emerging from some errand in the library. Linda was helping Mrs. Ketchem with the preparations for breakfast. As we turned into the transverse hall, we caught a glimpse of her in the dining room, as she set the grapefruit upon the table. And presently Ryker emerged from the dining room and joined us. I wondered what might have passed between him and Linda concerning their wedding of the day before. He said nothing that enlightened me, but his face seemed a trifle pale beneath its tan.

"Ryker," Jerningham said, "Nilsson and I have come to a decision about Linda. We think that at the time she killed Malachi she had been hypnotized by Ram Singh, and was not in the least to blame. We agree that she may go away and rest. But first we want to be perfectly sure about the hypnotism. Ram Singh has promised, in a spirit of bravado I think, to hypnotize her again this morning. If he can do so, we'll have our proof and be convinced."

"You don't think there is any danger to her in that proceeding?"

"We'll all be right there," Jerningham said. "I don't believe he can do her any harm."

"I suppose not," Ryker said thoughtfully. "I don't know much about hypnotism, and I'd rather not meddle with it. But if she must be hypnotized before you'll let her go—I hope Ram Singh succeeds."

He left it at that, and Jerningham excused himself and went off through the dining room to look for Linda. I gathered from his manner that he did not want my company. So I stayed with Ryker, trying to conceal my own excitement and anxiety, lest he might guess how much more was scheduled to happen than Jerningham had indicated, and might, in his fears for Linda, put a fatal obstacle in the way of Jerningham's plans.

Presently, Linda came and summoned us to breakfast. Obsessed as I was with the impending ordeal, I found the thought of food grotesquely irrelevant. Why eat, when no one knew how many of us would be alive at the end of the next hour? I took my place with the rest and went through the motions of eating, but I can remember nothing about the meal. My impression is that nobody spoke and none of the food had any taste. At any rate, the meal was quickly over.

From that time on, events seemed to move in a relentless procession. I remember Jerningham rising suddenly to his feet and asking us with quiet authority to adjourn to the library. I remember a feeling of mild astonishment at the discovery that he had herded Mrs. Ketchem into the room along with the rest of us. I remember the grimly imperturbable face of Nilsson as he ushered in Ram Singh, who bore himself like a king entering his audience chamber, rather than a murderer confronted by his judges.

I remember the enigmatic courtesy with which Ram Singh asked Linda to seat herself on the davenport, and the celerity with which David and Ryker preempted the space on either side of her. And the air of hostility with which Mrs. Ketchem, not having been asked to sit, proceeded to do so, settling herself in the larger of the fireside chairs. I remember being glad that Jerningham, weary as he was, did not take the other big chair, but remained standing between Nilsson and me, at one end of the davenport.

I remember the successive waves of irrational dread that swept over me as, one by one, the heavy black velour curtains were drawn across the windows by Ram Singh's lean, brown hand, and the room grew darker, and darker, and darker, and darker still. I remember the ghostly effect of his white-robed figure moving through the darkness till he took his stand on the hearth. I remember the unexpected scratch of a match, and the little sudden golden flame that sprang into flickering life, transferred itself to the wick of a candle standing on the mantel shelf, and steadied into a tiny, shining blade of light that stabbed the darkness.

"Look at the flame!" Ram Singh commanded Linda softly. "Look at the flame!"

I remember the odd slow quality of his voice, at the same time soothing and inflexible.

"Look at the flame. It is burning higher—higher—It is growing brighter—brighter—Look at the flame."

I remember the strange way in which that tiny dagger of light seemed to dominate the room, throwing all else into impenetrable shadow,—even the carven bronze of Ram Singh's face.

"Look at the flame. There is no other light in the world. There is only darkness around you. There is only darkness beneath you. Darkness—and the pit of sleep—the pit of sleep."

I remember how the voice itself seemed to come from the formless dark of empty space.

"Look at the flame. It is high above you—high—high—You are sinking away from it—down deep in the dark—down deep asleep—down deep asleep——"

The voice was irresistible, inexorable. I grew conscious of a great weariness. The lids of my eyes were heavy and dry.

"Look at the flame. It is higher and higher—brighter and brighter—Too high—Too bright—It dazzles your eyes—It blinds your eyes—Shut out the light—Shut your eyes—And sleep!"

I remember that I shut my eyes against the intolerable brightness of the candle flame.

And after that,—I remember nothing more.

Nothing, that is, until I came dazedly to myself, to find Jerningham shaking me viciously, but silently, with the fingers of his good hand gripping the back of my collar. Under the merciless treatment, my mind and my vision cleared at the same time. Nothing in the room had changed,—and the candle flame had shrunk once more to its real size.

In the dim light of that single candle, Ram Singh's dark face was a sardonic mask of triumph.

"Is the Sahib enlightened?" he asked softly.

Jerningham hesitated for the space of one long breath.

"Linda!" he said.

There was no answer.

"Linda! Do you hear me?"

"Yes," she answered tonelessly.

"Did Ram Singh order you to kill Malachi Trent?"

"No."

"Did anyone order you to kill him?"

"No."

"Did you kill him?"

"No."

"Did you help to conceal the killing?"

"No."

"Do you know who killed him?"

"No."

"Show us where you were when he was killed."

Mechanically she rose and went to the window seat at the side of the room. The curtains were still drawn. For an instant a sheet of daylight entered the darkened room, as she parted the curtains and stretched herself out upon the upholstered seat. Then the curtains fell together again and hid her from our sight.

"Is the Sahib enlightened?" Ram Singh inquired ironically.

Jerningham made no answer.

"David!" he said, in a tone of authority. "Do you hear me?"

"Yes," David answered, with a voice as dull as Linda's.

"Did you kill Malachi Trent?"

"No."

"Do you know who killed him?"

"No."

"Show us where you were when he was killed."

As mechanically as Linda had done, David rose from the davenport and left the library. Nilsson followed to observe, and came back a moment later.

"Just inside the room across the hall," he reported under his breath. "As he told us in the first place."

"Is the Sahib enlightened?" Ram Singh asked for the third time.

The question stretched my already taut nerves to the breaking point. To travel as long a road as we had traveled,—only to have it end in a blank wall,—and then to be taunted with the state of our enlightenment!

But Jerningham was imperturbable.

"Mrs. Ketchem!" he said, with a ring of command. "Do you hear me?"

"I'm not deaf," she crackled with malicious amusement.

"Nor asleep, apparently," was his dry rejoinder.

"Of course, I'm not asleep," she said acridly. "I didn't look at the candle. The rest of you can let him order you around if you like. But no heathen can tell *me* where to look—nor anything else!"

Her wrinkled old face was grotesque in the candle light.

"And neither can you!" she finished pointedly.

Again a silence filled the room. I heard Nilsson's feet shift a trifle on the floor.

"Ryker!" Jerningham said. "Do you hear me?"

"Yes," Ryker answered mechanically, and I realized for the first time that he too had looked at the candle flame too long.

"Then show us," Jerningham said, and his voice was suddenly casual, "show us what you were doing when Malachi Trent was killed."

Absently Ryker rose and started toward the door. But when he reached the spot between the door and Malachi's desk he stopped, hesitated, as if at a loss. He rested one hand uncertainly on the back of Malachi's chair.

And then, subtly, his bearing changed. He stiffened where he stood. When he turned again in our direction, it was with his usual decisive self-assurance.

"How," he demanded, in his crispest tones, "did I get over here?"

Jerningham's hand closed over my wrist in warning.

"You walked there, under hypnosis," he answered coolly, "after telling us why you murdered Malachi Trent and tried to murder Linda."

for one eternal moment, no one moved or spoke. I had need of Jerningham's steadying grip upon my wrist, for a dizzy sense of unreality swept over me, as though his astounding words had turned the world upside down. Before I had more than begun to grasp their implication, Ryker's cold voice cut the silence.

"You have," he said, "most rotten taste in jokes."

Without answering, Jerningham crossed the dim room and drew back the heavy curtains, letting the daylight flood in. Linda was still lying unconscious upon the window seat, but he never glanced at her. He turned and stood with his back to the windows, studying Ryker's face in the full light.

"It's no joke," Jerningham said at last. "You told us, under hypnosis, what you would never have told under any other circumstances,— the truth!"

I began to see what Jerningham was driving at, and marveled at the heroic dimensions of his bluff.

With a bewildered gesture, Ryker turned to the rest of us.

"What's the man raving about?" he demanded. "Is he hypnotized himself?"

"Don't worry about me," Jerningham said, laconically. "I didn't look at Ram Singh's candle flame. But you did,—or you wouldn't have answered my questions with such gratifying candor."

Ryker cast a swift glance at Nilsson's face. But Nilsson had risen to the occasion. He wore a look of grim amusement that made me wonder for a moment whether Ryker might not actually have betrayed himself as Jerningham pretended.

It made Ryker wonder too.

"Of course I don't know what I may have said," he conceded, with a careless shrug. "If you can hypnotize a chap and make him do anything you say, you can probably as easily make him answer 'Yes' to anything you ask. But—" his voice hardened,—"if you've resorted to hypnotism in order to make me the goat of your latest crazy theory,— you've carried your playacting a little too far."

Jerningham shook his head thoughtfully.

"No. My mistake all along has been that I haven't gone far enough. I took you and your devotion to Linda at face value,—even when I was trying the hardest to keep an open mind."

"I should hope so!" Ryker said crisply.

Jerningham's white face beneath the bandage assumed a look of chagrin.

"And the humiliating thing is," he continued, "that now, when you've told us the truth, I realize it's simply been staring us in the face. I don't understand how we could have been so blind!"

His voice took on the tone with which he embarks upon a purely intellectual argument.

"For instance, my last 'crazy theory,'—that Ram Singh perpetrated the murder through Linda, in vengeance for the theft of the ruby,—had one fatal defect, which we should have seen at the start. It didn't account for the destruction of Malachi's will. We've been extremely dense, all along, about the significance of that will. We thought it incriminated David, since he was the natural heir who was being disinherited. And after we discovered its contents, we thought it incriminated Linda. We never thought of the obvious fact,—that there was in existence a previous will, giving Malachi's millions to some third person who was determined to keep them even at the cost of murder.

He made a gesture of impatience.

"What's more," he said, ruefully, "we were actually *told* about that previous will,—if we'd just had the wit to understand. There was a line in that diary of Malachi's you burned, to the effect that at last he had found the perfect way to dispose of Linda. And Linda herself told us Malachi had threatened, about the time of that entry, to make a will in her favor, telling her she needn't be grateful, because the will would contain a clever condition, and he wouldn't mind her enjoying his fortune 'for as long as she had it'. We should have guessed that the clever condition was her marriage—her marriage to some unscrupulous man who'd take pains that she shouldn't live to enjoy her fortune long."

He made Ryker an ironical little bow.

"Malachi is to be congratulated on his resourcefulness. But of course, as you told us yourself, he had a gift for putting his hand on an efficient scoundrel when he needed one."

Ryker shrugged his shoulders with a carelessness which did not match the steady gleam in his pale gray eyes.

"I observe," he said sarcastically, "that you are manifesting your usual childish enthusiasm for your latest pet theory. But except for an evident intent to be insulting, your remarks are beyond my humble comprehension."

"The only thing you don't comprehend," Jerningham told him dryly, "is the completeness with which you betrayed yourself just now. Since you don't remember what you said, suppose I summarize it for your benefit. Then you'll know whether I'm giving you a theory or a demonstration."

There was a tense silence throughout the room. Nilsson and I hardly breathed. Ryker was outwardly indifferent, but his fate was hanging on Jerningham's words, and he knew it.

"You wanted Trent's millions," Jerningham went on, with such calm, cold certainty that I was tempted again to doubt whether it could be a bluff. "Your chance of getting them depended on three things,—your marriage to Linda, her subsequent death, and Malachi's earlier will, which gave you his estate, once those conditions were fulfilled. Your marriage to Linda had been blocked once by her unexpected refusal, but Ram Singh had guaranteed to make her keep her word, and you were confident it could be done. You were also sure you could attend to the trifling detail of her subsequent death. But when you found, Sunday night, that Malachi had changed his mind and was writing a different will, you were up against it. You had either to relinquish all hope of the Trent millions, or strike down Malachi before the new will could supersede the old. And you chose to strike— depending on your wits to cover the murder and see you through."

Ryker was standing motionless, his hand still grasping the back of Malachi's chair, his eyes never leaving Jerningham's face.

"Your theory fascinates me!" he said. "Pray go on."

"In a way, it's not our fault," Jerningham proceeded thoughtfully, "that we failed to understand such an extraordinary crime. We assumed, reasonably enough, that the murder of Malachi was of some direct benefit to the murderer. Whereas it was only preliminary, really almost incidental to your main plan,—and quite useless to you unless the other two thirds of the program could be carried out. We never dreamed the murderer was gambling in futures as recklessly as that. Of course you knew you could count on Ram Singh to make Linda marry you, but once that was done you were obliged, single-handed, not only to kill her before she could protest against the bogus marriage, but to do it in the guise of accident or suicide. Your solution of that problem was, I concede, a stroke of pure genius."

Ryker still waited, motionless, but the hand that gripped the chair-back was growing white at the knuckles.

"You did it all by word of mouth. When Ram Singh had hypnotized Linda, as she slept, and ordered her to go through the marriage ceremony, he left her, still hypnotized, alone with you. And before you brought her downstairs to the wedding, you dictated to her a farewell note implying suicide, and gave her the peremptory order to walk the ledge to her death. Would you mind telling us how you hit upon that method of disposing of her? Was it suggested by David's good night wish that we should walk out of our windows in our sleep and break our necks?"

Ryker disdained to answer.

"At any rate, it was a masterstroke," Jerningham went on. "Coming, as it did, before Linda ever waked up and learned she was married, it was a perfect example of that maxim of your discreet counselor, Lord Bacon, that 'when matters have once come to the execution, there is no secrecy comparable to celerity'. If Linda had taken one more step last night, and fallen to her death as you meant she should, the Trent millions would have been yours."

I was watching Ryker's unmoved face with absorbed attention, and I noticed a curious thing. For a fraction of a second, at the mention of Lord Bacon's name, his gaze flickered from Jerningham's face to the lowest row of books on the shelves behind me.

"So far as I can see," Jerningham finished, "you made only one mistake. That was in choosing us three to establish your alibi. If you hadn't brought back with you a first rate detective, and a unique observer, and a crazy playwright, you'd never have needed the alibi, for the cry of murder would never have been raised. However, you came very close to rectifying that mistake on two occasions. It was just your hard luck that Ram Singh knew how to save Mac from the poisoned arrow, and that my overcharged shot gun left enough of me intact to—ask the questions which you answered just now with the confiding candor of hypnosis."

Ryker took out his cigarette case, and selected a cigarette with calm precision. It was characteristic of the man that now as always his lighter worked on the first snap. He took a puff or two before he spoke.

"I knew you had a gift for melodrama," he told Jerningham. "But it is now apparent that your true field is comic opera."

He took another puff.

"Of course, I have no way of telling," he continued with consummate coolness, "how much of this latest piffle of yours you may have succeeded in putting into my mouth, while I was looking at Ram Singh's candle flame. But it doesn't matter a whit. No court, nor jury, would put the least faith in an alleged confession made under such circumstances."

"Perhaps not," Jerningham conceded with quiet significance, "unless the confession led to the finding of corroborative evidence."

Ryker's cigarette hesitated on its way to his lips.

"You see," Jerningham said, "you told us all about Malachi's previous will. When we offer that will in evidence, nine tenths of your confession is substantiated."

Again Ryker's eyes flickered. Was it to the same spot, the lowest row of books behind me? I could not be sure. But with a sudden wild inspiration, I turned and knelt to see what might be there.

I could have shouted aloud with triumph at what I saw. Side by side among other ponderous tomes stood two fat quarto volumes comprising the works of Francis Verulam, Lord Bacon. My hands were shaking with excitement as I pulled them out.

I might as well have been alone in the room, for all the sound that was made while Lord Bacon's pages fluttered beneath my fingers. But when at last I halted, where an extra sheet of paper lay between the leaves, I heard from someone a quick intake of breath.

I plucked forth the paper.

"Here is the will," I said, and my own voice sounded like the voice of a stranger in my ears. "It's dated last May, and in Malachi Trent's handwriting, but there aren't any witnesses."

"Don't need 'em in Pennsylvania," Nilsson spoke up. "Not if you write your will in your own hand."

Jerningham's eyes were blazing with suppressed triumph.

"Read it, Mac!" he commanded. "Read the Commonweath's Exhibit A."

I took one look at Ryker's stony face, and obeyed.

" 'May 19th, 1928.

" 'This is my last will. I give and bequeath my entire estate to the Media Title and Trust Co., to hold in trust and pay the income thereof to my beloved niece, Linda Marshall, for one year, in case she shall not later than a week after my death marry my business associate Heldon Ryker, in whom I repose great faith and confidence.

" 'At the end of one year, I direct my trustee to pay over my entire estate to my said niece.

" 'In case of the death of my said niece before the expiration of the said year, I direct my trustee to pay over my entire estate to the said Heldon Ryker.

" 'In case my said niece shall not marry the said Heldon Ryker, then I give and bequeath my entire estate to the B——w Hospital for the Hopelessly Insane.

" 'Malachi Trent   (Seal)' "

There was a silence in the room, broken at last by Jerningham's voice.

"Perfect," he said ironically. "Did a man ever sign a neater death warrant? Everything to Ryker, in whom Malachi 'reposed great faith and confidence,' on condition that Linda should marry him—and die within the year. . . . Nilsson, there, at last, is your case."

"It's a preposterous case," Ryker said suavely. "If you try to prosecute me, I'll call all three of you to swear to my alibi. You were with me every minute of the time that Malachi was being murdered. You even heard me talking to him over the telephone from the tea room where we met."

"Accurately put," Jerningham commented, dryly. "We heard you talking over the telephone. We didn't hear Malachi. We couldn't have heard Malachi, because he was already dead. That telephone call was faked. You never took your finger off the hook!"

"So that's the theory?" Ryker mocked us, lightly.

"And is it a part of the theory that I was in two places at once? Or did I leave my astral body inside the library, to bolt the door behind me as I left, and to tip over the clock at the time I returned with you?"

"You didn't need an astral body for that," Jerningham answered, relentlessly. "You bolted the door and you tipped over the clock yourself from the outside."

"But that's impossible on the face of it!" Ryker retorted.

"Is it?" Jerningham's voice was mocking now. "Then you shouldn't have told us how you did it! Very simple, really. Even I could do it with one hand!"

For an instant, his haggard features relaxed into a grin.

"Let me demonstrate the remaining one tenth of the Commonwealth's case," he said. "The grand finale of my comic opera consists in the repetition of a scene from Act I, which we missed owing to our late arrival. Nilsson, see that none of the cast decamps before the end of the play."

He strolled over to the closed door and stood regarding it.

"You were lucky," he said to Ryker, "in the type of bolt you had to deal with. It slides so easily that you can work it with one finger— from the inside."

He reached out with his forefinger, touched the tiny knob that projected from the bolt, and flicked the bolt back and forth, back and forth, in its channel.

"But to go out through the door and leave it bolted on the inside," he continued, "requires an elaborate piece of mechanism,—to wit, a piece of cord."

He turned to Malachi's desk drawer, and Ryker stepped back a pace out of the way, his eyes hard and watchful. The scissors and ball of green cord were lying in the drawer, as we had observed them Sunday night. Jerningham cut himself a two foot length of cord. Holding this piece by its two ends, he dropped the loop thus formed about the tiny knob that projected from the bolt. Then still holding the two ends, he stepped out through the door and drew it shut after him, so that all we could see was the loop of cord, both its ends disappearing through the crack of the door.

"Now!" Jerningham said, from beyond the door.

The cord stretched tight. The bolt began docilely to slide along in obedience to the steady pull. Presently, shot to its fullest extent, it stopped with a little click.

"Locked?" Jerningham inquired, from beyond the door.

"It's locked all right," I said. "At least it would be if anyone had screwed the socket back on the door casing after Sunday night's performance. But—the cord is still there to betray how you did it."

"Not for long," Jerningham answered.

He dropped one end of the cord and pulled the other, and the loose end fluttered its way around the knob and out the crack of the door.

"There!" he said through the closed door. "End of Scene 1. The door is now locked, ready for David to break in during Scene 2. The curtain will fall for thirty seconds to denote the passing of three quarters of an hour while Heldon Ryker drives to the Gray Goose Tea Room, and returns with three strong knights and true, to rescue the Maiden in Distress. Beginning of Scene 2. I pray you, fix your eyes upon the clock."

I heard the front door open, as he stepped out on to the porch. Ryker, standing by Malachi's desk, turned to look at the clock. So did

I. And before my eyes—slowly—uncannily—the clock began to move—to bow—to topple—farther—faster—till the crash of its impact reverberated in the room. For an instant the library faded from my sight, and I stood again at the door of Cairnstone House in the dark, hearing that crash for the first time, without knowing what it might portend.

I knew now well enough what it portended. Yet it cost me a distinct effort of will to throw off the sense of the uncanny, and force myself to look for the prosaic mechanical device that Jerningham must have employed. Even so I nearly missed it.

A long loop of green cord was snaking a stealthy retreat across the floor, vanishing beneath one of the black velour curtains. That curtain covered the window that opened on the front porch. Apparently the cord was going out that window. But the window was closed, I knew. Closed and locked and sealed so tightly that we had not been able to open it.

With a sort of dull unbelief, I watched the last of the cord disappear under the curtain. And then a single sound brought me enlightenment. It was an unmistakable sound,—a sound I had heard a thousand times in my life.

It was the click of the flap of a letter slot, dropping into place.

The letter slot in the window sash!

The letter slot that opened out on to the porch, within arm's reach of the front door.

No wonder Jerningham had said that the truth had stared us in the face.

I looked at Ryker, and the fury in his face appalled me. The mask was off, and the killer that was in him glared undisguised. He had moved, as though unconsciously, into a position of defense behind Malachi's desk. There was no one at his back, nothing but the fallen clock and the heavy black curtains that still shrouded the front windows. And Malachi's great flat-topped desk was a barrier between himself and the rest of us, who were standing almost in the center of the room.

But though he faced us, across the desk, he was not looking at us. He was watching, over his right shoulder, the door through which

Jerningham must presently return. And his left hand,—the hand he used when he wanted speed and accuracy, was buried in the pocket of his coat. Suddenly I knew why.

I opened my mouth to cry a warning. And that same instant the door swung open and Jerningham stood on the threshold.

The melee that followed was dazzlingly swift.

There was a gleam of blued steel as Ryker's left hand jerked from his pocket.

There was the double crash of two shots,—so close together that not until I saw Ryker's gun spinning through the air, and Jerningham standing unmoved, could I believe that Nilsson had fired in time.

There was Nilsson's leap across the intervening space,—gun thrown aside,—to take his man rough and tumble.

There was a sickening instant when Ryker, with precision incredible in the face of that charge, whipped Malachi's revolver from the half open desk drawer.

There was the flash of Nilsson's dive across the desk, and the jar as he and the killer went down together.

I caught up the automatic Nilsson had dropped, and rushed with Jerningham to where the two men struggled. David, roused by the shots from his long hypnosis, was on our heels. But Nilsson had no need for any of us. He rose almost immediately from the scuffle with calm satisfaction on his face, and Malachi's revolver in his grasp. Methodically he recovered Ryker's lost weapon, pocketed both guns,— and dusted his hands.

Ryker rose more slowly, with an unaccustomed awkwardness in his movements,—and a pair of steel bracelets glinting on his wrists.

Jerningham was looking at Nilsson with an odd expression.

"Thanks, Carl," he said. "That makes twice."

"Perfect chance to finish him," Nilsson growled, "and his damned gun stopped my bullet!"

"Just as well," Jerningham answered. "That was pretty work at the end."

He tossed a small handful of cartridges on the desk.

"I emptied the revolver of Malachi's this morning," he said, "when

I was in here arranging the scenery. I needn't have worried, though."
He grinned. "Your methods are positively disarming."

Nilsson grinned back.

"I can depend on my muscles," he admitted. "I'm not so proud of
my brains!"

Jerningham drew a long sigh.

"Nor I of mine! But it's over at last. And we caught him in time to
save Linda! That's the thing that matters most."

I glanced at Ryker. There was a little smile upon his lips that made
my blood run cold.

"Have you saved her?" he asked, softly.

With a sudden sick misgiving I turned to look at her, where she
lay deep in sleep upon the window seat. She was lying very, very still.
Too still.

David was first to reach her side. In a frenzy of concern he gathered her into his arms, shaking her, kissing her, calling her name, trying again and again and again to stand her on her feet. It was no use.
Nothing availed to break that sleep which seemed, with each passing
moment, more and more like death.

Ryker watched with cruel triumph in his thin smile. His face was
flushed. His eyes had a queer look.

"What's the matter?" he taunted Jerningham. "Not so completely
master of the situation as you thought? Can it be that you've failed in
the thing that matters most? That she isn't going to wake—at all?"

Jerningham turned upon him.

"What do you mean?" he demanded, with sharp anxiety. "She's
all right. It's nothing but an ordinary hypnotic sleep."

"No doubt! No doubt!" Ryker mocked him, with sardonic enjoyment. "Still—A few moments ago you tipped over the clock and fired
a couple of pistol shots in your little comic opera,—and she continues
to 'sleep'! Is that quite—ordinary?"

To David, working desperately over Linda, the words meant
little,—if indeed he heard them. To me, they were a vague menace.
To Jerningham they carried a ghastly significance.

"What was it?" he demanded, hoarsely. "Morphine?" Ryker
shrugged.

"How do I know?" he countered. "You said she wrote a suicide note. She probably took whatever was most—convenient. But if it did happen to be morphine—a real dose, say, of ten grains or so—how unfortunate that you should have had her hypnotized! Without the complication of the hypnotic sleep, you might have detected her state in time to save her life. But now———"

He broke off, enjoying the patent misery on Jerningham's face.

"Now that you've allowed her to sleep undisturbed for half or three quarters of an hour, I'll wager nothing can wake her short of Gabriel's trump. Sad, is it not? The great Jerningham in his omniscient wisdom seems to have contributed directly to her death! And she trusted you so implicitly. Sad—sad!"

The flush on Ryker's face was deepening, darkening. I could guess what a flame of fury burned behind the man's self-control, what bitterness of thwarted malice found expression in the mocking words.

But Jerningham was past caring for mockery. He snatched up the phone, and in a voice I could not recognize as his, called Dr. Lampton's number. From my place at his side I could hear the bland squeak of the operator's answer.

"The line is busy na-ow."

Jerningham thrust the instrument from him in despair.

"I ought to have known," he said wretchedly, "that you'd strike again as soon as you learned your original scheme had failed. I did suspect it, too—I thought of poison when I saw you come from the dining room this morning before breakfast. But I thought I was clever enough—Oh, what a fool!—a fool!"

There was an instant's silence. Then Ram Singh's voice cut in, cool and impassive.

"The Sahib admits he is a fool?"

"A damned, reckless, meddling, cocksure fool!" Jerningham groaned, in the bitterness of his spirit.

"Then the Sahib has at last attained enlightenment," Ram Singh said, gravely.

His dark gaze shifted to Linda. She was lying limp in David's arms, as oblivious now of his despair as she had been of all his frantic efforts to wake her. There was unmistakable compassion in Ram Singh's look. With a majestic step he moved to David's side and laid one sinewy brown hand upon the girl's unconscious forehead.

"You have been deep in the pit of sleep. Too deep," he said, in a voice so compelling that I felt it might reach almost to the gates of death. "Too deep to move—to think—to will to return. *But not too deep to obey.* You will rise from the pit—up—up—up to the light of day,—*and wake!*"

I held my breath and prayed for a miracle.

Her eye-lids fluttered, opened. She stirred, and lifted her head. She looked a bit startled, but quite herself, and her first act was to slip a slender, confiding arm around David's neck.

I heard behind me an inarticulate cry of amazement from Ryker. He was gazing at her in dismay, as at one unwelcomely risen from the dead. His face was darkly suffused with blood, his breathing slow and labored.

When he spoke, there was an unwonted thickness in his speech.

"Jerningham," he said, with some difficulty. "You said—you, suspected me—before breakfast. What—did you do?"

The whole room waited for Jerningham's answer.

"I switched the grapefruit at your place and Linda's."

Ryker's breathing was growing slower and more labored. He was staring at Jerningham now, but his eyes were not quite in focus, and the pupils were so contracted that the eyes looked lighter than ever. He rested his shackled hands on the desk before him as if for support.

"Then—I—ate—Linda's—grapefruit?" he asked, thickly.

"You did," Jerningham answered. "Was it poisoned, or was it not?"

With infinite effort, Ryker drew himself erect, scorning the support of the desk. He swept the room with one defiant look. But his glance passed above our heads, and I knew we were no more than dim shapes in the fog that closed about him.

"*Was* it poisoned, or was it not?" Jerningham demanded.

By sheer strength of will, Ryker compelled his heavy tongue to shape an answer.

"None—of—your—damned—business!" he said.

And stumbling, lurching, like a man drunk with sleep, he forced his feet to carry him out of the room and up the stairs. Nilsson followed, grimly watchful to the end.

The rest of us stood in silence, till the stumbling foot falls passed out of our hearing in the hall above.

"The man is dying," I said at last, uneasily.

"Yes," Jerningham said. "He committed his second murder after all. And this time—" his voice rang like a steel blade,—"this time we shall not interfere."

Two hours later we telephoned Dr. Lampton that Ryker had committed suicide.

The little doctor came at once, looking very grave indeed. He acquiesced in the suicide theory, confirmed our guess that the poison used was morphine, and promised to make out a death certificate accordingly. But his confiding friendliness was a thing of the past. He kept his thoughts to himself, and they did not seem to be cheerful ones.

As Jerningham and I saw him to the door, he put one question.

"Mr. Jerningham, how much longer do you expect to stay in this house?"

"We're leaving today." Jerningham answered wearily. "All of us, the living and the dead."

The plump little doctor gave him an odd look.

"I'm glad," he said. "I've never known any place to be so unlucky. First Mr. Trent is killed by a fall. And then you four, who came here right after his death, are the victims of accident after accident and finally—suicide. I wonder——"

The little doctor's expression grew odder still, as he studied our faces.

"No, it's a preposterous notion," he decided finally, leaving his thought unspoken. "Preposterous! And yet—I'm very glad indeed you're going."

We stood in the doorway and watched him drive away.

"Jerningham," I said, "it's dawning on him that things are not what they seem! Maybe we should have told him the truth."

"What! Weakening already?" Jerningham reproached me. "When

I've just talked myself hoarse convincing Nilsson and the rest of them that *nobody* must be told?"

"Oh, I know we've all promised to keep still," I said gloomily, as we returned to the library. "But it's not going to work. The minute the will is probated——"

"The will?" Linda caught the last words, and looked up quickly from the hearth, where she had been burning the rest of the poisoned arrows, and a few of Malachi's papers which we had agreed to destroy. "What about the will?"

"Why, the will must be probated," I explained, "so that you'll get Malachi's estate."

"*I?*"

The idea seemed to strike her like a blow. Apparently, despite all the explanations in the past two hours, we had not pointed out that very practical upshot of the matter.

"Why yes! We showed you the will. Malachi left you his whole estate on condition you should marry Ryker. And you did,—so it's yours."

She shivered, in spite of her nearness to the blaze.

"I never thought of that. Let me see it—again."

I handed her the will. She read it through slowly. Then, with one swift movement, she stooped and consigned it to the flames.

"But Linda!" I cried, in dismay. "It was worth millions!"

"I think she's quite right," Jerningham put in quietly. "The whole estate will go to David under the intestate laws."

"And all I have will be Linda's," David added, "as soon as we can get away from this damned place and find a license and a minister. When can we go?"

"Now," Jerningham said. "The sooner you take Linda out of here, the better. We'll look after the last details."

He spoke steadily, but there was gray exhaustion in his face.

"*I'll* look after the last details," Nilsson corrected him, with brusque concern. "You go on out and sit in the car till I come. You're *through!*"

Jerningham went, with a sigh of pure relief.

Nilsson turned to David and Linda.

"Ram Singh can stay for a few hours, and close the house," he said. "That is, if you're still sure you want to let him keep the ruby."

"Good Lord, yes!" said David. "The ruby—and the house too, if he'll take it! They're neither of 'em any good to *us*."

I joined Jerningham in the car outside. We could hear Nilsson's big voice arranging something over the telephone. Presently David and Linda stopped beside us to say goodbye.

"I'm not thanking you," David said to Jerningham. "There aren't words enough. But if you ever have any use for a few odd millions——"

"I'll ask for them," Jerningham promised cheerfully.

Linda smiled and said nothing. But her smile was not quite steady. And her eyes were wet.

We watched them drive away. We waited for Nilsson. After a while he joined us, competent and imperturbable, showing no marks of strain or relief from strain.

But with his foot upon the starter he paused for a last look at Cairnstone House.

"I wouldn't mind another war——" he said at last.

The starter whined. The engine picked up. The car began to move.

"—but God save us from another Armistice Day celebration like this!"

THE END